MURDER AT THE PUPPY FEST

At first glance, the room appeared empty.

But after my gaze had rocketed around the interior, sliding over paneled walls, museum-quality paintings, and an enormous mahogany desk, it finally dropped to the floor.

There I found what I'd been looking for.

A man was lying on the rug beside the desk. His body was on its side facing away from me. One arm was extended outward, fingers stretched as if he'd been reaching for something when he fell. I couldn't see the man's face, but even so I knew who he was. Judging by the grey cast to his skin and the utter stillness of his body, I was pretty sure I wouldn't be meeting Leo Brody today after all . . .

Books by Laurien Berenson

A PEDIGREE TO DIE FOR
UNDERDOG
DOG EAT DOG
HAIR OF THE DOG
WATCHDOG
HUSH PUPPY
UNLEASHED
ONCE BITTEN
HOT DOG
BEST IN SHOW
JINGLE BELL BARK
RAINING CATS AND DOGS
CHOW DOWN
HOUNDED TO DEATH
DOGGIE DAY CARE MURDER
GONE WITH THE WOOF
DEATH OF A DOG WHISPERER
THE BARK BEFORE CHRISTMAS
LIVE AND LET GROWL
MURDER AT THE PUPPY FEST
WAGGING THROUGH THE SNOW
RUFF JUSTICE

Published by Kensington Publishing Corporation

MURDER AT THE PUPPY FEST

LAURIEN BERENSON

KENSINGTON BOOKS
www.kensingtonbooks.com

KENSINGTON BOOKS are published by

Kensington Publishing Corp.
119 West 40th Street
New York, NY 10018

All Kensington Titles, Imprints, and Distributed Lines are available at special quantity discounts for bulk purchases for sales promotions, premiums, fund-raising, and educational or institutional use. Special book excerpts or customized printings can also be created to fit specific needs. For details, write or phone the office of the Kensington special sales manager: Kensington Publishing Corp., 119 West 40th Street, New York, NY 10018, attn: Special Sales Department Phone: 1-800-221-2647.

Kensington and the K logo Reg. U.S. Pat. & TM Off.

ISBN-13: 978-1-4967-0344-6
ISBN-10: 1-4967-0344-8
First Trade Paperback Printing: July 2017
First Mass Market Printing: June 2018

eISBN-13: 978-1-4967-0343-9
eISBN-10: 1-4967-0343-X
Kensington Electronic Edition: July 2017

10 9 8 7 6 5 4 3 2 1

Printed in the United States of America

*For every little girl who grew up wishing for a puppy
of her own.
My wish came true and I hope yours did too.*

Chapter 1

"Hey!" cried Davey. "Did you see that?"

Twelve years old and curious about everything, my son Davey doesn't miss a trick. I was driving. I had my eyes on the road ahead of us.

I was also frowning as I ran through the day's shopping list in my mind. I'd picked up Davey at soccer camp an hour earlier, and we'd since made stops at the pharmacy, the hardware store, and the dry cleaner, before grabbing dinner supplies at the supermarket. Now that we were halfway home, I was beginning to suspect that I'd forgotten something vital.

I glanced Davey's way. After a day spent running around in the hot summer sun, he'd been drowsy only moments earlier. Now he was sitting straight up in his seat, his hand thrust out the open window. To my surprise, he was gesturing frantically toward the other side of the road.

That wasn't like Davey at all. Usually I'm the frantic one in the family.

"See what?" I asked.

"That car!"

A dark green compact car was coming toward us in the opposite lane. As it flew past, I caught only a quick impression of a man hunched low over the steering wheel. A second person was sitting beside him in the passenger seat.

Nothing about the small sedan struck me as notable. Ours were the only two vehicles on the quiet, suburban road. Even so, if Davey hadn't said something, I wouldn't have noticed it at all.

"What about it?" I asked him.

"Those guys. Didn't you see them? They just dumped that dog!"

"*What?*" Suddenly, Davey wasn't the only one sitting up in his seat. He had my full attention now.

"Mom, you have to pull over."

I was already doing that. With blinker flicked on, I let the Volvo coast to the side of the road. "What dog? Where?"

"Look. He's over there."

There wasn't time for me to look at anything. Before the car had even stopped rolling, Davey was already throwing off his seat belt. With a burst of youthful agility, he opened his door and scrambled out. I hurried to follow suit.

"Wait for me," I yelled after him. "Look both ways!"

Right. Like that was happening.

I caught up to him as he reached the grassy verge on the other side of the road and I grabbed his hand.

"What?" Davey looked down in surprise.

He held his younger brother Kevin's hand all the time. Mine, never. At his age, a gesture of affection like that has been beneath his dignity for several years.

"Wait," I said quietly as I pulled Davey to a stop. "Give him a minute. We don't want to scare him."

The dog was about twenty feet away from us, sitting on the narrow strip of grass between the road and an old stone wall. His front legs were splayed wide apart. His head hung low, and a long pink tongue lolled out of the side of his mouth as he panted heavily. The poor guy must have tried to chase after the car that had left him behind; he looked exhausted.

He was small to medium in size and couldn't have weighed more than twenty pounds. His smooth coat was mostly white, dotted with black and brown spots. He had a rounded head and a skinny body. One ear stood straight up; the other hung down over his cheek. A black patch covered one eye.

It was clear that the dog had noticed us. He lifted his head and eyed us warily. Under the circumstances, his response was understandable. But I was still determined to proceed with caution.

I'd relinquished my grip on Davey's hand, but now I reached over and held my son back. He lived in a house filled with Standard Poodles. He assumed that every dog was as friendly and outgoing as the ones he knew at home.

"Tell me what you saw," I said.

"I noticed the car because it pulled over and stopped. I thought maybe something was wrong. But then a guy opened the door and threw that dog out. Just tossed him on the ground. Then the car took off again. They didn't even look to see if he was all right."

"Bastards," I said under my breath.

Davey usually calls me on any lapses in language. This time, he nodded in agreement.

"He landed on his side in the grass," he said, and I heard the quaver in his voice. "Then he jumped up and started running. Even after those idiots dumped him, he still wanted to go with them."

"They're all he knows," I said with a sigh. "He thinks he belongs with them."

This time, it was Davey who took my hand. He squeezed my fingers hard. "We *have* to help him. We can't just leave him here."

"Don't worry," I said. "We'll get him the help he needs."

Our hometown of Stamford, Connecticut, is a lively city situated on Long Island Sound in lower Fairfield County. North Stamford, where Davey and I live with my husband, Sam, and three-year-old Kevin, has managed to retain much of its bucolic appeal despite downtown growth in both commerce and industry. Out where we are, houses are still spaced wide apart and traffic isn't plentiful.

I had no intention of treating the little dog as heartlessly as his owners had. Davey and I would *not* be the second and third people that day to abandon him by the side of an empty road.

"Cool," said Davey.

It isn't every day that the mother of a preteen boy can make her son smile. That made two good reasons why we were going to be rescuing the spotted dog. Now I just had to figure out what our next move should be.

Davey lifted a hand and brushed damp, sandy-brown bangs up off his face. I knew there was a tube of sunblock in his backpack; I'd placed it there myself. But after a day spent running around in the sun, his nose and forehead were pink. There was also a smear of dirt on the back of his neck. Still dressed in his soccer gear, my son was badly in need of a shower.

"That dog looks pretty upset," he said. "Plus, I think he's scared of us."

"That's why we're going to stay here for now. We'll give him a minute to think about things before we approach him."

"Maybe we should call Aunt Peg."

Of course Davey would suggest *that* course of action. Faced with a canine conundrum, just about everyone I know would immediately think of consulting my Aunt Peg.

Margaret Turnbull enjoyed near-legendary status in the dog show community. A successful breeder and exhibitor of Standard Poodles for decades, she had handled numerous Cedar Crest Poodles to top year-end awards. Now in her mid-sixties, Aunt Peg had a flourishing career as a dog show judge and she hadn't lost a single step. Not only that, but she still managed to keep the rest of us on our toes as well.

In addition to her many accomplishments in the dog world, my aunt was a woman who simply *gets* dogs. She possessed the rare ability to understand instinctively what they were thinking and feeling. Poodles had been Aunt Peg's lifelong companions, but canines of all shapes and sizes were drawn to her, in part because she made it clear that she returned their appreciation and respect in full measure.

By contrast, I didn't even own my first dog until I was in my thirties. Which meant that I'd occasionally been known to rely on Aunt Peg's canine acumen to remedy my own shortcomings. It wasn't a perfect solution. You try living in the shadow of a legend and see how you like it.

"No," I said firmly. "We don't need Aunt Peg. You and I are perfectly capable of handling this on our own."

"Okay." Davey didn't sound convinced. "But if we're handling this, how come we're over here and he's all the way over there?"

Most days, I'm happy that I've raised a child who knows how to ask good questions. Other days, not so much.

"I just want to consider the best way to approach him," I said. "That little dog just had something terrible happen to him. The last thing we want to do is frighten him further. If he feels threatened by us, he could bite. Or he might turn around and run away."

Davey squatted down and held out a hand. "Here, pup. Come on, boy. We're nice people. We just want to help you."

The spotted dog cocked his head to one side. He was listening to us. He just wasn't sure yet that he believed what we had to say.

"A dog that skinny must be hungry," I said. "Let's try offering him some food. What do you have left over from lunch in your backpack?"

"Most of a turkey sandwich," Davey replied without taking his eyes off the dog.

"Why didn't you eat your sandwich?"

"I was too hot. The lunch break was short. I ate my cupcake."

Wonderful.

"And all those baby carrots you always put in even though I told you I'm the only kid who gets vegetables for lunch."

I supposed that counted for something.

"You stay here and keep an eye on him," I said. "I'll be right back."

It only took me a minute to run back to the Volvo and find Davey's sandwich, squashed beneath a pair of shin guards at the bottom of his backpack. The turkey and whole wheat bread were warm and had mashed together into a soggy lump. Our offering didn't look very appetizing, but I suspected that the little dog wouldn't care.

As I trotted back across the road, I saw that while I'd been busy inside the car, Davey had moved farther down along the grassy verge. The distance between him and the dog was now cut in half. In response, the dog had risen to his feet. Though his gaze remained fixed on Davey, he appeared half-poised to flee.

"I thought I told you to stay where you were."

"You were taking too long to think about things."

"I was trying to keep you safe."

"From him?" Davey scoffed. "What could he do? That guy's tiny."

The dog wasn't *that* small. Although, compared to the Standard Poodles Davey was used to, I could see how he might not be impressed by this dog's size. Standards are the largest of the three varieties of Poodles. When my dogs stand next to me, their heads are level with my waist. Standard Poodles are intelligent, fun-loving dogs and a constant source of entertainment. Poodles not only make their owners laugh, they also challenge their people to out-think them.

By comparison, the skinny little spotted dog watching us intently through narrowed eyes didn't look like much.

"He may be small, but he still has sharp teeth," I said. "And he's clearly frightened. We don't want to push him into doing something he doesn't mean to do."

Davey reached over and took the baggie out of my hand. "Let's see if he likes turkey. Maybe that will convince him that we want to help."

The plastic crinkled in Davey's hands as he withdrew the sandwich. The small dog lifted his ears. Then he tipped his muzzle upward and sniffed experimentally.

He was definitely intrigued. That was good.

"Break off a piece and toss it to him," I said.

Davey did as I'd requested. The dog watched the half-sandwich fly through the air. It landed in the grass no more than a yard from where he stood. Abruptly the dog's weight shifted forward. He looked down at the morsel of food, then quickly up at us. His mouth opened slightly, his tongue flicked up and down.

The spotted dog still didn't trust us, but he was tempted.

"Go on," I said softly. "You know you want it."

Before I'd even finished speaking, the dog leapt forward. He pounced on the sandwich and gobbled it down in one swift bite. As he retreated back to where he'd been, I got my first look at his tail. It was short and thick and tipped in black.

"That worked," Davey said with satisfaction.

"Do it again," I told him. "This time, throw the food a little closer to us."

The piece of sandwich had barely landed before the dog bounded toward us and snatched it up. Instead of scooting away from us, the small dog stood his ground. He stared intently at the last piece of turkey in Davey's hand. His skinny body quivered with eagerness.

"Poor guy," said Davey. "He must really be hungry."

"Let's sit down on the grass, we'll look less threatening if we're smaller. Now put the last piece here." I indicated a spot just two feet away. "Let's see what he does."

The dog didn't even hesitate. He gobbled up the last of the sandwich and quickly swallowed. Then he raised his head and looked at us curiously, waiting to see what we would do next.

Close up, the spotted dog looked even worse than he had from afar. Most of his ribs were clearly visible, as were the points of his shoulder blades. His legs and feet were crusted with mud and his toenails were overgrown. There was a ring of red, irritated skin around his neck where much of the hair had been rubbed off. Several scrapes were raw and oozing. It looked as though he'd recently been wearing a collar that was several sizes too small for him.

I growled softly under my breath. Horrible as this day's experience had been for the poor dog, it didn't appear as though his previous life had been much better. And yet despite all he'd been through, the expression on the little guy's face was hopeful. He even gave his stubby tail a gentle wag.

A lump rose in my throat. For a moment, I couldn't seem to draw in a breath. Once again, I found myself humbled by a dog's infinite capacity to forgive and offer trust.

"I'm out of food," Davey said glumly. "Oh, wait!" He dug a hand into the pocket of his shorts and pulled out a half-eaten protein bar.

I didn't even want to know where that had come from. Or how long it had been in there.

"Hold out your hand," I said. "See if he'll take it from you."

The small dog stretched out his neck, lifted his muzzle, and whisked the food out of Davey's fingers. He swallowed it in two quick gulps. Then he took a step forward and sniffed Davey's empty hand. Realizing there was nothing more there for him to eat, he sidled over to me and had a look around. Slowly, I lifted my fingers and scratched beneath his chin.

The dog stiffened at my touch but didn't draw back. After a minute, he began to relax and lean into the caress. He even moved closer so his slender body could press up against my legs.

"I think he likes you, Mom." Davey grinned delightedly at our success.

"I think he likes both of us."

The look on my son's face was every bit as hopeful as the dog's had been. "So now what do we do with him?"

Poor skinny little thing. It wasn't as if we had a choice.

"We take him home," I said.

Chapter 2

Once we'd overcome his initial reticence, the spotted dog attached himself to us like we were his new best friends. He followed us across the road and jumped into the car as soon as Davey opened the door. He looked around alertly as we got ourselves settled, then proceeded to make himself comfortable on Davey's lap for the ride home.

"For a scrawny dog, he's pretty cute," Davey said.

I'd barely driven a mile and the little guy was already asleep. His body was cradled by my son's legs, and Davey's hand rested comfortably on the dog's back. Beneath his fingers, the narrow rib cage rose and fell in a steady rhythm. Once again, I marveled at the fact that the dog could be so trusting, especially after the way his last car ride had turned out.

"It's not his fault he's scrawny," I said. "It looks like it's been a while since he had a good meal."

"We can fix that." Davey paused, shooting me a quick look out of the corner of his eye to gauge my response. "Can't we? *Please?*"

"You know we have five dogs already."

"Yeah, but . . . we have room for one more."

I didn't want to make any hasty promises, but I was thinking the same thing. Until recently, our pack of Standard Poodles had numbered six. My second husband, Sam, had brought three Poodles with him to our union five years earlier. Davey and I had contributed two: Faith and Eve, a mother and daughter pair. Then we'd added Davey's show dog, Augie. But two months earlier, we'd lost Casey, Sam's oldest bitch, to a fast-acting cancer. Her passing had left a hole in all our hearts. One that none of us had been in a hurry to fill.

And now this little dog had found us.

"Besides," Davey said, "look at him. He's not even half as big as a Standard Poodle. He could fit anywhere."

I gazed at the two of them and sighed.

Davey knew I was wavering. How could I not be?

"He *needs* us, Mom. He doesn't have anyone else."

The dog wiggled his shoulders and curled his body into a tighter ball. Eyes still shut, he snuggled deeper into Davey's lap and looked utterly content. It was as if he knew exactly how to seduce me to his side.

"Let's see what Sam says, okay?"

"Sam will *love* him," Davey said happily. "Trust me."

Sam's an even softer touch than I am. I suspected Davey was right.

Our house is in a quiet neighborhood whose wide streets and well-kept lawns are shaded by mature trees and neatly trimmed hedges. Colonial in style, like most of those around it, the house is set back from the road for privacy. Fortunately, the setting also allows for a fenced backyard spacious enough to accommodate the antics of five rambunctious Standard Poodles.

When I pulled into the driveway, Aunt Peg's minivan was parked in the turnaround next to the garage. My stomach gave a small flip, a response similar to the one you might have when unexpectedly encountering a hornets' nest.

Most of the time, I adored Aunt Peg, but she was a woman of many facets. She could be brilliant, devious, discerning, generous, and manipulative. And that was just on her good days. Peg ruled over her small portion of the world with a firm hand. She also had a Machiavellian talent for exploiting other people's weaknesses—a skill that was bolstered by a firm belief in the value of her own opinions.

As you might imagine, she and I don't always see eye to eye.

I frowned at Davey. "Did you call her after I told you not to?"

"No way." He shook his head vehemently. "Maybe she guessed something was up. Aunt Peg is like Severus Snape. She has special powers."

As I stopped the car at the back of the driveway,

the little dog awoke. He stood up, balancing himself nimbly on Davey's legs, and took a curious look out the window.

Quickly, Davey pulled him back. "We can't let Aunt Peg see Bud. He's just a mutt. She won't like him."

I'd been reaching for my door handle. Now I stopped and looked back. "*Bud?*"

"Yeah." Davey grinned. "Bud. That's his new name."

"Since when?"

"About five minutes ago. I came up with it while you were driving. Don't you think it suits him?"

It did, though I was loath to admit it. Once you named a dog, he was yours forever. On the other hand, wasn't that decision already pretty much made?

Davey gave the dog a gentle squeeze. "Look at you, Bud. You're a good boy. You like your new name, don't you?"

The dog wagged his black-tipped tail in response. In fact, he wagged it so hard that his whole body undulated with the effort. It had probably been a long time since anyone had spoken to him kindly, poor guy.

"Hey Bud?" I tried out the name myself.

That canny little dog spun around in Davey's lap and pricked his ears in my direction. He was prepared to like anything we had to offer.

"See?" cried Davey. "He knows his name already!"

More likely, he knew that luck had landed him in a good spot and he was ready to do whatever it took to stay there. But hey, who was I to argue with reasoning like that? I have Standard Poodles. I love a smart dog.

The side door to the house opened, and Sam stuck his head out. The Poodles had probably announced our arrival as soon as we'd pulled in.

"What are you guys doing out there?" he called. "Do you need help with the groceries?"

Damn, the groceries. I'd forgotten all about them. Thank God I hadn't bought ice cream.

Sam didn't wait for an answer. He shut the door behind him and headed our way. Davey lifted Bud into his arms and exited the other side of the car. I took a moment to watch Sam approach and appreciated the view.

Now, in mid-summer, my husband's dark blond hair had lightened to the color of sun-washed wheat. Sam had an easy smile and an athlete's trim physique. Even better, he moved with the grace and quiet confidence of a man who understood the world and was content with his place in it. Not for the first time, I acknowledged silently that the day we'd met had been the luckiest day in my life.

"Is everything okay?" Sam asked as he drew near.

"Sort of." I pushed open my door and stepped out of the car.

"Sort of?" A look of concern flashed across his face. "What's up?"

"We have an unexpected guest."

Even though I'd cautioned Davey that Sam's approval was needed before any permanent decisions could be made, that didn't stop my son from giving a whoop of delight as he came skipping around the car. Sam barely had a chance to realize what was happening before Davey danced to a halt in front of him, reached up, and deposited the skinny little dog into his stepfather's arms.

"Meet Bud," Davey said happily. "Isn't he the greatest?"

Sam peered downward uncertainly. Mud from Bud's legs was already streaked across the front of his shirt. "The greatest what?"

Bud widened his expressive eyes, tipped his muzzle upward, and licked the underside of Sam's chin. I swear that little dog must have been related to P.T. Barnum because he certainly knew how to reel in a sucker.

"Dog," Davey crowed. "Bud's a dog."

"I can see that," Sam agreed. His fingers reached up to fondle the dog's ears. "Who does he belong to?"

"About that—" I began.

"He belongs to us," Davey said. "We found him by the side of the road."

"Davey saw someone throw him out of a car," I said. "They just tossed him in the weeds and sped away."

"Are you serious?" Sam looked back and forth between us. "That's terrible."

"What's terrible?" asked Aunt Peg, coming up to stand beside us.

Intent on gauging Sam's reaction, I hadn't even noticed her approach. Aunt Peg was six feet tall and walked like a football linebacker. You'd think she wouldn't be able to sneak up on people, but there she was.

Before I could answer, Aunt Peg saw the wide

smile on Davey's face. She followed the direction of his gaze to the spotted dog in Sam's arms.

"Terrible?" she said again. Automatically, her hand reached out to pat the dog's head. "I must say he doesn't look like much, but I wouldn't call him terrible."

"We weren't talking about the dog—" I began.

"His name is Bud," Davey announced at the same time.

"Bud? *Really?*" Aunt Peg was not amused. "What a plain name. Is that the terrible part?"

"No," Davey chortled. "It's a perfectly good name. And he already likes it."

Aunt Peg turned her narrowed gaze on the small dog. "From the looks of him, he'd be apt to like anyone who said a kind word to him."

"Somebody dumped Bud by the side of the road," Davey told her. "I saw them do it."

"My word. That's criminal! Did you see their license plate? We'll report them to the police. People like that should be made to answer for their sins."

"No," I admitted. "No license number. We stopped and picked up the dog instead."

"Bud," Davey reminded us. Not that anyone had forgotten. "His name is Bud."

"Who's Bud?" a small voice piped up. Three-year-old Kevin, Sam's and my son, had come to join the party in the driveway.

Sam looked at Aunt Peg. "I thought you were watching him for me while I stepped outside."

"I *am* watching him," she replied. "See? He's right there."

Dogs enjoy Aunt Peg's undivided attention. Young children are another matter entirely.

"Really?" I said to Sam. "You left him with Aunt Peg?"

"I thought I'd only be outside for a minute. How long does it take to carry a bag of groceries into the house? I had no idea someone was going to put a stray dog in my arms and then want to have a conversation about it."

There was that.

"Besides," Sam added, "Faith's inside too. You know she wouldn't let anything happen to him."

Kevin tugged on the hem of my shirt. He looked up at me with beguiling blue eyes that were just like his father's. With his blond curls and chubby cheeks, he looked like a cherub in a Renaissance painting.

"Who's Bud?" he asked again.

I leaned down and picked him up. From that vantage point, Kevin could see the spotted dog for himself. But when he reached out a questing hand to give Bud a poke, I quickly pulled him back out of range.

Kev blew out a delighted breath anyway. "Pretty dog!"

"That child needs higher standards," Aunt Peg said.

"He's only three," I told her. Obligingly Kevin held up three fingers in support of my claim. "He loves all animals."

"Are you calling our new dog ugly?" Davey inquired.

"*Your* new dog?" Aunt Peg swung her gaze his way. "When did that happen?"

I didn't have an answer for that. Apparently no one else did either.

It was Kev who broke the ensuing silence. "Can't live here," he said firmly. "Not enough hair."

"I have a thought," said Sam. "Why don't we move this discussion inside?"

"I have another thought," Aunt Peg announced. "Before we do something rash, let's consider the likelihood that the little interloper you've brought home is loaded with fleas."

Involuntarily, I took a step back. *Fleas.* Yuck. The mere mention of the pesky insects made my scalp itch. In a home with normal dogs, fleas were an inconvenience. But for Poodles who were destined for the show ring, hair was a precious and ever-protected commodity. And fleas were a disaster in the making.

"Let's have a look." Sam flipped the little dog over in his arms. We all leaned in and peered at his stomach. The evidence that Aunt Peg's guess was correct was right in front of us.

"Eww," I said, pulling away.

"Eww," Kevin echoed. "Bud has peas. We don't like peas."

"That settles it," Aunt Peg announced. "That dog is not going inside the house."

"Not yet at any rate." Sam was unfazed. "Give me half an hour and I can fix this."

We're Poodle people. We're experts at giving dogs baths.

While Sam attended to Bud, the rest of us unloaded the car. As soon as we walked in the door, five Standard Poodles came and swarmed around our legs to welcome us home. Deftly, Faith nudged her way through the pack and pressed her nose into my hand.

Faith is big and black, and absolutely gorgeous. She had come to me as a gift from Aunt Peg and was the first dog I'd ever had the privilege to own. Faith has dark, soulful eyes, an empathetic nature, and a great sense of humor. Her entry into my life had changed everything. Before, I'd had no idea what I was missing. Now I couldn't imagine living without her.

Faith sniffed my fingers, then gazed up at me with a puzzled expression on her face. Meanwhile, the other four Standard Poodles—bitches Eve and Raven, and the other two dogs, Tar and Augie— were eagerly exploring the strange-dog scent they'd found on Davey.

"It's just Bud," he told them. "You'll meet him soon."

"Or not," Aunt Peg muttered under her breath.

While I put away the food, she got out a handful of peanut butter biscuits from the pantry and passed them around. Davey grabbed a couple of apples from the bowl on the counter, and he and Kevin left to find something more interesting to do than listen to grown-ups talk. Hopefully Davey was on his way to the shower.

That left just me and Aunt Peg.

I cut right to the chase. "Why are you here?"

"I'm surprised you even have to ask." Aunt Peg pulled out a chair at the kitchen table and sat down. "Because of Puppy Fest, of course."

"What about it?"

"Why wasn't I invited?"

I took a bottle of green tea out of the refrigerator, opened it, and had a long, cold swallow. "You ought to be asking Claire that. It's her event."

"That's precisely why I'm asking you. Claire is the one who neglected to include me."

Claire is the newest member of our extended family. On New Year's Eve, she'd married my ex-husband, Bob, and moved into his house on the other side of Stamford. My relationship with Bob is still a work in progress, but Claire and I had hit it off immediately. The fact that she was now Davey's stepmother made it important that we get along, but even without the family connection I would have loved Claire anyway.

"I read about the event yesterday in the *Greenwich Time*," Aunt Peg said. "Apparently it's going to be broadcast on local TV. I even have a passing acquaintance with its sponsor. So imagine my surprise when I discovered that Puppy Fest was being organized by a member of my own family."

So help me, there was a small, mean part of me that was happy there was one thing in the world that Aunt Peg didn't know.

She glared at me across the table as I sat down opposite her. "Would you please explain why Claire didn't ask for my help?"

"I'd imagine she thought you'd be too busy to get involved. Plus, you know . . ."

Aunt Peg lifted a brow. She was going to make me say it.

"Your thing is purebred dogs."

Puppy Fest was a charitable event sponsored by Puppy Posse Foundation, a local dog rescue whose mission was to provide aid for at-risk dogs in Fairfield and Westchester Counties. Modeled after television's famous *Puppy Bowl*, the event featured two teams of adorable, adoptable puppies in a faux competition. The puppies would chase toys and create cute canine mayhem on a stage constructed to look like a pint-sized football field.

Puppy Fest was sponsored by wealthy philanthropist Leo Brody, founder and chief benefactor of Puppy Posse. The event was scheduled to take place the following day at his waterfront mansion in Belle Haven. Claire, who worked as an event coordinator, had been hired by Mr. Brody to set up and manage the whole affair.

"My thing indeed," Aunt Peg snapped. "Just because I happen to be involved in the dog show world doesn't mean I don't have an interest in the welfare of all dogs."

Well, sure. But when it came to the canines she chose to live with, Aunt Peg was a bit of a snob. If I hadn't realized that previously, her reaction to Bud's appearance certainly would have tipped me off.

"Most of the puppies at Puppy Fest will be mutts and mixed breeds," I told her. "The purpose of the event is to raise money for Puppy Posse and to raise awareness about the plight of abandoned dogs." Then I paused, struck by a sudden thought. "Wait a minute. *You know Leo Brody?*"

"Of course," Aunt Peg replied, as if being acquainted with a man whose face I'd seen on magazine covers was nothing unusual. "He's made his home in Greenwich for many years. We've crossed paths on a number of occasions. Not only that, but one of his daughters shows dogs. Libby Rothko? She has Dalmatians."

I shook my head. Suddenly I felt as though the conversation had taken a detour into fantasy land. "Puppy Fest isn't a social occasion," I said. "It's going to be a lot of work for everyone involved."

She didn't look convinced. "What's your job?"

"Claire asked me to be a puppy wrangler." She hadn't had to twist my arm. Who in their right mind would turn down a job like that?

"I see. I hoped I'd be needed, but apparently I'm not. That being the case, I trust you will convey my disappointment to Claire." Aunt Peg pushed back her chair and stood. "One more thing. It wouldn't be the worst idea to turn that little dog over to Leo's foundation. I'm certain they'll do right by him."

"Do right by who?" asked Sam, coming in through the door.

The Poodles jumped up to greet him. I did the same. Okay, maybe the one I really wanted to see again was Bud. But to my surprise, Sam's arms were empty.

"Where's Bud?" The name rolled off my tongue easily—as if it belonged there. As if the spotted dog with the floppy ear was already on his way to becoming a member of the family.

"For now, I set up an ex-pen for him in the garage. He'll be happy there. He's got a bed, a chew toy, and a bowl of cold water. I think it's better if we keep him away from the Poodles until we've had a chance to get him thoroughly checked out by the vet."

Of course. I should have thought of that myself.

"The boys and I will take him to the animal hospital tomorrow while you're at Puppy Fest."

"Aunt Peg seems to think that we might want to drop him off at Puppy Posse," I said.

"That's one idea." Sam's gaze scanned my face, and I realized that he was looking for reassurance that we were in agreement. In the short time they'd been together, Bud must have charmed Sam too. "But it wouldn't be my first choice."

"Mine either," I said.

Aunt Peg shook her head. "If you two truly intend to have that dog take up residence here, you should leave him to be neutered when you take him to the vet tomorrow."

"That's not our decision to make," said Sam. "Not yet, at any rate."

I looked at him in surprise. "What do you mean?"

"Think about it, Mel. We can't just decide to keep this dog without making a good faith effort to locate his previous owners."

"His previous owners threw him out of a car!" I said hotly.

"I know that's what you saw." As always, Sam was the voice of reason. "But there could be another explanation. Maybe those men stole Bud from someone else. Maybe there's a heartbroken family looking for him."

"You've been watching too many Disney movies," Aunt Peg sniffed.

"Could be, but I don't want to make a decision about keeping him until I've had a chance to contact animal control and the local shelters. He's not wearing a collar, but I'll have the vet check for a microchip. We probably ought to place a notice on Craigslist too."

"But—" I began to object. Then my voice trailed away.

One of the things I loved about Sam was his sense of fair play. And now I knew he was right. But that didn't make me feel any better about it.

"Sorry," he said. "But it's up to us to do the right thing by him."

Even though I'd told Davey that Bud couldn't stay without Sam's approval, somehow I'd already begun to think of him as ours.

"I guess so," I grumbled.

Chapter 3

I like to think that if Leo Brody had known when he awoke on Saturday that the day would be his last, he'd have elected to spend it just the way he did—sitting on the floor of his home and playing with puppies.

Puppy Posse Foundation was one of many charitable organizations Mr. Brody supported, but I'd read that it was his favorite. His affection for dogs was a well-documented fact. Leo Brody and I had that much in common. Unfortunately, after that, all similarities between us ended.

I was a special needs tutor at Howard Academy, a private school in Greenwich. I spent weekends with my family, either at dog shows or on outings to kid-friendly places like Tod's Point or the Norwalk Aquarium. Evenings I was home early. Most nights, I was in my jammies by eight, sacked out on a couch with Sam, the kids, and a passel of Poodles.

By contrast, Leo Brody lived the kind of life that was covered extensively in the media. His financial dealings and social engagements filled the pages of the *Wall Street Journal, Vanity Fair,* and *Town and Country.* I wasn't entirely sure where his money had come from—all I knew was there was a lot of it and he enjoyed giving it away to worthy causes.

At ten o'clock the next morning, however, when I drove to the sheltered coastal neighborhood in Greenwich where Leo Brody lived, I wasn't thinking about his fame and fortune. Rather, it was Claire who was on my mind. She had asked for my assistance and I was happy to comply. The previous December, Claire had spent an entire day at the Howard Academy Christmas Bazaar, dressed in an elf costume for me. By comparison, I was getting off easy.

Leo Brody's house wasn't difficult to find. Due to its setting on a promontory of high, level, land overlooking Long Island Sound, I was able to see the mansion's roofline from a quarter mile away. Tall brick gateposts, shaded by a pair of leafy dogwood trees, marked the entrance to the estate.

The gates themselves were open, but a security guard was just inside, standing at the foot of the long gravel driveway. I knew that Puppy Fest was a huge undertaking; Claire had been working on the arrangements for several months. Between the TV crew coming to film the event, caterers who'd be feeding everyone, and the Puppy Posse employees who were bringing the event's participants from the rescue, there would probably be people coming and going all day long.

I stopped next to the guard, who checked my

name against his list, then instructed me where to go. Slowly, I drove the length of the driveway, taking my time and savoring the view.

The rambling, three-story house in front of me was constructed of red brick. Black shutters and white trim accented the dozens of windows that sparkled in the morning sun. The central portion of the home, already imposing in size, had two long wings reaching out from it on either side. A widow's walk with a small, enclosed cupola stood sentinel on the gabled roof.

As I neared the house, a smaller driveway angled off to one side. A discreet sign read SERVICE ENTRANCE and an arrow pointed to the back of the building. Out front, all was quiet. The rear of the palatial home, however, was a hub of bustling activity.

Two white vans with the logo of a local TV station were parked side by side, and a crew was busy unloading their contents. A large cargo truck had commandeered the prime spot just outside the open door to the house. Half a dozen people were unpacking the large plywood sets that would make up the event's playing field and backdrop. Two catering trucks were idling toward the back of the parking area. One driver was out of his vehicle, gesturing angrily as he complained about the entrance being blocked.

Not my problem, I thought as I drove to the far end of the lot and parked beside Claire's Honda hybrid. At least not until I'd checked in with Claire and found out what she wanted me to do first.

I walked inside the house through the open door and immediately came to a stop. The narrow passageway in front of me was clogged with large men, stacked boxes, crates on dollies, and a jumble of assorted gear and equipment.

Stuck at the end of the line, I raised my voice above the din. "Does anybody know where I might find Claire Travis?"

Nobody answered. In fact, almost no one paid any attention to me at all. When one man glanced back and shrugged, I saw that he was wearing earbuds.

Slipping past, I maneuvered my way to the front of the unruly crowd. There, a bottleneck had formed with people and paraphernalia trying to squeeze through in both directions. I spotted a small opening and slithered through.

Almost immediately, I came upon a doorway that led to an enormous kitchen. Things looked slightly less hectic in there so I ducked inside. Anything was better than the chaotic hallway behind me.

A quick scan revealed a swinging door on the other side of the kitchen. Dodging between a restaurant-quality stove and a center island whose gleaming steel countertop was piled high with everything from fragrant rolls to fresh raspberries, I made a beeline for the next exit. Nobody paid any attention to me as I went barreling by. I hit the door, pushed it open, strode through . . . and stopped again.

Now I was standing in a beautifully appointed formal dining room. Visible through an ornate arched entryway was a grand, two-story foyer. In contrast to the area of the house I'd just left, here everything was peaceful. Too peaceful. Feeling suddenly like an interloper in Mr. Brody's private space, I turned back to reenter the kitchen.

Then I had a better idea. Away from all the commotion, I could hear what I was doing. I pulled out my phone and called Claire.

She picked up right away. "Where are you? Are you here yet?"

"I arrived five minutes ago. I'm near the kitchen. It's a madhouse over here."

"It's a madhouse everywhere." I heard her sigh. "Thanks for coming early. I'll take all the help I can get. Come to the ballroom. It's in the west wing."

"There's a *ballroom*?" I said without thinking. Then I looked around. Of course the house had a ballroom. "Right. I'll be there in a minute. Do you want to give me directions or can I see it on Google Earth?"

"Excuse me," a male voice said from behind me. Whoever he was, he sounded annoyed. "Can I help you?"

I looked over my shoulder. The man who'd spoken was standing in the foyer. Dressed in linen pants and a crisp button-down shirt, he had a pudgy build and thinning brown hair. The perplexed look on his face accentuated deep frown lines that bracketed either side of his mouth. I guessed him to be about ten years older than me, probably in his mid-forties.

"Um . . ." I said. "No?"

"No what?" asked Claire.

"Are you lost?" asked the man.

"Yes . . ."

"Yes *what?*" Now Claire sounded exasperated. I didn't blame her.

"Call you right back," I said.

I shoved the phone in my pocket, walked over, and introduced myself. "I'm here to help Claire Travis with Puppy Fest," I said. "Except that I can't seem to find my way to the ballroom."

"This house tends to have that effect on people. It's in the other wing. Come with me. I'll show you where you need to be."

"Thanks."

As we walked across the entrance hall, I didn't know what to look at first: the marble floor in a geometric design beneath my feet; the wide, curving, staircase that led to a second-floor balcony; or the crystal chandelier that hung high above my head. A spacious living room, visible through open double doors, merited only a quick glance before I followed the man down another hallway, this one leading us past a library and a music room.

"The west wing was added onto the original house fifty years ago," my escort told me. "The home's previous owner liked to throw parties and he wanted the ballroom situated so that it overlooked the Sound. That's why it's a bit of a hike."

Whoever the man was, he certainly knew his way around the place. "Do you work here?" I asked.

"No." He glanced over at me. The question seemed to amuse him. "Actually I used to live here. Leo Brody is my father."

He might have started with that information, I thought irritably. Maybe about the time that I'd introduced myself. Not only that, but he still hadn't told me his name. Maybe I was just supposed to know?

"Sorry," I said.

"No problem."

The man stopped and pointed to the left. "Just walk around the corner. The ballroom is the first door on the right. You can't miss it."

"Thank you, I appreciate . . ."

My thanks was delivered to empty air. Mr. Brody's son had turned his back to me and was already striding away.

I stared after him briefly. Maybe my remark about his working in the house *had* been a problem after all. Or perhaps the Brody family didn't feel the need to worry about manners when dealing with the hoi polloi.

"You're here for Claire," I said under my breath, then repeated the words like a mantra. "You're only here for Claire."

"Oh my," said Claire. "If you're already talking to yourself, you'll be absolutely insane by this afternoon."

I whirled around. Why did I always seem to be facing the wrong way in this house?

Claire was taller than me, and also thinner. Her long, dark, hair was straight and frizz-free and her honey-toned skin and brown eyes gave her a vaguely exotic look. Standing side by side, we probably resembled Mutt and Jeff.

"Some people might call me half-cracked even on my best days." I would have given Claire a hug except that she had a phone in one hand and a clipboard in the other. She was holding the latter in front of her like a shield.

Claire grimaced. "Please don't make me discuss your Aunt Peg. I simply don't have time today to do that topic justice."

"She did ask me to convey her disappointment to you," I mentioned.

"Of course she did. What now?"

"You didn't ask her to help with Puppy Fest."

"And that's a problem why?"

"Actually, I'm not entirely sure."

"Excellent," Claire said briskly. "Then let's move on. Are you ready to get to work?"

"Of course. Just tell me what you want me to do."

I followed Claire to the ballroom. Once inside, I immediately saw why that location had been chosen for the event. The room was vast and mostly empty of furniture. Between its high ceiling and the row of glass-paneled French doors that opened onto an outside terrace, the ballroom was flooded with natural light.

Claire and I walked around the room, keeping to the edge of the floor and stepping carefully over scattered tarps and thick, black wires. A construction crew was assembling the rectangular playing field near one end of the hardwood floor. A group of technicians was working on a sound system. A row of freestanding lights had been pushed back against the wall. Beside them, two men were unloading even more gear.

Despite the level of activity all around us, the mood in the room was calm and purposeful. Everybody had a job to do, and all were prepared to do their assignments well.

My gaze stopped on an oversized folding table that

was littered with old coffee cups and surrounded by empty chairs. A man wearing a suit and tie and wire-rimmed glasses was standing beside it. Brandishing a microphone in one hand and a sheaf of papers in the other, he appeared to be repeating a list of football terms.

"Who's that?" I asked Claire in a low tone.

"Trouble," she muttered. Then she turned to me and her expression brightened. "Want to make him your first assignment?"

"Maybe." Based on her initial assessment, I wasn't about to commit until I knew more. "What would I have to do?"

"Convince him to put the playbook down and step away from the microphone. In fact, if you could get him out of the room entirely, that would be a huge bonus."

"What's the catch?"

"Well, for starters, he won't be easy to budge. He'll probably pull rank and tell you to get lost."

I turned Claire around and steered her through the closest set of French doors. Outside on the terrace, we could speak without being overheard. "I'm guessing there's more to the story than that. Why don't you start at the beginning?"

"The man with the mic is Fred Brody. He's one of Mr. Brody's sons."

Another one. Apparently the place was crawling with them.

I spared a glance back inside. Mic Man was still practicing his elocution. "So Fred Brody is serving as commentator for Puppy Fest?"

"Heavens no. And that's the problem."

"Okay." I waited for her to continue.

Instead, Claire said, "How much do you know about Leo Brody?"

"Mostly just what I read in magazines or see on TV. He's a self-made millionaire who attends charity events, serves on boards, and donates money to worthy causes. He loves dogs. Is there anything else I need to know?"

Claire lowered her voice to a whisper. "He also loves women."

That didn't seem like a bad thing.

"Good for him?" I tried.

"He's been married three times."

"He sounds like a busy man." I found myself whispering as well. "Why do we care?"

"Because those three marriages have produced nine children."

"*Nine?*" I might have shrieked a little at that.

"Nine," Claire confirmed. "And most of them have shown up today. As if I don't already have enough to do, this place is suddenly overrun with Leo Brody's relatives. It's not just the children—who, by the way, are actually adults—there are grandchildren running around too."

"What are they all doing here?"

"Sucking up, apparently." Claire lifted a hand and raked back a strand of silky hair that had fallen forward over her face. "I'm sorry, did that sound rude?"

"Kind of," I admitted.

Claire doesn't have a mean bone in her body. Not only that, but her job routinely places her in high-stress situations. I'd seen her soothe difficult clients with more tact and aplomb than I could ever muster. Normally she breezes through challenging events without ever losing her cool. So this level of agitation was definitely out of the ordinary.

"Puppy Posse is Mr. Brody's pet charity, and Puppy Fest is their signature event," she said. "Because of that, his whole family turns out to show their support. Unfortunately, nobody warned me about that aspect ahead of time. I was hired to plan and execute a large event with a lot of moving parts. But Mr. Brody never said anything about my having to wrangle a dozen of his relatives at the same time."

"I get that having them show up unexpectedly is a nuisance," I said. "But this is their family home, so you can't exactly throw them out. Can't you just ignore them?"

"I wish! None of them attended the advance meetings. Nor have they asked about arrangements that have already been made. Instead, they're all just suddenly *here,* determined to pitch in and help out in whatever manner they think is best. Regardless of whether they know what they're doing or not. Take Fred, for example. He's decided that since he once performed in a high school play, he should serve as the announcer for the puppy bowl game."

"Is he any good?"

"I have no idea. But the point is, I also don't care. Mr. Brody has gone to a great deal of trouble and expense to produce this event. It's the most important fundraiser and PR vehicle on Puppy Posse's annual calendar. The puppy bowl will be broadcast *live* over local TV. This isn't amateur hour, and we can't afford for things to go wrong just because a bunch of family members want to make a good impression on Daddy."

"I see your problem," I said. "Do you want me to have a chat with Fred?"

"I've already tried that." Claire frowned. "Like the rest of his family, he likes to talk and hates to listen."

"What if . . . ?" I stopped and considered.

"Please tell me you have a good idea. I'll love you forever if you take Mr. Brody's relatives off my hands so I can get back to doing my real job."

"When the show opens, before the actual game starts, who's doing the introduction?"

"Oliver Gregson, the same man who'll be doing the live play-by-play during the game. He's a professional announcer."

"Mr. Brody didn't want to introduce his own event?"

"No. He was definite about that. The paparazzi take his picture all the time but Mr. Brody almost never appears on camera if he can help it. Besides, the intro is only a few scripted lines about Puppy Posse and all the wonderful work they do. The point is to get right to the game."

"So few lines that maybe even a non-professional could handle them without flubbing?"

Claire stared at me for a moment. Her eyes widened. "Melanie Travis, you're a genius."

That made me laugh. "Not even close. But I deal with seven-year-olds for a living. I've learned how to come up with creative solutions."

"Do you think Fred would go for that?"

"All you can do is ask. But based on the way he's over there struggling with his football terminology, I bet he might actually be relieved to accept an offer that gets him off the hook without losing face."

"Come on." Claire grabbed my arm. "You're coming with me."

"You're the one in charge," I said. "What do you need me for?"

"You persuaded me. Now you can work your wiles on Fred."

Wiles? She had to be kidding.

"Besides"—Claire grinned—"you've been able to put up with Peg all these years. After that, dealing with the likes of Fred Brody should be a piece of cake."

Chapter 4

Convincing Fred Brody to limit his contribution to performing the introduction turned out to be easier than Claire and I had expected. Our success might have had something to do with my musing about the unpredictability of puppies, and then casually mentioning that *I* would never be brave enough to host a live broadcast over which I had so little control.

Five minutes later, Fred had the short script for the intro in his hand and he'd gone back to rehearsing. It was a toss-up who looked more relieved about the switch: him or Claire.

"I knew there was a reason I asked you to come today," Claire said with a smile. She was steering me toward a closed door at the end of the room.

"Puppies," I reminded her. "You promised me I could play with puppies."

"We're on our way now. The puppies are in the

salon next door. They arrived shortly before you did. A couple of Puppy Posse employees are getting them settled, and then we'll just have to keep them calm and quiet until game time."

"How many puppies are there?"

"Lots." Claire consulted a note on her clipboard. "Jane, the director of Puppy Posse, told me they were bringing twenty-two."

"Wow, that's more than I expected. Are they all going to take part in the game?"

"I don't think so, but that's not up to me. Did I mention that Jane is one of Leo Brody's daughters?"

I shook my head.

"She's the one making all the decisions concerning the puppies. I know she brought extras in case some that are scheduled to play don't work out. Obviously we want all the puppies to be happy and animated during the game. So those that are intimidated by the lights, or the noise, or the commotion going on around them, will have to be quickly switched out. And that's something we won't find out until we're up and running—and broadcasting live."

"Some challenge," I said.

"Tell me about it," Claire grumbled.

As we reached the door to the salon, I paused and looked back. Even without turning around, I could tell that the level of activity in the ballroom had intensified since we'd entered ten minutes earlier. I watched a nearby worker drag a piece of heavy equipment into place and heard the loud rasp as it gouged the hardwood floor.

Claire and I both winced.

"I assume there are other options," I said. "Why does Leo Brody hold Puppy Fest in his house?"

"I have no idea. If it were up to me, we'd be in a television studio in downtown Stamford. Maybe he likes the convenience. But who knows? A man with his resources can do whatever he wants, even if it sounds illogical to the rest of us. And it's not like he's going to have to deal with all this chaos. That's my job."

"Yes, but—"

Claire reached past me, turned the knob, and opened the door to the salon. "Why don't you ask him yourself? Last time I saw Mr. Brody, he was in here sitting on the floor, playing with the puppies."

The room we entered felt small and intimate compared to the large expanse of space we'd just left. It was furnished like a cozy parlor with linen-covered chairs, a wide, overstuffed sofa, and matching Queen Anne accent tables. With its plush carpeting and floor-length drapes, the salon didn't look at all like the kind of place I'd have picked to house twenty-two playful, probably unhouse-broken puppies.

But then again, what did I know about the lifestyles of the rich and famous? I wouldn't have opted to hold Puppy Fest in a ballroom either.

A dozen medium-size crates were lined up against one wall of the room. Most were open and empty. Some of their previous occupants were asleep on the rug. Others were busy exploring their new surroundings. Though squeaky toys and rawhide chips were scattered around the floor, one puppy was lying beside an upholstered chair leg, chewing happily. Automatically, I leaned down and scooped him up into my arms.

"Thank you! I should have caught that." A harried-looking young man hurried over and took the errant puppy from my hands. "I'll put him back in his crate for a rest."

"Will, this is my friend, Melanie Travis," Claire said. "She has lots of experience with puppies and she's here to help out."

"Great to meet you." Will nodded in my direction as he leaned down and placed the puppy inside an open Vari Kennel. "And I'm glad you're here. We can use the extra hands."

"Where is everybody?" Claire looked around. "Jane? Mr. Brody? And aren't you supposed to have another helper or two?"

"Mr. Brody was called away. Something about a phone call. Jane's outside on the terrace where we've set up the ex-pens." Like the ballroom beside it, the salon had French doors that opened to the outdoors.

"Jack, who was scheduled to be here, called in sick this morning." Will didn't bother to hide his annoyance at that turn of events. "Lucy just ran to the bathroom, and yes, we're still waiting for two or three more people to show up."

"I don't understand," said Claire. "Why didn't the rest of the crew come over from Puppy Posse at the same time you did?"

"Well . . . because they're not exactly employed by us."

Claire flipped back several sheets of paper on her clipboard. She ran the tip of her finger down a list on the page. "I don't see a notation about that. Where are they coming from?"

"Claire?" The glass-paneled door that led to the terrace opened, and a woman came striding briskly into the room. She was younger than me, but not by much, with a strong build, short, spiky hair, and a no-nonsense demeanor. "Is there a problem?"

Then she stopped and stared at me. "Who are you?"

"Melanie Travis." I smiled and stuck out my hand. "You must be Jane."

"I am." She grasped my fingers and squeezed them so hard that I nearly gasped. When she released my hand, I found myself taking a step back.

"Why are you here?" Jane asked.

"I came to help out—"

"Who told you that we needed your help?"

"Jane," Claire said in a conciliatory tone. "Melanie is a friend of mine. She has lots of experience with dogs and puppies. I asked her to stop by."

"Then you've done your duty," Jane said to me. "And now you can be on your way."

"You really want me to leave?" I lifted a hand and gestured around the room. "You and Will are outnumbered here nearly a dozen to one. Where are the rest of your assistants?"

"I'm sure they're on their way."

"They should have been here already," Claire pointed out. "I was assured that Puppy Posse would have everything to do with our puppy participants under control. Will, do you have phone numbers for the missing handlers?"

"Umm . . . no?"

He looked over at Jane. So I did too. Then I

thought about something Claire had said earlier and guessed what the problem was.

"You hired family members," I said.

"I didn't have to *hire* them," Jane snapped. "They were coming anyway. Puppy Fest is a Brody family institution—we all pitch in and help out. Not that you would know anything about it."

Thank goodness for that, I thought. The more time I spent in this house, the happier I was to have no connection to the Brody clan. And considering how crazy my family was at times, that was saying something.

Claire checked her notes again. "I have some names here. Megan Brody?" She glanced up.

"That's Ron's daughter," Jane told us. "She and her sister, Ashley, are both coming."

"Trace Richland?" Claire read aloud.

"Trace?" Will stared at Jane. "You asked *him* to come?"

"He volunteered. You know he loves dogs. He's been a big help to us at Puppy Posse."

"Sure," Will muttered. "When he shows up. There's a reason the other employees call him 'Without a Trace.'"

I bit back a smile. Jane did not look amused.

"That was uncalled for," she said.

Will didn't apologize. Instead, he picked up two puppies who were playing next to his feet and left the room.

"I guess it's a good thing I'm here," I said into the silence that followed.

Claire gave me a grateful smile.

"That remains to be seen," said Jane. "Try not to get in the way."

She reached down for a couple of puppies, then followed Will out to the exercise pens on the terrace.

"I don't think I made the best first impression," I said to Claire.

"Don't mind Jane. She can be a bit of a control freak. But when she sees how useful you are, I'm sure she'll warm up to you."

Maybe, I thought without conviction. But I doubted that I would warm up to her.

"Now that you're settled," Claire said, "I need to keep moving. You'll be okay here, right?"

"Absolutely. I'm surrounded by puppies. What could be better than that?"

After Claire left, I checked to make sure that the two water bowls sitting on a waterproof pad near the wall were both full. Then I crossed my legs and sat down on the floor. Ten puppies were loose in the room and when I patted my knees, I was quickly swarmed by warm, wiggling bodies. Several puppies climbed into my lap. One jumped up and tried to grab my hair. Two others began to chew on my shoelaces.

I was interested to see that several of the puppies looked like purebreds. I picked out a Cocker, two likely Labs, and one mostly Beagle. The rest were a variety of shapes, sizes, and colors. Every single one was adorable. Not only that, but they were all happy, healthy, and obviously well socialized.

Kudos to Puppy Posse, I thought, *for doing such a nice job with them.*

I hadn't realized that Jane had reentered the

room until I heard her speak. When I looked up, she was standing over me.

"I imagine they're not up to your usual standards," she said stiffly.

I expected Jane to sit down beside me. When she didn't, I removed the puppies from my lap and gently disengaged the little terrier who was tangled in my laces. Then I stood up too. Jane had already moved away. Now she was looking at the water bowls. There was probably no point in telling her that I'd already done that.

"What are you talking about?" I asked.

Jane replied without turning around. "I'm sure you know."

"If I did, I wouldn't be asking."

"You're related to Margaret Turnbull."

"So?"

Jane ignored my question. Instead, she picked up a puppy who was asleep on the rug and placed him inside an open crate. Then she deftly separated two puppies who were squabbling over a toy. She was good with dogs, I had to give her that.

"Do you know my Aunt Peg?" I asked.

"Nope, never met the woman. But Libby told me all about her."

Libby? I thought. Then the memory cells kicked in. Leo Brody had a daughter named Libby who showed Dalmatians.

"Your sister," I said.

"Half sister," Jane corrected.

"Older or younger?"

She shot me a withering look. "Does it matter?"

"No, not really. I was just curious."

"You and everybody else."

I almost laughed. Did Jane think I was trying to dig up information to sell to the tabloids? Did she honestly think that the tabloids cared which one of the sisters was older?

"Apparently you knew exactly who I was when we met earlier," I said. "Why pretend differently?"

"This is my house. I can do whatever I want."

Seriously? I'd had conversations with third-graders that were more mature than this.

"I thought this was Mr. Brody's house," I said. At her age, it seemed odd that Jane wouldn't have moved out of her father's home by now. "I didn't realize you lived here too."

"You weren't kidding when you said you were curious."

The door that led to the hall opened and a young African-American woman came in. Dressed in jeans and a polo shirt, she had braided hair and a beautiful smile. Before I could introduce myself, Jane stepped between us.

"Lucy, there you are . . . finally. Take Tandy and Rex outside to the ex-pen, would you?"

"Of course." Lucy picked up the puppies and skirted past us.

"I'm not your enemy, Jane," I said when we had the room to ourselves once again. "I get the impression that you'd already formed an opinion of me before we even met."

"Let's just say that I know everything I needed to know."

"Like what?" Now I *was* curious.

"I've been to dog shows, okay? I know what you people are like. The only kind of dog that matters to you is one with special parents and a fancy pedigree. Never mind all the inbreeding—not to mention the over-breeding—it takes to produce your perfect champions."

"So it isn't just me you despise. It's all breeders of purebred dogs."

"Look around," Jane said shortly. "This is the end result of what you people do. An over-abundance of defenseless, abandoned puppies. The unwanted dog problem is huge. Do you ever stop to think about that when you plan your upcoming litters?"

"I've only ever had one litter," I told her. "Standard Poodles. Both parents are champions, which means that they have correct conformation, plus the intelligence and great temperament that dogs need to be successful in the show ring. Not only that, but both parents have had all their genetic testing done to ensure that they're healthy and to give their offspring the best chance of being healthy too."

Jane looked like she wanted to say something. I didn't give her a chance.

"There were six puppies in the litter. I kept one and Aunt Peg took another. The remaining four went to homes on Aunt Peg's waiting list, and I can guarantee you that none of them were unwanted. Some of the people on that list had been waiting more than a year."

Jane shook her head. "Screw the list. Those people should have just picked up a puppy from their local animal shelter. I'm sure there would have been plenty to choose from."

"Lots of people prefer to own a specific breed of dog," I said. "Sometimes due to past experience or maybe because of the job that they want the dog to do. You can't fault them for that."

"Why not?" Jane snapped. "Pound puppies and rescue dogs have just as much going for them as your pedigreed dogs do."

"I never said they didn't." I thought of Bud, who was hopefully on his way to the vet right now. "But you're not giving conscientious breeders enough credit. Does the shelter offer a health and temperament guarantee? Does it teach new owners how to groom and handle their puppy? Would it let them meet the puppy's parents, or offer to take it back at any time if they aren't able to keep it?"

"Look around." Deliberately, I repeated the words Jane had said earlier. "There isn't a single puppy in this room that came from a responsible breeder of purebred dogs. What you have here are the results of negligence, accidents, and just plain stupidity on the part of pet owners. People who are too lazy to walk their dogs or fence their backyards. Those who refuse to spay and neuter their pets. Or who think that letting their bitch have a litter with the dog next door will teach their children the facts of life. *That's* where these puppies came from."

I expected Jane to fire back another volley. I was readying another argument in reply. Instead, we were both startled into silence when the door was flung open and two teenage girls came bounding into the room. One was blonde, the other brunette, but both shared the same pale blue eyes and scattering of freckles over their cheeks.

"Hey, Aunt Jane! Here you are. We've been looking all over for you."

As one, Jane and I dove to the floor, both of us quickly scooping up recumbent puppies in the energetic teenagers' path. The brunette hopped to one side out of the way. The blonde just giggled at our hasty maneuver.

"Not so loud," Jane told them. "We're trying to keep things quiet in here so the puppies will rest until it's time for them to perform."

"Sure. Sorry." The blonde was still grinning. "Whatever you say." Her gaze slid my way. "We haven't met. I'm Ashley. This is my sister, Megan. Leo Brody is our grandfather. I guess you work at Puppy Posse with Aunt Jane?"

I took a moment to enjoy the affronted expression on Jane's face, then said, "No, I'm just here for the day, helping out. Jane and I met a few minutes ago. I'm Melanie Travis. Are you two twins?"

"Good guess," said Megan. "Not everybody catches that because we're not identical."

"You look alike to me." The puppy I'd picked up—a tan-colored female with long silky hair and big paws that promised growth to come—was asleep in my arms. Megan appeared to be the calmer of the twins so I asked her if she wanted to hold a puppy.

"Sure. Whatever." She held out her hands. "He won't, like, pee on me or anything, will he?"

"I doubt it." Will and Lucy had been popping in and out of the room, exchanging the puppies in the ex-pens for those that were playing inside. I was pretty sure this puppy had been a recent arrival. "And he is actually a she."

"She. Cool." Megan received the puppy into her arms. "Does she have a name?"

I looked at Jane for help.

"It's Delilah," she said.

"Delilah?" Ashley chortled loudly. The puppy opened her eyes and lifted her head. "Hey, look! She likes me."

"Shhhh," Jane said softly

The rebuke didn't have the slightest effect. Ashley was now bouncing around the room on the balls of her feet. She peered into an open crate, then kicked a ball across the room. It hit a table leg, ricocheted off, and came flying back.

When Jane had requisitioned these two family members to help out with the puppies, she'd clearly overlooked the fact that Ashley might need a caretaker herself.

"Ash," Megan said, her voice firm. "Sit."

"Sit." Ashley sank down on the couch. She held her arms up in front of her, wrists cocked downward to make her hands look like paws. "Stay. Beg."

Megan reached into a bag of treats on a nearby tabletop. She pulled out a puppy biscuit and tossed it at her twin. Ashley bounced up and caught it in her mouth. I heard the treat crunch as her teeth bit down on it.

Wow. And I thought my family was nuts.

Ashley swallowed, then said, "So where's Leo? I thought he'd be here. We only came today because we wanted him to see us."

My first thought was: *she calls her grandfather Leo?*

My second: Ashley and Megan hadn't come to the Puppy Fest to see Mr. Brody. They'd only shown up so that he could see them. Apparently Claire had been right about that.

Out of the corner of my eye, I caught Jane staring at me. She looked like she could guess what I was thinking. Once again, she looked annoyed.

Or maybe irritation was just Jane's habitual expression. Because I'll tell you what. I'd be cross too if I had to deal with these people every day.

Dressing up like an elf was nothing compared to how this was turning out. By the time Puppy Fest was over, Claire was going to owe me big time.

Chapter 5

"I need you to do something for me," Jane said. Hopefully she wouldn't tell me to get lost again. "Sure," I said. "That's why I'm here."

"Would you run over to the kitchen and get some bottled water?"

And just like that, I was demoted from puppy handler to waitress.

"How many bottles do you want?" I started counting heads. "One for everyone?"

"Oh, it's not for us." Jane was biting back a smirk. "It's for the puppies."

"The puppies," I repeated.

"I don't want to upset their little stomachs with town water."

She had to be kidding. Everyone I knew who lived in lower Fairfield County drank *town water*. Including me and my family. And our little stomachs were just fine, thank you very much.

"Bottled water," I said, just to make sure that we were on the same page. "For the puppies."

"You got it. I'm sure there's some in the kitchen. We'll need at least twelve bottles. Just tell them I sent you."

As if I wouldn't even have the ability to speak up for myself.

"It's a long way to the kitchen," I said sweetly. "Are you sure you don't want to write that down for me?"

"Nah." Jane was already turning away. "I'm pretty sure you can remember it."

Over on the couch, Ashley was grinning like a baboon. Taking a cue from her aunt's behavior, she was clearly enjoying my discomfort. She raised her hand and waggled her fingers. "Ta! Try not to lose your way."

Insulted by a girl whom I'd just watched eat a dog biscuit. I was pretty sure my day couldn't sink much lower than that.

A workman in the ballroom directed me to a back hallway that bypassed the family rooms I'd inadvertently entered earlier. The passage was a reasonably direct route to the kitchen and other working areas of the house. An hour had gone by since I'd made the trip in the other direction. By now, everything was unloaded and the crews had moved on. My trip to the kitchen was swift and unimpeded.

There, the catering staff was putting together various elements of the lunch that would be served buffet style to the on-site crews. Once prepped, it would be available whenever people had a chance to come and grab a bite to eat. At least a dozen people were working in the crowded room, all attending to tasks that looked more important than the errand that had brought me into their domain. Loath to interrupt the flow of frenzied activity, I hovered briefly in the doorway and looked for an opening.

"You there." An apron-clad man, busy filling a huge serving bowl with creamy potato salad, paused and pointed his spoon at me. "What do you need?"

"Bottled water," I said.

"One bottle?"

"No, twelve. It doesn't have to be cold."

Several heads swiveled in my direction. Obviously my request was more entertaining than food prep.

"Twelve bottles?" The man frowned. "Who's it for?"

"Jane Brody. She wants it for the puppies."

"What puppies?"

Well, crap. If the caterers didn't know the purpose of the event for which they'd been hired, I didn't have time to stand there and explain it to them.

Thankfully, I didn't have to.

"Are you kidding me?" A man who'd been standing with his head poked inside a sub-zero refrigerator straightened and turned around. "It's Puppy Fest today!"

He had dark, curly hair and broad shoulders that tapered to a narrow waist, and when the man turned and I saw his face, I felt a small jolt of recognition. I'd seen those same narrow features and light blue eyes several times already today. Apparently members of the Brody family shared several identifying characteristics.

Aunt Peg would have been fascinated by that. If Leo Brody were a dog, we would have said that he was prepotent.

"You must be another one of Mr. Brody's sons." I walked over to where the man stood. "I'm Melanie Travis. I'm helping out with the puppies."

"Right you are. I'm Joseph Brody. Call me Joe." Unlike his sister, his handshake was firm but not painful. "So you need a dozen bottles of water, is that right?"

"I'm not sure *need* is the correct word," I told him. "But, yes, that's what I was sent down here to retrieve."

"You'll have to watch out for Jane. She has a wicked sense of humor."

Not in my company, she didn't. In the time I'd spent with Jane, I had yet to see evidence of any humor at all.

"Don't let my sister push you around," Joe said. "She'll send you on a snipe hunt if you let her."

"I'll do my best."

"Good girl. Now come with me and I'll show you to the pantry. If we have bottled water, that's where it would be."

As I followed him across the beautifully appointed kitchen, Joe talked to me over his shoulder. "Have you met my father yet? Puppy Fest is his favorite day of the year. He likes to introduce himself personally to everyone who's come to help out."

"No," I admitted. "I haven't even seen him."

"Too bad then, you just missed him. He was

here a few minutes ago nabbing half a sandwich. Dad loves to eat. He'll grab just about anything around here that isn't nailed down. Ahh, here we are."

Like everything in Leo Brody's house, the pantry was enormous. When Joe flipped on the switch, track lighting revealed shelves on three sides of the rectangular room stocked with everything from canned food, to baking supplies, to dry goods. My family could have lived in there for a month without missing a meal.

"I see you're ready for the apocalypse," I said with a laugh.

"Never hurts to be prepared. And speaking of which, look . . . two cases of bottled water." Joe picked up half a flat and handed it to me. "Can you carry that all right?"

"Sure, no problem. Thanks for your help."

"Glad to be of service." Joe started to leave, then turned back. "A word of advice?"

"Sure."

"Jane likes to be in charge. "Don't let her bully you."

The warning sounded as though it was based on experience. With nine children from three different mothers, I wondered where Joe and Jane fit in the hierarchy of the family.

"I don't have much choice in the matter," I told him. "My only job today is to take orders."

"Oh well." Joe grinned. "Then I guess you're out of luck."

I carried the water back to the salon. Upon my arrival, Jane glanced at me with disinterest and waved vaguely toward a corner where some other supplies had been stacked. I dumped the bottles there—no surprise, the errand hadn't been an emergency—then headed outside to the terrace to see if any help was needed.

Two exercise pens had been set up in the shade of the house, their floors lined with a thick layer of newspaper. There were currently three puppies in each, including Delilah, whom I'd last seen in Megan's arms. While I was gone from the room, both twins had disappeared. And as far as I could tell, Trace had yet to show up.

I might not be Jane's first choice as assistant, but at least I was there. It seemed to me that should have counted for something.

Lucy and Will were lounging in the shade while they kept an eye on the puppies. "Everything under control out here?" I asked.

"Just great," Lucy replied. "Puppies are a breeze." She gave me an uneasy look and I wondered how much of my conversation with Jane she'd overheard. "You know, unlike people sometimes."

"We didn't have a chance to meet earlier," I said. "I'm Melanie—"

"Why is everyone standing around talking?" Jane interrupted. She leveled a glare in my direction. "You said you were here to make yourself useful."

"What do you need?" I didn't snap out an impatient *"now"* at the end of that sentence, but a careful listener might have heard it hanging in the air between us.

Both Will and Lucy pointedly looked away.

"I want you to go find Caroline."

"Okay." I paused. "Who's Caroline?"

"Caroline? *Caroline Richland?*"

I shook my head.

"As curious as you are about my family, surely you've seen her picture somewhere."

So then another Brody relative. Possibly another sister.

"I saw her half an hour ago," Will volunteered. "She was outside the living room. I asked if she was ready to come and kiss the puppies, and she said there were a few other things she had to do first, but that she'd be along shortly."

"That's Caroline." Jane was annoyed again. "Always running on her own schedule and figuring everyone else will wait. She needs to be here now. It's time."

So help me, I couldn't resist asking. "Time for what?"

"To kiss the puppies," Jane told me. "Weren't you listening?"

Well, sure. But I'd only half-believed what I was hearing.

"It's tradition," Lucy explained. "Before every Puppy Fest, Mrs. Richland kisses each of the puppies for luck. You know, so they look really cute on TV and get adopted."

"Does it work?" I asked.

"Oh, who knows?" said Jane. "It's probably just a silly superstition. But Caroline likes to make a big deal out of it. She says it's her contribution to the event's success. And our father humors her, just like he's always done. The rest of us plan, and prepare, and work our fingers to the bone, and then Caroline shows up at the last minute and blows a few kisses, and everyone tells her how special she is."

Jane abruptly stopped talking. She looked at the three of us and frowned. "Not that I'm jealous or anything."

No, of course not, I thought.

Suddenly the mission didn't seem like such a chore. I had no desire to go back inside the small, stifling room with Jane. "What does Caroline look like?"

"Tall and blond," Jane said. "Bone-thin, perfect manicure, flawless makeup."

Not that she was jealous or anything.

"She's wearing a red suit," Will added helpfully. "And"—his hand flapped in the air as he searched for the right words—"high heels. That's what you call them, right? They were red too."

"Oh, just ask anyone." Jane frowned. "Everyone knows who Caroline is."

"Will said he saw her near the living room," I said.

"Then start there."

"So it's okay if I wander around the rest of the house . . . ?"

"If you're only going to wander," Jane said shortly, "you'll never find Caroline in time."

"That isn't what I meant—"

"Enough arguing already. Just go."

So I went. The living room was empty, as were the next two rooms I peered into. The mansion had more rooms than I would have known what to do with, but Leo Brody seemed to have had no problem filling all that space with furniture. I paused and took a closer look. Probably antiques.

The only people I ran across in my travels were one maid and two men who appeared to be guards, positioned unobtrusively to watch over the private areas of the house during the day-long event. All shook their heads when I described Caroline.

Suddenly Jane's advice to *just ask anyone* wasn't sounding particularly helpful. Especially since I could hear a clock ticking in my head. The game was due to start in ten minutes. Puppy Fest was being broadcast live. The show would go on the air whether or not Caroline had performed her traditional duties.

Maybe Caroline was carrying a cell phone, I thought suddenly. And Jane would have her sister's number. My hurried progress through the house slowed, then stopped altogether.

Damn. Joe had warned me and I hadn't listened. Jane had sent me on a snipe hunt.

And I'd fallen for it. *Idiot.*

It was a good thing Caroline hadn't actually needed to be retrieved because by the time I made it back to the salon, the broadcast was already starting next door. As I hurried past the ballroom, I saw that the lights were on, the cameramen were filming, and Fred Brody was welcoming the audience to the Third Annual Puppy Fest sponsored by the Puppy Posse Foundation of Stamford, Connecticut. To his credit, Fred didn't trip over a single word.

Jane and her assistants now had four more minutes of relative calm while a pre-taped profile for each of the puppy players was shown to the viewing audience. The game would consist of two thirty-minute halves, with a ten-minute break in the middle and a five-minute wrap-up afterward. Jane had already decided the order in which the puppies would appear. A schedule was taped to the back of the door between the two rooms.

I opened the door to the salon and slipped inside. The first person I saw was my supposed quarry, Caroline Richland. She was hard to miss. From the top of her impeccably coiffed head to the toes of her Christian Louboutin shoes, the woman was so perfectly put together that the very air around her seemed to glisten.

And she was indeed kissing puppies.

Jane, Will, and Lucy were facilitating. The three of them had formed a canine assembly line and they had the process down to a science. Will lifted each puppy from the floor. Jane held it while Caroline applied her lips to the puppy's muzzle. Then Lucy carefully wiped away any lipstick stains before putting the puppy back down.

I wouldn't have believed it if I hadn't seen it.

As I stood there watching the spectacle, Jane caught my eye and winked. Or maybe I imagined that.

A monitor had been set up in the salon so we could follow the game's progress. Now we all saw that the profiles were coming to an end. It was time for the first group of puppies to make their entrance.

As Caroline exited the room, Jane thrust a

chubby black-and-tan bitch into my hands. As I tucked her under my arm, Jane placed one of the Labs in my other hand. Since Megan and Ashley—not to mention Trace—were still MIA, I'd finally been promoted to the position of puppy handler. Yippee.

"Missy and Jackson," Jane said. "They're the last two to go in. Just follow us and do what we do."

That sounded easy enough and it was. Ninety seconds later, all eight puppies were on the playing field. They went scrambling from one end of the large structure to the other, running, jumping, and tossing toys in the air. A whistle blew and the game began.

Lucy and Will returned to the puppy room. Jane remained behind, standing out of range of the cameras and watching the action live. For the moment, everything seemed to be under control. Claire was on the other side of the playing field. Clipboard hugged tightly against her chest, she was chewing on her lip as she watched the game on a monitor. I walked around to join her.

Claire saw me coming and silently beckoned for me to follow her. Together, we walked halfway down the large room. Close enough so Claire could still see what was happening, but far enough away that a wide-ranging microphone wouldn't accidentally pick up our conversation.

"*Where have you been?*" she whispered. "I checked on the puppies five minutes before the broadcast began and you weren't there. You're supposed to be helping Jane."

"I *am* helping Jane," I said with a grimace. "I'm

doing everything she tells me to. Unfortunately, most of it has nothing to do with puppies. Jane's had me chasing all over the building, running errands for her."

"That sounds like a waste of your talents. But I guess if that's what Jane thought she needed . . ." As she spoke, Claire stood up on her tiptoes. She surveyed the crowded room with a preoccupied frown.

"What's the matter?" I asked.

"I just realized that Mr. Brody isn't here. He told me earlier he was excited about watching the game live. I assumed he'd appear when it started. But I don't see him anywhere. Do you?"

I'd only ever seen Leo Brody in pictures and on TV, but I was certain I'd recognize him. I pulled over a straight-backed chair, climbed up on the seat, and had a look around.

"I don't think he's in the room," I said after a minute.

That wasn't what Claire wanted to hear. She exhaled a loud sigh. "I was so pleased when we started right on schedule. But now Mr. Brody is missing the game. I'm sure he meant to be here. He must have lost track of time."

Claire's gaze swung my way. Her eyes narrowed. "Did you just say that you've been running all through the house?"

I nodded.

"Good. Then you already know your way around. That'll help."

"Help what?" I asked cautiously.

"Someone has to find Mr. Brody and let him

know that Puppy Fest has already started. And I'm in charge so I can't go."

Wonderful, I thought. This quest had all the makings of another snipe hunt.

"I'll bet Mr. Brody has a cell phone." Never let it be said that I don't learn from my mistakes. "Why don't you give him a call?"

Claire's glare was withering. "Do I *look* like the kind of person who would have Leo Brody's private number?"

There was that.

An image of Claire in the elf costume popped into my head. I closed my eyes briefly and gathered my strength. "Where should I look first?" I asked. "Where would you expect Mr. Brody to be if he's not here?"

"Try his office. I get the impression that Mr. Brody lives for his work. I don't think he ever puts it entirely aside. I'll bet he got sidetracked by a phone call or an email."

"Office," I said. "I'm on my way. Where is it?"

"The other side of the house. East wing on the ground floor. I met with him there when I interviewed for this job. The room has an outside entrance, but I'm sure you can get there from inside the house too."

East wing, I thought. My head swiveled to the left. Claire sighed. She grasped my shoulders and repositioned me so I was facing the other way.

My sense of direction was notoriously bad. I could get turned around in the produce section of the supermarket.

"*East* wing," she said again.

"Right. I heard you the first time. That's where I'm going."

Spurred by Claire's worried expression, I left the room at a jog.

This wouldn't be like looking for Caroline, I told myself. I was in Mr. Brody's house, attending *his* event. If he wasn't in his office, surely there would be someone around who knew where he was. And the upside? Having been five minutes behind Leo Brody all day, I was finally going to have the opportunity to meet the man.

Now that I had my bearings, it was easy to follow the back hallway until it deposited me outside the kitchen. Lunch was now set out on a wide countertop, and a dozen people were milling around the room. Some were already eating; others were just beginning to fill their plates. My gaze sped over the assembled group. The catering crew was there, along with a bunch of workmen and even a guard or two. But Mr. Brody wasn't among them.

I crossed the kitchen and cut through the dining room to the foyer. This time, I went in the opposite direction from the one I'd taken earlier. My footsteps muffled by a thick Persian rug, I followed another wide hallway past an array of opulent rooms. The sheer size of the house seemed staggering to me. I had no idea what one man—even one with a big family—would do with so much space.

The corridor angled to the right as I left the central portion of the house and entered the east wing. Several rooms opened off this extended hallway. The door to the first was slightly ajar.

I'd almost reached it when I heard a loud gasp. Almost immediately, it was followed by a shriek of alarm. Startled, I hesitated. My breath jammed in my throat.

"Noooo!" a woman cried out. The plea ended on a strangled sob.

For a shaky moment, it felt as though my heart had stopped beating. I was half-tempted to turn and run. Instead, I rounded the corner and looked inside the room.

Chapter 6

At first glance, the room appeared empty. But after my gaze had rocketed around the interior, sliding over paneled walls, museum-quality paintings, and an enormous mahogany desk, it finally dropped to the floor. There I found what I'd been looking for.

A man was lying on the rug beside the desk. His body was on its side, facing away from me. One arm was extended outward, fingers stretched as if he'd been reaching for something when he fell. I couldn't see the man's face, but even so, I knew who he was. Judging by the grey cast to his skin and the utter stillness of his body, I was pretty sure I wouldn't be meeting Leo Brody today after all.

Above him, crouched over the body, was an attractive middle-aged woman. Blond curls fell forward over her face, not quite obscuring features whose skin was too tight to be entirely natural. There was a slash of bright red lipstick on the woman's mouth, and her voluptuous figure was encased in a formfitting leather suit. *Leather.* In summer, no less.

"What happened?" I asked.

The woman's head snapped up. "Who the hell are you?" Her shrill voice and combative stance stopped me in my tracks.

"Melanie Travis. I'm here working on Puppy Fest. I was sent to find Mr. Brody. *What happened?*" I asked again. This time, the question was edged with steel.

"I don't know," the woman wailed. "I just found him like this."

"When?" I hadn't seen her in the hallway as I'd approached. I wondered how long she'd been in the room.

"Not even a minute ago," she said quickly. Too quickly for my taste. "No more than that."

"Is he . . . dead?"

The woman bit her lip, staining her teeth with blood-red lipstick. She stood up and backed away. "I think so."

I stepped forward and knelt down gingerly beside the body. Mr. Brody's skin was cool to the touch as I slid my fingers along the back of his neck to the artery beneath his jaw. As I'd suspected, no pulse beat beneath my fingertips.

There was no point in running for immediate help. Instead, I reached in my pocket and pulled out my phone.

"What are you doing?" the woman demanded.

I rocked back on my feet and stood up. "Calling nine-one-one."

"No! Put the phone away! You can't do that."

"Do you have a better idea?"

"Yes. No." She turned and stared out the window behind her. "Wait a minute. Let me think."

"Think about what?" The phone was still cradled in my palm. Unless she came up with a good answer, I was using it.

"You have no idea. . . ."

"You're right," I said, when her voice trailed away. "I don't. For starters, who are you?"

"Becca Montague. Leo and I are . . . we were . . . friends."

Her telling pause and the emphasis she placed on the last word told me everything I needed to know about their relationship. As did the smug look on her face and the defiant set of her shoulders that dared me to contradict her.

"A friend would want the authorities here as soon as possible," I said. My finger began to press buttons.

"No!" Becca came flying across the room and tried to grab the phone away from me. "Leo would hate this kind of publicity."

One hand held her at arm's length. The other finished dialing. "Leo won't know," I told her. I glanced downward, then immediately regretted that decision and lifted my eyes again. "And he won't care."

"You'll be sorry you did that," Becca snapped. She shoved past me and strode out of the room.

Quickly I completed the call. Then I backed deliberately out of the office, being careful not to touch anything.

If I kept my gaze averted from the body on the floor, the room looked blessedly normal. A book lay open, spine up, on a reading chair near the window. Several file folders were neatly stacked on Mr. Brody's desk. A pair of reading glasses was perched on top of them. Sitting on a nearby credenza was a plate of cookies and a half-empty glass of milk.

Nothing appeared to be out of place. Nor did anything I saw in the office point to a probable cause of death. Mr. Brody was an older man—maybe he'd had a heart attack. Perhaps one minute he'd been sitting at his desk, finishing up some work before heading over to watch his beloved Puppy Fest, and the next he'd simply been gone.

As I reached the doorway, I realized that I'd been holding my breath. Suddenly it felt great to exhale. I looked up and down the corridor outside the office. It was empty. Becca Montague had disappeared.

I wondered if it was too much to hope that she had run away to summon assistance. One of the security guards would have been best, but right that moment, I would have been happy to see anyone at all.

"Hello?" I called out.

No one replied.

My second attempt was louder. Much louder. "Help!" I screamed. Then I added, for good measure, "I need help here!"

This time my plea had the desired effect. Almost immediately, I heard the sound of footsteps hurrying in my direction.

"I'm coming, miss," a male voice answered. "Where are you?"

"Outside Leo Brody's office. Please hurry!"

A man with buzz-cut hair, wearing a plain dark suit and shiny shoes, came flying around the corner. Judging by the combative expression on his face, he was fully prepared to confront whatever kind of problem might lie ahead. Then he saw me standing by myself in the hallway and slid to a stop. Warily, he looked around.

"What's wrong?" he demanded.

Silently I gestured into the room.

Sizing up the situation in a glance, the guard thrust out an arm and motioned me back. "Stay out here."

"I've already been inside the office," I told him. "Leo Brody is dead."

The guard swiftly confirmed my conclusion for himself. Then he looked back at me. "What happened?"

"I have no idea. He was like that when I got here two minutes ago. A woman was in the room with him."

"Who?" The word snapped out like a gunshot.

"Becca Montague. She said that she and Mr. Brody were friends."

"Where is she now?"

"I don't know. She left when I said I was going to call nine-one-one."

"And did you?"

"Yes. The dispatcher said she would send help right away."

The guard had taken out his phone. Now he slid it back in his pocket and stood up.

"What's your connection here? How did you happen to find the body?"

"I came today to work on Puppy Fest—"

He stared at me suspiciously. "That's taking place in the west wing. In fact it's going on right now. What are you doing all the way over here?"

"I was sent to find Mr. Brody and let him know that the game was in progress so that he could come and watch."

"Sent by whom?"

I've been interrogated by the police before. It's not a comfortable position in which to find yourself. This inquiry by the security guard felt much the same. On the other hand, I understood his reaction. Though I suspected he'd been hired to watch over the valuables in the house rather than its occupants, the fact remained that Leo Brody had died on his watch.

"Claire Travis. She's the woman in charge of Puppy Fest."

The man nodded sharply.

At least he recognized Claire's name. That was something.

"Why did she send you?"

"Claire asked me to come today and help out. We're friends. Actually, she's family. . . ."

His brow lifted, requesting clarification.

"Claire is married to my ex-husband."

"And you're friends," he muttered under his breath. He didn't sound as though he believed me.

Frankly, I didn't care. I had bigger things to worry about.

"Look," I said. "I'm a little busy right now. I'm supposed to be helping with Puppy Fest. Since you have everything under control here, I'm going back to the ballroom."

"It would be better if you stayed until the authorities arrive."

"The game will be over by then." I started to walk away. "If you need me, I'll be in the west wing."

"What's your name?" the guard called after me.

I stopped again. "Melanie Travis."

"Do you have any ID?"

"Not on me. I needed to have my hands free today for the puppies. I locked my purse in my car."

"Then you'd better—"

"No," I said, sounding every bit as exasperated as I felt. "I just found a dead body, okay? And even before that, I wasn't having a great day. There's somewhere else I really need to be right now. So I'm not going to stand here and argue with you about it. Do you know Claire Travis?"

"I know who she is."

"Claire will vouch for me. If you can't find me, look for Claire."

"Wait." The man held out his hand, fingers beckoning. "Let me see your phone."

I took it out and handed it over. He scrolled through the list of contacts until he found the number listed under "Home." He wrote it down on a piece of paper, then handed the phone back. "Okay, you can go now."

"Thank you," I said. I didn't add, *It's about damn time.*

I ran all the way back to the other side of the house. I wasn't sure whether I was running toward my obligations or away from what I'd just seen. Either way, it was a huge relief to be able to leave the whole horrible business in the security guard's capable hands. He would know all the proper steps to take, and I could get back to what I was supposed to be doing.

As I flew around the last corner into the west wing, I glanced down at my watch. Twenty minutes had passed since I'd left the ballroom. By now, the first half of the game would be nearly finished. Claire would probably be livid about my prolonged disappearance.

Claire. Realization suddenly stopped me in my tracks. I was going to have to break the news to her about Leo Brody's death. *Damn.*

She must have been waiting anxiously for my return because as soon as I stepped into the ballroom, Claire came hurrying over.

"Where's Mr. Brody?" She peered around behind me as if hoping that he would magically materialize.

"Claire," I said in a low voice. "We have to talk."

"Is he on his way?"

"No, he's not."

Her face fell. "What do you mean? He has to be here. This is his day. This is *his event*! Do you know how many hours I've spent working on Puppy Fest so that everything would be perfect?"

I shook my head. There was no point in answering.

"And now Mr. Brody *doesn't even bother to show up?*"

"Claire, there's a reason—"

"I don't care what the reason is." Claire growled under her breath. "Step out of the way, Melanie. I feel like punching something, and I would hate for it to be you."

We both heard the sound of approaching sirens at the same time. The ballroom was toward the rear of the house so their keening wails were muffled. Even so, it was clear that the emergency vehicles were closing in on our location.

"What's that?" Claire's anger was gone in an instant. "What's going on? Oh my God, is that why Mr. Brody isn't here? Is he hurt?"

I reached out and placed a comforting hand on her shoulder. "He isn't hurt, Claire—"

She shook me away. "Don't tell me he's being arrested," she whispered in a horrified tone.

"Claire, stop, okay? Mr. Brody isn't being arrested." I paused before continuing with the dire news.

"Then what?" she demanded.

"I'm afraid it's worse than that. Mr. Brody is dead."

"No. No, he's not." Claire stared at me in disbelief. "You must be wrong. I just saw him an hour ago."

"I found him in his office," I said quietly. "One of the security guards is there with him now."

"Which guard?"

I doubted that Claire cared who it was. Her brain was just casting around for any other piece of information so it wouldn't have to process the bombshell I'd just dropped on her.

"Beefy," I said. "Buzz cut. Shiny shoes."

"That's Clark. He seems to be a good guy."

When he isn't asking questions, I thought.

"I only met the security detail in passing. Mr. Brody took care of that part. There's a firm he uses. . . ." Claire sucked in a deep breath. "Are you sure Mr. Brody is dead?"

"Yes."

"And Clark thinks so too?"

Another time I might have protested the implication that my own word wasn't enough. Now I just told her what she needed to hear. "We both checked. I'm sorry."

"What happened? Mr. Brody looked great for his age, but I know he was in his seventies. Did he have a stroke? A heart attack?"

"I don't know," I told her honestly. "As soon as I found him, I called for help. The dispatcher said she'd send the police and an ambulance. That must be who we just heard. They'll figure out what went wrong."

We both glanced toward the other end of the room. Nobody else appeared to have been disturbed by the sirens. If indeed they'd noticed them at all.

The game's first period was nearing its end. A large time clock, positioned above the playing field, ticked steadily downward. During the half-time break, a pre-recorded promo about the good work the Puppy Posse Foundation was doing would be broadcast to the viewing audience. Volunteers were already busy manning the phone lines, accepting donations and steering potential adopters to the Puppy Posse website. Despite what had happened on the other side of the house, inside the ballroom everything was proceeding smoothly.

"So now what?" I said.

Claire looked surprised by the question. "We keep going. We have no choice. It's a live broadcast. It has to go on to the finish."

"Aren't people going to wonder where Mr. Brody is?"

"Hopefully no one will notice," Claire said with a frown.

I don't think either one of us believed that.

"What are you going to do if the police show up?"

"I'll worry about that when it happens. In the meantime, I have a game to run."

Claire strode back to the other end of the ballroom. I followed more slowly behind her. When she veered off toward the phone bank, I slipped back through the connecting door that led to the salon.

Will and Lucy were out on the terrace. Jane was alone inside the room. I watched as she gently placed two tired puppies back inside a crate. She latched the door shut, then glanced up and saw me.

As she straightened, she was already radiating anger. "I guess I should have known better than to count on you for anything."

"Sorry," I said. Though the woman didn't know it yet, she had just lost her father. Compassion moderated my tone. "I was called away."

"I guess that must have been more important than doing your job."

"It was, actually."

"So now what? Are you here to work or not?"

"I'm here to work," I said.

Jane barked out directions and I followed them. I refilled water bowls. I picked up soiled newspapers from the bottoms of the ex-pens and replaced it with fresh. When the game started up again, I helped ferry replacement puppies back and forth between the adjoining rooms. And through it all I kept my head down, obeyed orders, and said as little as possible.

"I guess that break did you some good," Jane said toward the end of the game. We'd just delivered the last set of puppies to the playing field and finally had a few minutes to catch our breath. "You're a lot more useful now."

I didn't say a word. Instead, I turned away and stared out the French doors. Not even Jane's taunting could tempt me to discuss where I'd been and what I'd seen while I was gone.

Forty-five minutes had passed since I'd left Clark waiting outside Leo Brody's office. Slightly less since Claire and I had heard sirens. I knew there would have been plenty for the authorities to do upon their arrival. Still, it couldn't be long until they made their way to our location.

As if my thoughts had conjured his presence, a uniformed police officer entered the other end of the ballroom. He paused in the doorway and took a look around, as if uncertain who to approach first. A moment later, Will came bursting out of the salon. He gazed wildly around the room, located Jane, and came hurrying toward us.

I backed away as he leaned in close and whispered something in Jane's ear. Having delivered his message, Will turned and ran. He looked like he couldn't get away from us fast enough.

Jane spun toward my direction. "What did you *do?*" she demanded. "There's a policeman in the salon. Will said he's looking for you. You're wanted for questioning."

"I didn't do anything—" My forceful denial was interrupted by the other officer who had crossed the room with quick, purposeful strides.

"Are you Jane Brody?" he asked.

Suddenly she looked uncertain. "Yes, I am."

"I'm going to need you to come with me."

"Why?" Jane's gaze skittered in my direction. "What's happening? What is this about?"

"Just come with me, ma'am. *Please*?"

As I watched the two of them walk away, the clock on the playing field ran down to zero. Aside from the wrap-up to be delivered by Oliver Gregson, Puppy Fest was officially over. Perfect timing.

Jane was on her way to receive bad news. My prospects weren't looking great either.

I went back to the salon to confront my own troubles.

Chapter 7

The police officer waiting for me in the salon had red hair and looked about twelve years old. That, plus the fact that his uniform was too big for him, lessened the effect of the officious smirk on his face. He introduced himself as Officer Sammit.

Since apparently we weren't sharing first names, I identified myself as Ms. Travis.

Officer Sammit was not amused by my reply. He made no attempt to hide his opinion that we were not starting off well. I figured that was his problem.

Will and Lucy stood at the edge of the room, watching the exchange with bug-eyed fascination. Now that Puppy Fest was over and most of the work was finished, Megan and Ashley had reappeared too. That was a good thing. Since Jane and I were both needed elsewhere, the more helping hands in the salon, the better.

"Jane was called away," I said to Will.

He nodded uneasily. His Adam's apple bobbed up and down in his throat.

"I don't know when either one of us will be back." I gazed around the room, addressing my question to everyone. "Can you guys handle everything here on your own?"

"Sure," Lucy replied. "No problem."

"You might start by retrieving the puppies that are still in the ballroom," I said.

Four young people went scrambling past us and disappeared through the doorway. I wished I could go with them.

"Let's go," said Officer Sammit. "Detective Young is waiting for us in the library."

Anxiety over the events of the past hour must have made me giddy. I was half-tempted to inquire whether Colonel Mustard was in the conservatory. Fortunately I caught myself in time. Officer Sammit didn't seem like the kind of guy who could take a joke. At least not while he was on duty.

Sammit set a brisk pace and I matched my steps to his.

I've had quite a few adventures in my life, and as a result I've probably had more contact with the police than most people. From my point of view, those interactions have not always proceeded smoothly.

Detective Raymond Young and I had crossed paths six months earlier when he was investigating the suspicious death of a petty thief and I was trying to locate a missing dog. At that time, I'd been struck by both his intelligence and his willingness to listen to what I had to say. I could only hope that his takeaway from our prior meeting had been the same as mine.

I had passed by the library earlier, catching a quick glimpse of floor-to-ceiling bookshelves, wide windows, and cordovan leather furniture. But now, when I entered the room behind Officer Sammit, I saw nothing but the tall black man seated in one of two wing chairs that flanked a massive fireplace.

Detective Young rose to his feet and gestured for Sammit to leave us. He and I met in the middle of the room.

For a moment, the detective stared at my face. All at once I remembered his piercing brown eyes. And how it had sometimes felt as though he could look right through me.

"We've met before," he said. "Haven't we?"

"Yes, last December. At Howard Academy."

"That's right. The missing dog. I thought your name sounded familiar. Please, have a seat. I have some questions for you."

The cushions on the leather chair opposite his were plump and inviting. Carefully I perched on the edge of the seat. I had no intention of getting too comfortable. Or of letting down my guard.

It turned out that was a good thing. Because Detective Young's first comment was a doozy.

"I understand that you were the last person to see Leo Brody alive," he said.

"No, that's not true." The denial came out more forcefully than I'd intended. Nevertheless, I shook my head for emphasis. "I never actually met Mr. Brody. Not . . . um . . . before. However, I believe I was one of the first people to see him after he died."

Detective Young leaned back in his chair. I suspected he'd done it on purpose—pulling away to make himself appear less threatening. I wasn't fooled for a minute.

"Explain," he said.

"I was sent to find Mr. Brody. Puppy Fest had started and he was supposed to be in the ballroom watching the game. But he wasn't."

Young nodded. No doubt someone had already informed him of the charity event's purpose and format.

"Claire Travis is the woman running the event. She was busy in the ballroom so she asked me to locate Mr. Brody."

"Claire Travis." He repeated the name thoughtfully. "Any relation?"

"Claire is married to my ex-husband. She is my son Davey's stepmother."

The detective's brow creased as he considered that. Seriously, am I the only person in the world who has a cordial connection with her ex-husband and his new spouse?

"What kind of relationship do you and Claire Travis have?" Young asked.

"We're friends," I declared. "*Good* friends."

Even to my own ears, it sounded like I was trying too hard.

"So . . . why do you suppose she sent *you* to find Mr. Brody?"

If he was hoping to assign a sinister motive to that turn of events, Detective Young was bound to be disappointed. Clearly he had yet to meet Claire. I'd seen baby rabbits with more sinister intent.

"She sent me because I was available," I said. "And because she knew that if she asked me to do something, I would get it done."

He nodded again. I was probably supposed to find that reassuring. And maybe even encouraging. Like now would be a good time to spill my guts.

If I had any guts to spill, that is.

For half a minute, the detective and I both sat in silence.

"Tell me what happened next," he said finally.

"Claire said she thought Mr. Brody was likely to be in his office. So I went there to look for him."

"You knew where his office was, then? This man whom you'd never met?"

Now I did settle back in my chair. There might have been some slumping involved. And maybe even a sigh. I was beginning to feel seriously annoyed.

"This interview will go a lot faster," I said, "if you don't treat everything I say like it's a potential minefield."

Detective Young held up his hands, palms facing outward. As a protest of innocence, it left something to be desired.

"I'm just trying to get the facts straight in my mind. It will be easier for both of us if you tell me everything completely the first time. That way, I won't make any assumptions that might turn out to be wrong."

The statement was followed by another encouraging nod. If Young was ever ready to put the police force behind him, he could probably have a career in psychiatry.

"Claire told me that Mr. Brody's office was on the ground floor in the east wing. So I went to the other side of the house and started looking around."

"Did you see anybody else?"

"Just some people in the kitchen who were eating lunch. Mr. Brody wasn't among them, so I kept going."

"Then what happened?"

"I went through the front hall and crossed into the east wing. I'd almost reached Mr. Brody's office when I heard someone scream."

Detective Young steepled his fingers beneath his chin. "Who was it that you heard?"

"A woman. I found out later that her name was Becca Montague. From the doorway to the office, I saw that Leo Brody was lying on the floor. Becca was leaning over him."

"Was she touching him?"

I thought back. "I don't think so. But I'm not entirely sure about that."

"So Leo Brody was on the floor. A man whom you've never met. How did you know it was him?"

"I've seen his picture in magazines and on TV. It looked like him from what I could see. Plus, it was his office. So I made an assumption."

"And Ms. Montague, what was she doing when you got there?"

"Nothing. Maybe crying. I don't know."

"But she was right next to Mr. Brody."

"Yes."

At this rate, I was going to be in this room all afternoon.

"Had you met Ms. Montague previously?"

"No. Before today, I'd never met any member of the Brody family."

The detective's expression shifted briefly before resuming its bland countenance. "Ms. Montague, did she represent herself to you as a member of the Brody family?"

"At first she didn't say who she was. But when I said I was going to call nine-one-one, she got very upset and told me not to. At that point she told me that she and Leo were *friends.*"

"*Friends.*" Young repeated the word, using the same intonation I had.

I was pretty sure we were both on the same page, so I nodded.

"Did she tell you why she didn't want you to call for help?"

"She said that Mr. Brody would hate the publicity. She told me that I would be sorry for not listening to her."

"But you called anyway?"

I had no idea why the statement was posed as a question. I was quite certain the detective would be aware that I was the person who'd made the call.

Before I could answer, there was a quiet knock on the library door. I turned in my seat to see who might be joining us, but I needn't have bothered. Detective Young wasn't having any interruptions.

He quickly stood up and crossed the room. Opening the door no more than a few inches, he held a hushed conversation with whoever was outside. They spoke for several minutes. Long enough for me to become more than a little fidgety.

When he'd closed the door securely behind him and returned to his chair, I said, "I'm wondering how much longer this is going to take?"

Settling again in front of the fireplace, Detective Young seemed surprised by the question. "I see no reason to adhere to a timetable. The important thing is to gather as much information as we can."

"I don't understand. Mr. Brody didn't look . . ." I stopped and searched for the right word. "Injured. I thought he must have had a heart attack."

"How far into the office did you go?" Young asked. "Were you close to the body?"

"I touched it," I admitted.

Detective Young's brow lifted. He hadn't expected that.

"I asked Becca if Mr. Brody was dead. She said she thought so. I wanted a more definitive answer."

"Why?"

I should hope the answer to that was obvious. "In case he was still alive and there was some way I could help."

"Such as?"

I threw up my hands. "Running through the house and screaming for a doctor? Or at least someone who knew CPR."

"I see. So you checked for yourself. Where did you touch him?"

"Mr. Brody was lying on the floor facing away from me. I slipped my fingers under his jaw and felt for a pulse. If it wasn't a heart attack, what happened to him?"

Detective Young's narrowed gaze made it clear

he felt he should be asking the questions, not answering them. "We'll have more information after the autopsy is performed."

"But you must have a guess," I prompted.

In deference to the high-profile nature of the deceased, Young appeared to be choosing his words carefully. "We have our suspicions," he allowed.

I waited for him to elaborate. He didn't.

"Are you telling me that Leo Brody didn't die of natural causes?" I asked.

"No, I don't believe I said anything of the sort."

Detective Young looked at me and frowned. He was probably recalling our previous encounter. If so, he might also be realizing that I wasn't going to allow him to brush me off so easily.

"We have reason to believe that Mr. Brody suffered from anaphylaxis. His lips and tongue were swollen. Probably his throat too. He appears to have vomited shortly before his death."

Detective Young paused, giving me a moment to absorb the news. Then he said, "Several members of Mr. Brody's family have told me that he suffered from a severe peanut allergy. Were you aware of that?"

Slowly I shook my head. "I had no idea."

"If so, you were an anomaly. Apparently it was common knowledge among those who knew him and worked for him. This entire property is a peanut-free zone. Mr. Brody's allergy was a life-threatening condition, and he took great care to make sure that everyone around him was aware of it."

"But I *wasn't* around him." I was getting tired of repeating myself. "I never met the man."

"Yet you were here in his house."

"I was doing a favor for a friend."

"So you said. For Claire Travis."

I nodded. I'd been hoping the conversation would move forward. Now it appeared that we were going backwards.

"I've been told that Ms. Travis would most certainly have been informed of Mr. Brody's allergy when she was hired. The caterers tell us that they were given strict instructions about ingredients, food preparation, and even equipment that could be brought onto the property. So it seems unusual that you would be the only person in the house who wasn't aware of Mr. Brody's dietary limitations."

All at once it felt as though I was being accused of something.

"I'm sure I'm not the only person here who didn't know," I said sharply. "Was the television crew advised of Leo Brody's peanut allergy? And what about the workmen who assembled the playing field? Were they informed?"

"I don't believe so," Young conceded. "But none of those people had access to any food."

"Neither did I!"

"So you say. And yet you were seen in the kitchen at two different times this morning. Not only that, Ms. Travis, but despite your professed reason for being here, you were observed on several occasions leaving the area where Puppy Fest was taking place and entering private rooms in Mr. Brody's house."

I tried to summon an outraged reply. It didn't come. Instead I was simply speechless.

"Do you care to explain what you were doing?" Detective Young asked after a moment.

Even I was surprised by the words that came out of my mouth. "Do I need a lawyer?" I asked.

"That is, of course, entirely your decision. Although if I were you, I would prefer to keep this conversation on a friendly basis. All I am trying to do is gather information. I'm assuming there were good reasons for your actions this morning. And it seems to me that it would be in your best interest to tell me what those reasons might be."

Once again, Detective Young seemed to be choosing his words with great care. Belatedly, it struck me that this death would be handled differently from others I'd been involved in. Leo Brody's wealth, his prominence in the business world, and his media-friendly social life would change everything.

No wonder the detective was determined not to overlook a single detail. His actions would inevitably come under scrutiny too. He would want to be very sure of his facts and conclusions.

And it was just my bad luck to be standing in his way.

Despite Detective Young's assurances, I had no illusions about my role in this supposedly friendly conversation. The phrase *cannon fodder* suddenly seemed apt.

For the second time, there was a knock at the door. Again, the detective held a quiet conversation from which I was firmly excluded.

"New information?" I asked upon his return.

"Nothing you need to be concerned about. Now, getting back to your movements throughout the house earlier . . ."

"There's a simple explanation," I said. "The first time I passed through the kitchen was just after I arrived, and I was lost. The second time, I'd been sent there to pick up a supply of bottled water for the puppies. I didn't touch or go near any food on either occasion."

"Bottled water," Detective Young repeated. "For dogs?"

"That was Jane Brody's idea, not mine. Claire asked me to provide whatever kind of assistance Jane needed. And that's also why I visited the private part of the house—because Jane sent me."

"Sent you for what reason?"

"Jane wanted me to find Caroline Richland and bring her to the salon so that she could kiss the puppies before the game started."

Detective Young stiffened. "This isn't a joke, Ms. Travis."

"Crazy as it sounds, I'm not joking."

He shook his head. I wondered whether the detective was doubting my veracity or my sanity. Probably both.

"And did you manage to locate Caroline Richland?"

"No, but it turned out that Jane knew where her sister was all along. She didn't actually need me to find Caroline. She was just trying to get rid of me."

Detective Young glanced up. I'd regained his interest. "Why would she do that?"

"Though I didn't know it ahead of time, it turned out that Jane didn't want my help." I paused, then added, "She doesn't like people who breed purebred dogs. Or any dogs, for that matter."

"Jane Brody is the director of the Puppy Posse Foundation? Is that correct?"

"Yes."

"It seems odd that she would have a prejudice against a fellow dog lover."

I shrugged. That seemed like as good an answer as any.

"I find it an interesting coincidence that every time you were seen somewhere suspicious, it was at Ms. Brody's behest."

Detective Young appeared to be thinking out loud. I remained silent and listened while he worked things through.

"You're under the impression that she was finding excuses to keep you from the salon," he said slowly. "But what if there was another reason for her actions? Suppose she was trying to establish your presence in other areas of the house?"

At first I didn't understand what he was implying. Then suddenly I did, and I didn't like it at all.

"Are you saying you think Jane Brody was trying to make it look like I had something to do with her father's death?"

Chapter 8

"Not necessarily. I'm merely taking the time to consider any and all possibilities."

I shook my head. Every possibility seemed crazy to me. Then again, this entire day was beginning to feel surreal.

"For that to be true, Jane would have needed to know ahead of time that her father was going to die today," I pointed out. "But that can't be the case."

"Why not?" Detective Young sounded genuinely curious.

"Because Jane had a job that required her to be in either the salon or the ballroom. Surely someone—Will, or Lucy, or the Brody twins—can account for her whereabouts at the time of Mr. Brody's death."

"If only it were that easy to pin things down."

Oh. It should have occurred to me to wonder about this earlier.

"Where did Mr. Brody get the food that contained peanuts?" I asked. "You said that he was hyper-vigilant. So it's not like he would have put something in his mouth unless he thought it was safe."

"We're still looking into that. There was a plate of cookies and a glass of milk in Mr. Brody's office. We think that's the most likely source."

Of course. Now that he mentioned it, I remembered seeing both those things on the credenza.

"We showed the cookies to the catering crew, and they denied ever having seen them before. The plate came from a set of family china, but nobody we've spoken to has any idea how it came to be in Mr. Brody's office, nor where the cookies came from. We've sent the remaining cookies away to be tested."

"Were there fingerprints on the plate?"

Young shook his head. "No, unfortunately everything was smudged. There was nothing we could use. And it appears that the cookies could have been placed in Mr. Brody's office at almost any point this morning."

"Why would he have eaten a cookie if he didn't know where it came from?" I wondered aloud.

"Apparently it's not unusual for the cook to leave a snack in Mr. Brody's office. He was known to have a good appetite."

"But the cook didn't leave this snack for him?"

"No. In fact, he isn't even here. Because of all the commotion with Puppy Fest, he was given the day off. We've sent someone to talk to him, but as he hasn't been seen on the premises all day, I doubt that he'll have anything to tell us."

It seemed incredible that a man of Leo Brody's stature could have been felled by something so totally ordinary. "Wouldn't Mr. Brody have tasted the peanuts in his cookies?" I asked.

"Whole nuts, certainly. But these cookies appeared harmless. It's possible, however, that they might have contained ground-up nuts or perhaps a nut by-product. If that's the case, Mr. Brody could easily have eaten several cookies without ever becoming suspicious."

"Then it was an accident." I didn't bother to hide my relief.

Detective Young didn't agree or disagree. Instead, he merely said, "Right now, we're asking questions and keeping our options open. Complicating matters further is the fact that on this particular day the house has been filled with outsiders since just after 8 a.m."

"It's been filled with family, too," I mentioned.

Young glanced up. He waited for me to elaborate.

"Leo Brody has nine grown children, plus grandchildren. Many of them make a special effort to show up for Puppy Fest."

The detective looked at me with interest. "Is there a specific reason for that?"

"Puppy Fest is Mr. Brody's pet project. Apparently, it pleases him when his family joins in to help make the event a success." I would have left it at that. But when Detective Young gave me another one of his persuasive nods, I found myself adding, "If I were a cynical person, it might occur to me that buttering up the wealthy family patriarch could lead to significant future benefits."

To my disappointment, the detective didn't comment. Instead, he rose to his feet, signaling that our conversation had come to an end.

"Thank you for your cooperation, Ms. Travis. If you think of anything else I should know, please get in touch."

Detective Young started across the room. I stood up and followed. But before he could usher me out the door, I wanted a few more answers.

"What about an EpiPen?" I said. "Considering the severity of Mr. Brody's allergy, wouldn't he have kept something like that around?"

"He would and he did. There are numerous EpiPens placed around the house for easy access. We've checked on their whereabouts and all are accounted for . . . except the one that should have been in his right-hand desk drawer."

"Do you think somebody removed it?"

"That's one possibility."

Young reached for the knob and drew the library door open. Obviously he expected me to walk through it. Instead, I planted my feet and stood my ground.

"One last thing," I said. "Who told you that I was the last person to see Mr. Brody alive?"

"I don't see how that is pertinent."

"You would if you were me," I told him.

His arm, placed around my shoulders, pushed me gently though the doorway. "Thank you for taking the time to talk to me."

As if I'd been given a choice, I thought as the door clicked shut between us.

* * *

I never made it back to the ballroom. Instead I ran into Claire in the hallway. She was on her way to an interview with Detective Young.

"Sorry I had to run out on you again," I said. "What do you want me to do now?"

"I guess you may as well go home. Will and Lucy started packing up right after you left. By now, they're just about finished." Claire was one of the most cheerful, energetic people I knew, but now she looked totally drained. The day's events had clearly taken their toll. "What a mess this whole thing turned into. Have you been with the police all this time?"

"Yup. Detective Young is very thorough. I'm sure he'll have plenty of questions for you too." I reached out and laid a hand on her arm. "Think about what you're saying before you answer, okay?"

"What do you mean?" Claire's voice lifted. She cast a quick glance at the policeman escorting her to the library—Officer Sammit, who'd done the same for me. He averted his gaze, staring at the ceiling while he pretended not to listen in. "You're worrying me, Melanie. I don't have anything to hide."

"I don't either," I said firmly. "But it turns out that Mr. Brody didn't die of a heart attack."

She reared back. "Then what happened?"

"Detective Young will fill you in. But it wasn't natural causes. Something went very wrong while everyone was gathered here in Mr. Brody's house for Puppy Fest. So I think we all better be worried about that."

* * *

I took Claire's advice and went straight home.

It was mid-afternoon, and Sam and the boys had just returned from a successful visit to the vet. Their trip must have included at least one additional stop because Bud was wearing a new rolled leather collar. Davey was holding the end of a matching leash as the spotted dog capered up and down the driveway.

Kevin had been watching Bud's antics, but when I parked the Volvo on the edge of the turnaround and got out, he spun around and ran toward me with his hands outstretched. "Mommy home!" he cried.

What mother doesn't love a greeting like that?

"You're just in time," said Sam.

I caught Kev on the fly and swung him up into my arms. "In time for what?"

"We're about to introduce Bud to the Poodles."

"Great. So the vet gave him a clean bill of health?"

"As far as he could tell. We boosted all of Bud's vaccines to be on the safe side and ran a heartworm test. We also picked up some ointment for the sores on his neck."

"But here's the best part," Davey chimed in happily. "Bud doesn't have a microchip."

"No chips!" Kev clapped his hands in the air.

Davey and Kevin weren't the only ones who were pleased. At some point in the last eighteen hours, I had already begun to think of the little dog as ours.

"I put Bud's picture on the bulletin board at the clinic and posted a notice on Craigslist," Sam said.

"Animal Control doesn't have a report of any missing dogs fitting his description. And when I told the vet where Bud came from, he just shook his head and wished us luck with our new dog."

"So that means Bud is really ours," Davey prompted. "Right, Mom?"

"Right, Mom?" Kev echoed.

I looked at Sam. He lifted an eyebrow, deferring the final answer to me. That made me smile. Then suddenly we were both grinning.

"Yippee!" Davey was just as adept at reading parental silent language as Sam and I were. "Welcome home, Bud."

Sam and Kev went into the house to let the Standard Poodles out in the fenced backyard. Since they'd been cooped up inside for a while, Davey and I waited out front, giving the Poodle pack time to blow off steam and attend to business. When it was time to join them, I reached over and took the leash out of Davey's hands.

"Just a precaution," I said. "If Bud is going to be a new member of the family, we want this first meeting to go as smoothly as possible."

"You don't have to worry about that," Davey told me. "The Poodles like *everybody*."

"Yes, they do—but Bud is a wild card. We don't yet know him well enough to predict how *he'll* react. And a pack of big black dogs all checking you out at once can be pretty intimidating."

"Bud will love it," Davey said with enviable confidence. "In five minutes, they'll all be best friends. You'll see."

Faith was the first to approach when we entered the backyard. The other four Poodles were still racing around the other end of the enclosure, probably hot on the trail of a rabbit. Faith noted my appearance immediately. As soon as we came through the gate, she lifted her head. Her tail was already wagging as her smooth stride carried her across the lawn. She was so focused on me that it took her a few seconds to notice Bud.

When she did, the big Poodle slid to a stop. Then, ears pricked and head tipped to one side, Faith covered the last several feet between us more slowly.

"Good girl," I crooned. "Come and meet Bud."

Holding Bud on the end of a lead was like being attached to a tiny tornado. By the time Faith reached him, he was already standing up on his hind legs with his front feet frantically pawing at the air. He hopped up and down in place and woofed with excitement under his breath.

Bud and Faith came together and touched noses. Each dog eyed the other one curiously. Then abruptly Bud dropped back down to all fours. He barely hit the ground before he bounced back up and issued a short, sharp bark.

That was all it took to alert the rest of the pack to the fact that there was an interloper in their midst. As the four remaining Standard Poodles came racing toward us, I reached down and scooped Bud up into my arms. Not even slightly concerned about the oncoming horde, the skinny little dog whined and wiggled to be set free.

The guy was a small dog with a Napoleon complex. He clearly had no idea of his own size relative to the rest of the canine world.

"In a minute," I told him as the stream of Poodles eddied around us.

Bud's rounded head whipped from side to side. His stubby tail wagged furiously. He was so excited that he could hardly decide which way to look first.

One by one, we performed the introductions. Sam and Davey helped. While we were occupied with that, Faith nudged Kevin several steps away from the fray, then held him there, keeping him safe. Lord I loved that dog.

It only took a couple of minutes for everyone to calm down. Then I unsnapped the lead from Bud's collar, lowered the little dog to the ground and gently released him into the group. For a moment, nobody moved.

Then suddenly Bud dodged between the sea of legs to extricate himself from the pack. Once free, he took off like a shot across the yard. In a rapid flurry of activity everybody else—including Davey and Kevin—followed. Sam and I just stood and watched them go.

"I bet there's some Beagle in that dog," I said, considering. "And maybe a bit of Cattle Dog."

"I was thinking Bull Terrier with a smidge of spaniel," Sam replied.

"Did the vet tell you how old he is?"

"Young. He couldn't pinpoint his age exactly, but he guessed around eighteen months."

I watched as Tar, the older of the two male Poodles, flew underneath the tire swing, dodged around a tree trunk, and doubled back to the group—only to crash smack into Raven. Retired now from a successful show career, Tar was the silliest Standard Poodle I'd ever met. When the God of Canines was handing out brains, Tar must have been off somewhere digging a hole. Or maybe he was just lost. Tar always meant well, no matter what kind of trouble he was getting into. But honestly that dog didn't have a clue. Not even one.

"I hope Tar isn't a bad influence on Bud," I said.

Sam just laughed. "From the looks of Bud, I think that's more likely to work the other way around."

As if to prove his point, Bud leapt up and grabbed a mouthful of Augie's hair. Beside me, Sam stiffened. My response was less restrained. I shrieked.

Augie is our only Standard Poodle currently being shown. He wears the continental clip, one of two adult trims approved by the Poodle standard for the show ring. A mane coat of thick black hair covers the front half of his body. His hindquarter is mostly shaved to the skin except for two rounded rosettes of hair on his hips, bracelets on each of his lower legs, and a pompon on the end of his tail.

Augie is approaching his second birthday, and the long hair on his head, his ears, and his neck has been growing—protected and coddled—virtually since birth. The Poodle currently needed just five more points, including a major win, to finish his championship. There was no way I was going to let Bud ruin Davey's chances of accomplishing that feat.

Luckily Davey had seen what was happening and he was already on it. Moving quickly, he inserted himself between the two dogs and gently disentangled them. His fingers slid the hair out of Bud's mouth, separated the strands, and smoothed them back into place. Then he looked our way and gave us a jaunty thumbs-up.

Smart aleck.

Sam's shoulders relaxed. Mine did too. I slid my hand sideways and threaded my fingers through his. He squeezed my hand and pulled me closer.

"You got back earlier than I thought you would," he said idly. "How was Puppy Fest?"

Loath to let the day's events intrude on our current happiness, I didn't reply right away. Sam must have sensed that something was wrong, however. He grasped my shoulders and turned me to face him. Then he tipped my face up to his and said, "What?"

I closed my eyes briefly. "Leo Brody is dead."

"Damn. When?"

"Sometime earlier today, while we were getting everything set up for the Puppy Fest."

"How?"

I told him everything I knew, which wasn't much.

"What a shame," Sam said at the end. "It sounds like it was a very unfortunate accident."

"I hope you're right. Detective Young is keeping his options open."

"You've met him before, haven't you? As I recall, you were impressed with him."

"I was." I gazed out across the yard, making sure that everyone was minding their manners. "He's smart, he's thorough, and he isn't intimidated by the Greenwich elite. All of which should stand him in good stead now."

Sam nodded. "The news outlets are going to be all over this."

"Like moths circling a flame. Virtually everything Leo Brody did was news, and this is guaranteed to be more of the same."

"I'm glad you're well away from it," said Sam.

"Me too," I agreed.

Chapter 9

Aunt Peg has more skills than most people can claim, but cooking isn't one of them. So when she showed up late Sunday morning bearing lunch for all of us, I knew something was up.

Then again, it was Aunt Peg. Where she's concerned, something is always up.

It was the best kind of summer day: warm and sunny with a light breeze. Fluffy white clouds floated across a clear blue sky. Davey and Kevin were playing in their tree house. The Poodles and Bud were entertaining themselves in the backyard.

When Aunt Peg arrived, Sam and I were on the deck. I was settled on a chaise longue with a book. Sam was polishing his outdoor grill. Aunt Peg let herself in the back gate, greeted the dogs with more enthusiasm than she lavished on the human members of the family, then went inside the house and set about unpacking the supplies she'd brought with her.

What choice did we have but to follow?

Now, with the back door open so we could keep an eye on things outside, Sam and I were sitting at the kitchen table. Faith was lying at my feet. The three of us were watching Aunt Peg with some bemusement.

"She must have heard about Leo Brody," I whispered to Sam.

He nodded. "The story was on last night's news and in the Sunday papers. Peg probably wants the inside scoop."

"What's that?" Aunt Peg asked. She has ears like an owl. Standing at the counter, she looked back at us over her shoulder. "What did I miss?"

"Not a thing." Sam laughed. "You never do."

I started to rise. "Would you like some help?"

"I thought you'd never ask. I've brought sliced roast beef, rye bread, and something called quinoa salad. It doesn't look like much, but the man at the market said it's supposed to be good for you. Come and make yourself useful."

I should have expected that. *And* what happened next. I'd barely reached the counter before Aunt Peg had taken my seat at the table. Now *I* was in charge of lunch duty.

"Did I hear you say something about an inside scoop?" she asked.

"We assumed you want to talk about Leo Brody. Isn't that why you're here?"

"Perish the thought," said Aunt Peg. "I came to check on your progress with Bud."

If anyone was fooled by that declaration, I had a racehorse I wanted to sell them.

Aunt Peg leaned around so she could see out

the back door too. The mismatched canine crew was playing tag in the yard. "He appears to be fitting in rather well, doesn't he?"

Two days earlier, Aunt Peg had recommended we drop Bud off at Puppy Posse. So let's just say that I wasn't entirely convinced by today's turnaround. Life with Aunt Peg has made me suspicious of everybody's motives, particularly hers.

I grabbed tomatoes and mayonnaise out of the refrigerator, set out plates, and opened up the bread. "What changed your mind?" I asked. "On Friday, you thought we should get rid of Bud."

"Friday he had fleas," Aunt Peg replied. As if that made all the difference. "I take it he passed his vet check?"

"Flying colors," Sam told her. "Assuming no one shows up to claim him, I'll make an appointment in a couple of weeks to get him neutered."

Racing in pack formation, the Poodles came flying up onto the deck. They zoomed across the wood floor, dodging nimbly around lounge chairs and a picnic table, then jumped off the other side. His short legs pumping like pistons, Bud scrambled along behind.

"I can see some Boxer in that dog," Aunt Peg mused. "And maybe a dash of Whippet."

"We guessed Cattle Dog and Bull Terrier," I told her.

"Don't forget Beagle," Sam added. "And we're probably all right. I bet there are at least ten different breeds in Bud's lineage."

I formed a tidy mound of sliced tomatoes. "It doesn't matter who Bud's ancestors are. The important thing is that he found his way here to us.

When I came downstairs this morning, Kevin, Bud, and Davey were curled up on the couch together watching cartoons."

"There's nothing so grateful as a dog who's been rescued from a bad situation," Aunt Peg said. "That little dog has landed himself in deep clover. Don't doubt for a minute that he's aware of that. And speaking of Davey, I trust he's prepared to face some tough competition next week?"

The following Friday and Saturday, Augie was entered in back-to-back dog shows in Carmel, New York. Both shows had drawn major entries in all three Poodle varieties and the competition was expected to be top-notch.

"He and Augie are as ready as they'll ever be," Sam said easily.

Aunt Peg approached dog show competition with impassioned enthusiasm that bordered on zealotry. And she would love to be able to inspire a similar do-or-die fervor in Davey. So far he had resisted her efforts—once even going so far as to quit the sport when the pressure became too great. Sam and I were equally determined that Davey's dog show experiences should be fun rather than stressful. As a result, Sam and I spent a lot of time running interference.

"I could give Davey a handling lesson this afternoon," Aunt Peg proposed.

"Thanks, but that won't be necessary," I said.

"I'd be happy to come by and help scissor Augie on Thursday—"

"We've got it covered," Sam told her.

"In that case, you've given me no choice."

I put down the knife, stepped away from the

tomatoes, and turned to face the kitchen table. *Now what?*

"Since we've exhausted all other possible topics of conversation, I shall be forced to discuss Leo Brody's untimely demise."

Aunt Peg crossed her arms over her chest and looked unbearably smug. *You've brought this on yourself,* her expression said.

Maybe I'd been outmaneuvered. Or maybe it was simply time to bow to the inevitable. I set aside the lunch supplies and joined Sam and Aunt Peg at the table. This was a conversation I wanted to have behind us before we called the boys inside to eat.

Noting my return, Faith stood up and moved around the corner. When I was seated, she settled in beside me. I reached down and scratched behind the Poodle's ears. Now I was ready to talk.

"Start at the very beginning," Aunt Peg ordered. "And tell me everything."

"For that, you'd be better off talking to Claire," I pointed out. "She was the one in charge yesterday. I bet she knows more than I do."

I stopped speaking as Davey suddenly appeared in the open doorway. To my surprise, Claire was with him. My son was grinning like a magician who'd just conjured a rabbit out of a hat. Considering our topic of conversation, I felt pretty much the same way.

"Hey, Mom, look who just arrived."

"I was going to ring the front doorbell," Claire said. "But Davey saw me drive in and brought me back here. I hope that's okay?"

"Of course," I said. "Come on in. We were just talking about you."

Claire looked stricken. "Oh no. It's because I need to apologize, right? I am *so* sorry."

"Sorry for what?" Davey asked brightly. He likes it when someone's in trouble and it isn't him. "What'd you do?"

Quickly, I stood up and stepped between them. "Davey, where's Kev?"

"Digging in the sandbox."

"Why don't you go help him?"

"Because things sound more interesting in here."

Of course they do.

"Out you go." I shooed him through the door. "Lunch in twenty minutes."

"Lunch?" Claire blinked. She started to backpedal out the door. "This is even worse. I didn't mean to disturb a meal." Then her gaze found Aunt Peg and she wailed, "And you have company too!"

"Nonsense," Aunt Peg said firmly. "I'm not company. And neither are you. Now step inside and join us before I'm forced to chase you around the yard and bring you in here myself."

Fortunately, the threat of that potential mayhem did the trick.

Sam stood up and pulled out a chair. Claire came inside and sat. Her nose twitched up and down. "I smell roast beef."

"Aunt Peg brought it," I told her. "Are you hungry?"

"No, not particularly. But I'll make the sandwiches, if you like."

"Sit," Aunt Peg answered for me. Her outstretched hand forestalled Claire's rise. "We'll eat later. Right now I want to hear what you have to say about what happened yesterday."

I'd seen grown men quake when directed to perform by Aunt Peg. But Claire just let that stuff roll right off her. Perhaps because she didn't show dogs and felt no reverence for Peg's years of accomplishments, Claire was about the only person I knew who wasn't intimidated by Aunt Peg.

Or maybe it was because Aunt Peg actually likes Claire.

Sometimes I wonder what that would feel like.

Claire began the recitation. I broke in every so often to add details and embellishments. Though we'd been separated for much of the previous day, it turned out that our stories jibed remarkably well. Aunt Peg listened mostly in silence—a rarity for her. Apparently, Claire's narration merited a level of respect that one coming from me did not.

"So you're the one who found the body," Aunt Peg said to me when we were finished.

"No. Becca Montague was in Mr. Brody's office when I got there. *She* found the body."

Aunt Peg looked thoughtful. "Or maybe that was what she wanted you to believe. Suppose Leo was alive when she arrived? Indeed, she might have brought those cookies with her and shared them with Leo herself. When you walked in, maybe she was checking to make sure that the peanuts had produced the desired effect before making her escape."

We all pondered that for a minute.

Finally I shook my head. "I don't think so. Becca was very upset about what had happened. Almost hysterical."

"You would be too, if you'd just killed somebody," Sam pointed out.

"And don't forget, she tried to stop you from calling for help," Aunt Peg added. "I find that most odd."

"But what would she have had to gain?" I asked. "She's Mr. Brody's girlfriend, right?"

I glanced over at Claire, who shrugged. "I only ever met the man in a business capacity. I never ran across that Becca woman. And I'm pretty sure I would have noticed someone wandering around in a leather suit."

"Maybe she took out an insurance policy on Leo's life," Aunt Peg speculated. Once she gets hold of an idea, she hates to let go without a fight.

"Then that would make things easy," I said. "Detective Young will be all over her, and we'll be able to read about the conclusion of his investigation in tomorrow's newspaper."

"Speaking of Detective Young . . ." Claire's expression sobered. "That's why I came to talk to you. This is all my fault. If I hadn't asked you to help out at Puppy Fest, you wouldn't be involved in this terrible mess at all."

"You have nothing to apologize for," I said firmly. "I was happy to help and I'm glad you asked me. Besides, I'm no more involved in what happened than anyone else who was present in Mr. Brody's house yesterday. I wasn't singled out for special treatment. I'd imagine the police talked to everybody who was there."

"Yes, they did," Claire agreed. "Detective Young made sure of it. But I was surprised by some of the questions he asked me."

"Like what?"

"Of course I was happy to help in any way I could. Not that I had anything useful to tell him because I was working all the way on the other side of the house. So I figured that the detective and I would have a short conversation. Except that we didn't."

Aunt Peg's fingertips began to drum on the tabletop. She was impatient for Claire to get to the point.

I was too. "Claire, what did Detective Young want to know?"

"Well . . . mostly about you."

"Me?"

Claire nodded. "He asked me why you'd taken part in the event. And what you were doing at various times of the day. He was particularly interested in why I had picked you to send to Mr. Brody's office."

"That's no big deal," I said. In truth I found the detective's level of scrutiny a little alarming.

"That's not all," Claire mumbled.

"There's more?" So help me, Aunt Peg sounded pleased by this turn of events.

Once again, my hand left my lap and drifted downward. My fingers tangled in the dense curls on Faith's head as I patted her for reassurance.

She gazed upward and our eyes met. *How bad can things be when your dog loves you?*

"I told Detective Young he was being nosy," Claire said stoutly. "That was when he asked me if I was aware this was the third time that someone you knew had died under suspicious circumstances."

The third time was putting it mildly. Thank goodness the detective didn't know the full extent of my previous adventures.

"But I didn't *know* Leo Brody," I pointed out. "I never even met the man."

"But you were there," Claire said unhappily.

"If I were Detective Young, I'd probably wonder too," Aunt Peg reflected.

"You are *not* helping," I told her.

"So I'm really sorry," Claire finished. "I hope I haven't gotten you into any trouble."

Sam reached over and patted Claire's shoulder. "None of this is your fault. Nobody needs to get Melanie into trouble. She attracts problems like this all on her own."

Aunt Peg turned to address me. "So what are you going to do about *that?*"

I gazed out the open doorway. Davey and Kevin had left the sandbox and were engaged in a lively game of tag. Several Poodles and one small spotted dog were playing along too. In another minute, that hungry crew would come bounding into the kitchen looking for lunch. It was time to make the sandwiches.

I stood up and walked over to the counter.

"*Well?*" Aunt Peg demanded. She wasn't about to let me get away that easily.

When I turned back to the table, all three were staring at me. Faith was watching, too. "I don't intend to do anything. Leo Brody's death is not my problem."

Somebody snorted derisively under their breath. It might have been Sam. It could have been Aunt Peg. At least it wasn't me.

Chapter 10

I managed to keep my word for almost a week. Between Gymboree classes for Kevin, soccer camp for Davey, and two dog shows for Augie, coming up on Friday and Saturday, it was a busy week. Nevertheless I still managed to keep a close eye on the local news. Okay, to be perfectly honest, I made sure that I read anything and everything having to do with Leo Brody's death.

Surprisingly, there wasn't much.

An obituary in the *Greenwich Time* newspaper lauded Brody's achievements in the business world and his dedication to philanthropy. The Puppy Posse Foundation even got a brief acknowledgment. I learned which schools Leo Brody had attended, what clubs he belonged to, and about his military service during the Vietnam War. The obituary listed the names of Brody's three ex-wives, nine children, and six grandchildren. There was no mention of Becca Montague anywhere.

A small private funeral was held in Connecticut. Those who wished to contribute to their favorite charity were asked to make a donation in lieu of flowers. A memorial service for Leo Brody was scheduled to take place in New York City at the end of the month.

What I didn't see—despite some rather diligent searching when I thought no one was looking—was any mention of a police investigation. I probably should have been relieved by that. And yet the omission left me with a vague feeling of dissatisfaction instead.

We awoke Friday morning to the sound of rain lashing against the roof of the house. Even worse, the forecast predicted that the showers would continue throughout the day.

Sam and Davey had already devoted a considerable amount of time and effort to making Augie show ring ready—first clipping, then bathing, and then a meticulous blow-dry of the Poodle's thick coat. Add that to the necessity of keeping all that hair smooth and dry until the moment Augie stepped into the ring, and the prospect of a downpour at an outdoor dog show was definitely something to dampen the mood.

That being the case, it was a good thing that one of us had the resilience of a twelve-year-old. Davey flatly refused to be discouraged by the bad weather. Between the end of the school year, a vacation we'd taken to the mountains, and the start of the boys' summer activities, nearly two months had passed since we'd last been to a dog show. Impatient to compile the remaining points needed to finish Augie's championship, Davey was eager to get his dog back in the ring.

We packed up the car and set out early. Augie came with us, obviously, but we left the rest of the crew at home. The Poodles had the run of the house; Bud was currently locked inside a large crate in the kitchen. We'd discovered the hard way that the little dog loved to chew.

Owning Standard Poodles had obviously spoiled us in that regard. Told to leave something alone, they did. Bud had other ideas. Not only that, but he was a sneaky little dog. He'd snatch up a prize, drag it behind the couch, and destroy it there. My favorite pair of loafers had been the first casualty of Bud's clandestine activities. Now we crated him when we were out of the house. It just made things easier.

The trip to the show ground in southern Putnam County took just over an hour. Dog show exhibitors are a resolute and determined breed. We have to be because it's not unusual to drive hundreds of miles in search of good judges, elusive points, and major entries. By those standards, this show was taking place virtually around the corner.

Three enormous tents had been set up on the field in Veterans Memorial Park where the show was being held. Two of the tents formed wide center aisles for long rows of show rings that extended outward on either side of them. The third was the handlers' tent, where exhibitors congregated to ready their dogs to compete. Crammed with grooming tables, crates, generators, chairs, and ex-pens, it was also the best place on the show ground for socializing, hearing the latest gossip, and rehashing the day's results.

Sam pulled his SUV right up next to the tent so we could unload all of our gear without getting soaked. Augie danced on the seat with excitement as he watched us carry his crate and table under the tent and set them up. When his turn came, Sam gathered the big black dog into his arms, carried him swiftly between car and tent, and deposited him on the tabletop without his feet ever touching the ground.

In a house filled with dogs, Augie was the first Standard Poodle that belonged solely to Davey. Which meant that showing him to his championship was Davey's responsibility. Sam was guiding the two of them through the process. My assignment was to stay out of their way. By now, I had that part down pat.

As soon as Augie was on the table, Sam and Davey unpacked the grooming supplies and got to work. We had two hours before the start of the Standard Poodle judging, but they had plenty to do. First, Augie's coat needed to be meticulously line-brushed. Then the long hair on his ears would be unwrapped, and his comfortable, everyday topknot would be taken out and replaced by the tighter, precisely positioned version he would wear in the ring.

After that, Sam would help Davey apply the layers of hair spray that would make the plush hair on Augie's head, neck, and back stand up straight. Lastly, careful scissoring would add a finish, ensuring that all the components of the Poodle's trim presented a smooth and balanced appearance.

While Sam and Davey got started, Kevin and I

backed the SUV out of the unloading zone and drove it to the parking area on the other side of the big field. Rain was still coming down in sheets, and watching the windshield wipers slap back and forth put a huge smile on Kevin's face. That child adored water. Sometimes I swore he must be half fish.

A yellow hooded slicker, purchased with an inevitable growth spurt in mind, covered Kev's body from his head to the tops of his red rubber boots. As I locked the car behind us, he scampered over to the nearest puddle, bounced up in the air, and landed in the water with a loud splash.

Luckily I was standing just out of range. Otherwise I'd have gotten soaked.

"Come on, Kev, let's go." I held out my hand. "We need to get back to the tent. Davey and Dad are waiting for us."

"In a minute."

As Kevin jumped again and produced another impressive splash, my phone buzzed in my pocket. When I pulled it out, I saw Aunt Peg's name on the screen. Why wasn't I surprised?

"Where are you?" she asked without preamble.

"In the parking area. Kevin is jumping in puddles. Want to join us?"

"Surely you're joking."

"He thinks it's fun," I said brightly.

"Kevin is three." Her voice was dry. "A juice box can entertain him for half an hour. I have more important things to do."

"Like what?"

I waggled my fingers in Kevin's direction and he

came and took my hand. We started back across the park.

"Libby Rothko is here today showing her Dalmatians," Aunt Peg said. "Considering that you were there when her father died, I was thinking you might want to pay your condolences."

Leo Brady hadn't even been dead a week. And his daughter was at the dog show. Exhibiting Dalmatians. I couldn't decide whether I wanted to applaud her dedication to the sport of dogs or denounce her lack of respect for her father's memory.

Or maybe the whole thing was none of my business.

"Libby Rothko doesn't even know who I am," I said. "I doubt that she cares about hearing my condolences."

"Of course she does," Aunt Peg replied. "I told her that you'd be coming around to speak with her."

Just once, it would be nice if Aunt Peg would let me make my own choices. And maybe even my own mistakes. A little advice is a good thing. But Aunt Peg's version of guidance sometimes felt like a collar around my neck.

"I'm busy," I lied.

"Bring Kevin with you. I'm sure Libby would love to meet him."

I truly had my doubts about that. But anyway, care of my three-year-old son wasn't what I had been referring to.

"I'm heading back to the handlers' tent to help Sam and Davey with Augie," I said.

"Don't be ridiculous," Aunt Peg sniffed. "If they

don't need my help getting that dog ready for the show ring, they certainly don't need yours."

I wished I had a good answer for that. Unfortunately there wasn't one. Instead, I sighed and said, "When?"

"When what?"

"When is Libby expecting me?"

"Now would be good."

Of course it would.

"Where is she?"

"Libby has her crate set up next to the Dalmatian ring, and she's grooming a dog on top of it. It's ring eight. I'll meet you there."

I slid my thumb down to disconnect the call but Aunt Peg had beaten me to it. Having gotten what she wanted from me, she was already on to the next thing.

"See phone?" asked Kev.

My son held up his hand and I placed the device in it. He frowned at the dark screen, then rotated the phone sideways and had another look. It didn't help. Kev shook his head in confusion.

"Where's Aunt Peg?" he asked.

There was no way I could explain the magic of a wireless connection to a three-year-old. Especially since I didn't actually understand it myself.

"Aunt Peg had to go," I told him. "But we'll see her again in just a minute."

We'd been heading in the direction of the handlers' tent, but now I angled our progress toward the middle of the big field. Mid-morning, all the show rings were already in use.

It's difficult to be a dog show exhibitor on a rainy day, but it's no picnic being a judge either.

Almost all were wearing boots and hats. One judge
we passed on our way to the Dalmatian ring appeared to be entirely encased in clear plastic. Some
attempted to remain dry by standing beneath the
covered portion of their rings, but most were stepping out into the rain to get a better look at the
dogs they were judging. I half-expected to see
them shake off when they returned to the tent,
just like the canine competitors did.

Even on a sunny day, the tent-covered aisle between the rings would have been crowded with dogs
and exhibitors. That day, with spectators trying to
escape the weather as well, the narrow passageway
was a madhouse. Kev and I had barely gone three
yards before I leaned down and picked him up.

"Pat dog?" he asked, his head whipping around
as a pair of regal Salukis went gliding by.

"Sorry, not now." I hugged him to me. With all
the commotion, Kev would be much safer in my
arms. "Maybe later, after Augie is finished in the
ring."

Aunt Peg was six feet tall. Even in a crowd it was
easy to pick her out, and especially so in a crowd
like this one where most people were leaning
down looking at their dogs. Peg saw us coming
and lifted a hand high above her head to wave us
to her side. The broad beckoning gesture allowed
for no second thoughts. When Aunt Peg sum-
moned, attendance was compulsory.

The various members of the Brody family I'd
met the previous week had shared similar features
and coloring. I expected Libby Rothko to fit the
same physical model. I couldn't have been more
wrong.

Libby was tall and slender, and every bit as sleek as the Dalmatian that was sitting atop the crate beside her. Her sable-colored hair was pulled back in a tight ponytail, a hairstyle that accentuated her high cheekbones and olive-toned skin. Beneath dark, dramatic eyebrows, her eyes were a deep shade of brown. She was dressed in a sunny yellow suit that would provide the perfect show-ring backdrop for her liver-spotted Dal. No doubt it had been chosen for precisely that reason.

Aunt Peg performed the introductions. Libby and I shook hands.

Kev gave her a cheery wave. "Pat dog?" he asked hopefully.

The Dalmatian was wagging its tail in a friendly manner but I angled Kevin away anyway. Heaven forbid a passerby touch a Poodle when it's about to go in the ring. I knew that grooming requirements weren't nearly as exacting for a short-haired breed, but I wasn't about to take any chances.

Libby noted the evasive tactical move with approval. She ignored Kevin's question and said to me, "You're the woman who solves mysteries."

I guessed that meant I didn't have to wonder what she and Aunt Peg had been talking about before my arrival.

"I'm very sorry for your loss," I said. "I never had the pleasure of meeting your father, but I'm sure he was a wonderful man."

"He was." Libby nodded. "Dad was absolutely the best. He was a kind and gentle man who dedicated his life to trying to help others. And he didn't deserve what happened to him."

"No indeed," Aunt Peg agreed heartily.

"Were you there last Saturday?" I asked. I hadn't seen Libby at the event, but Leo Brody's mansion was huge. There had probably been any number of people present on that day whom I hadn't seen.

"Puppy Fest? Heavens, no." Libby blew out an indelicate snort. "As if I would have any desire to take part in that circus."

Aunt Peg and I shared a look.

"Why, Libby, you surprise me," Peg said. "The event was in aid of a very good cause. What didn't you like about it?"

"The cause itself is great." She reached up and smoothed back a strand of hair that had worked its way loose from the ponytail. "That wasn't the problem. It never is."

I waited for Libby to expand on what she'd said. Instead, the woman turned away from us and began to rummage through her tack box. Behind her back, I raised my eyebrows and aimed a pointed glare in Aunt Peg's direction.

My aunt is known for her ulterior motives. This time, however, it appeared that she had dragged us over here for nothing. Now that I'd paid my condolences, it was apparently time for Kevin and me to leave.

Then Libby yanked a slender brown show lead out of the box, turned around, and said, "If you were there, I guess you must have met my family."

"I met some of them. There seemed to be a lot of Brody relatives in attendance."

"Of course there were." She sounded annoyed. "That's the whole point, isn't it?"

"Yup," Kevin replied, nodding his head for emphasis. He likes answering questions, whether they're addressed to him or not.

Surprised, Libby flicked her gaze his way. "Out of the mouths of babes . . ."

"What point are you talking about?" Aunt Peg asked.

"Puppy Fest is supposed to be an extravaganza of Brody goodwill, but that's such a joke," Libby said grimly. "Everybody makes a big deal of showing up and pretending to be interested. It's pathetic. And it's all just a charade. You couldn't pay me to get mixed up in that again."

Chapter 11

Claire had alluded to something similar. But in light of what had happened, I found myself wanting to hear more. Especially from a source within the family.

"How is it a charade?" I asked.

Libby cast a quick glance toward the ring. Bulldogs were currently being judged. Dalmatians would follow. Seeing that she still had time to wait, Libby relaxed and leaned back against the edge of her grooming table.

As soon as she came within range, her Dalmatian stepped forward and rested his head on her shoulder. The dog's long pink tongue snaked out and licked the bottom of her ear. Kevin giggled with delight.

"Licked your ear," he chortled. "Funny dog."

Libby reached up to pat the Dal's cheek and smiled at Kev. "His name is Troy, and he would agree with you. He thinks he's pretty funny too."

Then she turned back to me, and her expression sharpened. "It's no secret that my father is . . . was . . . a very wealthy man."

Aunt Peg and I both nodded.

"Maybe you're also aware that he was married several times?"

Taking a page from Detective Young's playbook, I offered another encouraging nod.

"I come from a big family," Libby said. "Dad married his first wife, Wendy, right after college. They had three children, my older half-siblings. A decade later, my mother became his second wife, and my sister Caroline and I were added to the mix. Clarissa was wife number three. My parents were already divorced by the time she showed up. Clarissa popped out four more kids and probably would have kept going if my father hadn't divorced her too."

"Nine children is a lot," I said.

"Tell me about it." Libby snorted.

"Did you have a pleasant childhood?"

"Sure. When you're a child, you think the way you live is normal. And our lives were pretty idyllic. Everyone worked hard to make us believe that we were one big, happy family." Her hand cradled Troy's head, fingers scratching beneath the Dalmatian's chin. "If there were tensions between the ex-wives and Dad, we were unaware of it. The house was always filled with kids. There was always somebody around to play with. Back then, we never felt the need to compete with one another."

She paused to dwell on the memory for a bit, then said, "But of course we had to grow up. And now that we're all adults, we have a better understanding of how the world works. I guess it was inevitable that everything would change."

If Libby continued to beat around the bush, we wouldn't hear the end of the story before the Dalmatian judging started. Aunt Peg, silent as a clam, was no help. So I jumped in and got to the point.

"I assume we're talking about money," I said. "Even with a large family like yours, there must be more than enough to go around."

"There would be . . . if it was made available to us. But my father was always very strict when it came to finances. As kids, we all had chores to do each week. Anyone who slacked off didn't get their allowance, no excuses allowed. And once we got out of college, Dad sent us off to make it on our own. He said it wasn't right for him to continue to support us when there were so many people that needed help who hadn't enjoyed all the advantages we had."

"Leo had a point," Aunt Peg said. "That sounds like responsible parenting to me."

"I agree with you," Libby replied. "But I was in the minority. Other family members weren't happy about what Dad called his 'tough love.' They felt they'd been raised to expect a certain standard of living, and when it went away, well . . . they became pretty bitter about it."

Kevin was growing heavy in my arms. I took a look around, then set him down in the empty space beneath the grooming table, where he'd be hemmed in by our three sets of legs. Kev grabbed a Matchbox car out of the pocket of his slicker and began to push it through the grass. With luck, that would keep him entertained for a few minutes.

"What does that have to do with Puppy Fest?" I asked.

"My father adored Puppy Fest," Libby said. "It was his favorite day of the year."

"Of course it was," I agreed. "How could anybody *not* love puppies?"

"You would know the answer to that if you were a member of my family. Especially if you resented the fact that money you felt should be spent on your needs was going instead to support a bunch of mangy mongrels."

"Mangy mongrels?" Aunt Peg's voice rose.

"Those aren't my words, but I've heard them used often enough when my father wasn't around."

"I would think an attitude like that would make your family stay away from Puppy Fest rather than the reverse," I said.

"No, not a chance." Libby shook her head. "Puppy Fest became the adult version of the chores we'd had to do when we were kids. Show up and get a gold star for participation. Stay away and risk annoying the person who holds the purse strings."

Even if Puppy Fest was a self-serving opportunity for other family members, I still had to wonder why Libby hadn't attended the event. Her relatives' motives aside, Libby claimed to have a warm relationship with her father. That alone should have been enough to induce her to take part in the display of family solidarity.

Libby pushed off from the table and stood. The Best of Breed class in Bulldogs was filing into the ring. The Dalmatian judging would be starting shortly.

"I'm going to be blunt," she said.

"Please do," I shot back. Libby wasn't the only one who needed to be somewhere. Time was passing in my life too.

"I'm worried about what happened," she said. "The whole scenario doesn't make sense to me. Dad was too careful about what he ate. He *never* slipped up. And am I really supposed to believe that it was a coincidence that his EpiPen went missing just when he needed it most?"

"Those are all good questions. What do the police have to say about them? Have you talked to Detective Young?"

"Only briefly," Libby grumbled. "He was the one who told me that they'd established the cause of death and that it's what we all suspected. My father died of anaphylactic shock after ingesting ground-up peanuts. Young also informed me that without any indication of foul play, they won't be investigating further. The authorities have ruled my father's death a tragic accident."

That came as a surprise.

I knew I should have been relieved. That outcome signaled the end of the detective's nosy inquiry. But instead what I felt was a sharp stab of indignation on Leo Brody's behalf. The authorities might not have agreed with me, but I still felt there were questions that needed to be answered.

"Are you sure?" I blurted out.

"Of course I'm sure." Libby didn't look any happier about the conclusion than I was. "That's exactly what the detective said. I don't understand it. My father is gone. And just because he died after eating a cookie, it seems like nobody is taking this seriously."

"Maybe Melanie can help," Aunt Peg said.

For once Aunt Peg and I were in agreement. Having happened on the scene mere minutes too late, I also wanted to know the truth about what had transpired that morning in Leo Brody's office.

"That's a great idea," Libby concurred. In fact she spoke up so quickly I had a sneaking suspicion that she and Aunt Peg had already settled this between them.

So much for my momentary delusion that I was making my own choices. Apparently all Aunt Peg had needed to do was bait the trap. And then wait for me to fall in.

When Libby turned to face me, I saw that her expression was grim. "I'll never believe that my father's death was an accident. Those cookies were left in his office on purpose. And the worst part is that whoever put them there had to have known him very well indeed. That person was familiar with Dad's habits and routines. They knew he worked at his desk every morning—even on weekends. They knew that he loved to snack. *They even knew his favorite kind of cookie.* This hateful thing was done by someone my father trusted."

Libby was right to be angry, I thought. Those added details of what had taken place made Leo Brody's death seem all the more despicable.

"It sounds as though you mean to implicate your own family," I said.

Despite the accusations she'd made, I still half-expected a quick denial. It didn't come. Instead, Libby nodded.

"Good," she said instead. "I'm glad we understand each other."

In the ring, the Bulldog judge was passing out ribbons for Best of Breed, Best of Winners, and Best Opposite Sex. Libby slipped the grooming noose off over Troy's head and slid a slender chain collar on in its place. Then she lifted the liver-spotted Dalmatian off the table and set him down gently on the ground.

I hurried to ask another question before she left. "What about Becca Montague?"

Libby's head snapped up. "She's not important."

"She told me she and your father were friends."

"Oh, they were friendly all right. Becca showed up three months ago and she's hardly let him out of her sight since."

"Showed up from where?" asked Aunt Peg.

"Dad met her at a fundraiser for some worthy cause. One of those deathly dull charity dinners where everyone is either drunk or bored to tears. Becca latched on to my father like a barnacle on the hull of a boat. He has children older than she is. The two of them looked ridiculous together."

"Apparently your father didn't think so," I pointed out.

"What *he* thought of her doesn't matter anymore, does it?" Libby reached over and grasped my arm. Her grip was surprisingly strong. "Becca Montague is nobody. It's my family I'm concerned about. Go and talk to my siblings. Find out what the hell they were thinking. Start with my brother, Graham. He's always broke."

Before I could even begin to form a suitable reply, she was gone.

*   *   *

Aunt Peg and I didn't wait around to see whether or not Libby and Troy won. Half an hour had passed since Kev and I had left the handlers' tent. It was time to get back and see how Sam and Davey were doing with Augie.

Aunt Peg and I cast dignity aside as the three of us dashed between the two tents. We all got wet anyway. Kevin was the only one who thought that was just great. Ducking under the awning of the grooming tent, we threaded our way between the tightly packed handlers' setups. Sam saw us coming and smiled.

"Sorry that took so long," I said. "We got side-tracked by Aunt Peg."

"I figured it had to be something like that." He knew my aunt all too well.

Augie was currently lying upright like a sphinx on his grooming table. His mane coat was already line-brushed, and his bracelets and hip rosettes had been slickered. Now Davey was using a knitting needle to part the hair on the Poodle's head, forming the ponytails that would provide a framework for the structured topknot he would wear in the show ring.

The American Kennel Club currently recognizes one hundred and eighty-four different dog breeds. Those breeds are divided into seven groups: Sporting, Hound, Working, Terrier, Toy, Non-Sporting, and Herding. In most cases, a breed's group designation is determined by its original function.

Poodles, with three size varieties, belong to two different groups. Standards and Miniatures are judged in the Non-Sporting Group. Toy Poodles reside in the Toy Group. Bulldogs and Dalmatians are also Non-Sporting dogs, and the judge that was currently examining the Dalmatian entry would be judging Augie and the remainder of the Mini and Standard Poodles later.

"You're getting quite good at that," Aunt Peg said, leaning in for a closer look as Davey deftly slipped a small colored rubber band around a long skein of topknot hair.

"I've been practicing," Davey replied without taking his eyes off the task at hand. He looked relieved when Aunt Peg kept her itchy fingers at her sides and confined her participation to merely remarking on his progress.

We all relaxed—even Augie—when she took a step back from the table.

"Pretty soon Davey will be giving Crawford a run for his money," Terry Denunzio commented from the next setup over.

The Poodle breed is dominated by professional handlers, and Crawford Langley is one of the best. His Poodle presentation is superb, and his reputation is impeccable. He's been at the top of the game for decades. Crawford has the luxury of choosing which Poodles he wants to handle, and those he takes in the ring are almost always the ones to beat.

Terry is Crawford's assistant handler and his life partner. Terry's quick wit and boundless energy act as the perfect foil for Crawford's calm, dignified demeanor. Over the years, Terry has had more hairstyles and colors than a circus Poodle. Blond, he resembles the boy next door. Now with black locks and a hoop in his pierced ear, Terry's vibe was decidedly Goth. The look was a little dark for me, but he carried it off with aplomb.

Terry would be the first to tell you that he's a people person. You can translate that to mean that his concept of boundaries is a little sketchy. He's never seen a conversation that he doesn't want to eavesdrop on, or insert himself into. Terry is one of my best friends but there are times when I just want to smack him. And he almost always deserves it.

Now, however, I smiled gratefully in his direction. It would be a long time before Davey would approach Crawford's level of expertise, but it was kind of Terry to pay the compliment and boost Davey's confidence.

"Nope," said Davey. "Not going to happen. I promised I would finish Augie's championship, but then I'm hanging up my show leash and retiring."

Aunt Peg's eyes flew open wide. "You wouldn't dare."

I sidled her way and stepped on her foot. Aunt Peg winced and nudged me aside, but the move had the desired effect because she also clamped her lips together.

"Who's retiring?" Crawford asked. Returning from the ring with an Italian Greyhound tucked under his arm, he slid between two tables and a stack of crates and entered his setup. "Certainly not Davey. You're too young to retire."

"Too young," Kevin agreed with a giggle. "Young as me."

Davey leaned back and gazed downward around the tabletop. Kev was sitting in the grass at our feet.

"Nobody's as young as you," he told his little brother. "You're barely older than a baby."

Kev's face crumpled. "I'm *not* a baby. I'm a big boy!"

"Of course you are." Sam leaned down and scooped Kev up into his arms. "You're the second-biggest boy in the family."

"Big boy." Kev repeated the words for emphasis. "I have my own dog."

That declaration came as a surprise. We all turned and looked at him. Kev gave us a toothy grin, pleased to be the center of attention.

"Davey has Augie," he said with satisfaction. "And I have Bud."

I thought Terry's expressive eyebrows were going to fly all the way up into his perfectly coiffed hair. He turned away from the white Standard Poodle he was scissoring and swiveled in our direction. For the record, the swivel is a move that Terry has perfected. His swish is well above par too.

"You have a new Poodle named Bud? When did *that* happen?" Terry inquired, tamping down a grin. "And *who* came up with that wonderful name?"

Crawford slanted his assistant a look. "I don't hear anything wrong with the name. Not when you consider that we've shown Poodles named Bubbles, Twinkie, and Doll Face."

"Bud isn't a Poodle," I said.

In the silence that followed, you could have heard a knitting needle drop. Or a can of hair spray. Then, suddenly everyone was talking at once. Terry's voice rose above the rest.

"*What?*" His shriek was so high-pitched that dogs on the tabletops all around us pricked their ears

and turned to look. "You're branching out into a
new breed? I can't believe this is happening and
we're just hearing about it now."

"Not just one breed," Aunt Peg informed him.
"Many breeds."

That was enough to pique even Crawford's interest. He paused in the act of slipping the IG into
a crate. "Which ones?"

"Beagle, Boxer, Whippet, maybe some Cattle
Dog . . ." I said. "All rolled into one."

Terry's mouth fell open. His voice dropped to a
horrified whisper. "You mean he's a *mutt?*"

Crawford began to laugh. "That explains the
name."

"Hey," Davey complained good-naturedly. He'd
finished Augie's topknot and was standing the
Poodle up to be scissored. "I like that name. I
picked it myself. And it suits him."

"I'm sure it does," Terry agreed piously. "*Bud*
the mutt."

"Bud the mutt," Kevin echoed happily. The insult went right over his head. "He's my dog."

Terry patted Kev's arm. "And what a lucky
young man you must be." Then he propped his
hands on his hips and stared at the rest of us. "I
know there's a story here. Out with it."

Grooming a Poodle is busy work. While the fingers fly, the brain can be miles away. Or in this
case, the mouths. While Crawford and Terry put
the finishing touches on the three Poodles that
comprised their entry in Standards and Sam and
Davey went to work spraying up Augie's topknot
and neck hair, my whole family pitched in to tell
Bud's story.

"He has *spots*?" Terry said at the end. His tone implied that the mere thought was inconceivable. For a handler who specialized in solid-colored Poodles, maybe it was.

"He does," I confirmed. "And short hair."

"It's great," said Davey. "Bud will never need to be clipped. Or even brushed."

"When you put it that way, you make me wonder why we didn't get a smooth-haired dog sooner," I said wistfully.

Aunt Peg was having none of that. "That's easy," she declared. "Because wonderful as other dogs are, none can compare to a Poodle. And speaking of which, we'd better look sharp. If your judge is running on time, we have to get moving."

Once she pointed it out, I realized that other Standard Poodles around us were beginning to leave their grooming tables and head to the next tent with their handlers. Luckily there was a brief lull in the rain. On a day like this, a smaller Poodle could be carried to the ring tucked beneath its owner's raincoat. Standards had to make their way on foot through the wet grass. Augie's bracelets would suffer, but as long as his liberally hair-sprayed mane coat stayed dry, his trim would re-main intact.

Davey held Augie's leash. Sam took up a position on the Poodle's other side. Aunt Peg led the way, clearing a path through the crowds beneath the tent and giving no one a chance to jostle our immaculately coiffed entry. Kevin and I brought up the rear. When we reached the ring, the Puppy Dog class was already being judged.

As a fully mature, almost two-year-old dog, Augie

was entered in Open Dogs. On the day, it would be the third Standard Poodle class to be judged after Puppy and Bred-by-Exhibitor. It was also the class with the largest entry. There was a four-point major on the line, so the numbers were sizable in both dogs and bitches.

Davey had been showing Augie for more than a year. So far, the Poodle had accumulated ten points toward the total of fifteen he would need to complete his championship. He'd also won one of two mandatory "majors," meaning that he had beaten enough male Standard Poodles at a single show to earn three or more points. The number of points awarded was based on the amount of competition, and majors were *always* a coveted prize.

As we waited ringside, I checked out Augie's competition in Standard dogs. Most were being shown by professional handlers. Only one other Poodle would enter the ring with his owner on the end of his leash, and that woman was a skilled competitor who'd beaten me handily every time I'd shown against her. Not only that, but Davey was the only junior handler in the entire Standard Poodle entry. He and Augie would have their work cut out for them.

"It seems odd not to have Bertie here," Sam commented as the Puppy Dogs exited the ring. "I hope she's feeling okay."

Bertie Kennedy was my sister-in-law; she was married to my younger brother, Frank. A professional handler herself, she usually attended many more dog shows each year than we did. Now she was seven months pregnant with her second child, however. This pregnancy wasn't proceeding as smoothly as her first, so she was taking some time off from the pressures of the show scene.

"Bertie called yesterday to wish Davey luck," I said. "She's going stir-crazy just sitting around with her feet up, but other than that she's fine."

"Quit talking and pay attention," Aunt Peg said.

The single dog in the Bred-by class had been awarded his blue ribbon. The eight Standard Poodles entered in Open were beginning to form a queue outside the in-gate. Fingers threaded gently through Augie's narrow chain-link collar to hold him close to his side, Davey tucked his greyhound comb into his armband and checked to make sure that he had bait in his pocket.

Sam guided Davey into the line as it began to move forward and sent him off with a pat on the back.

"Have fun," I called after him.

Aunt Peg materialized beside Davey just as the pair was about to enter the ring. As usual, she managed to have the last word. "You show that Poodle like the good dog he is and come back a winner!"

But hey, no pressure, right?

Chapter 12

Black clouds rolled in and it began to drizzle again.

The Poodles in the Open Dog class lined up nose-to-tail underneath the tent, filling the long side of the enclosure. They'd been called into the ring in catalog order, which placed Davey second to last. That gave him plenty of time to get Augie correctly positioned before the judge took his first look at him on his initial pass down the line.

I watched the judge check out the first half-dozen entrants in the big class. Then he came to Augie. To my dismay, his gaze barely even paused. Instead, it slid right past the big black dog to the Standard Poodle standing behind him.

This was the first time I'd ever seen this judge and already I didn't like him. As he lifted his hands palms-up and the handlers prepared to gait their dogs around the ring for the first time, I leaned in close to Aunt Peg and said, "Who is that guy anyway?"

"Ricardo Vega," she whispered back, adhering to ringside etiquette that dictates all conversation about the judging take place in a low voice. "He's from South America."

"He didn't even look at Augie!"

"That was just the first glance." Even as she spoke to me, Aunt Peg's eyes remained riveted on the ring. "He'll pay attention when he sees how well that dog moves."

I wasn't so sure. A judge has less than two minutes to evaluate each dog, and first impressions are important. Davey had done exactly what he was supposed to do upon entering the ring. He'd had Augie stacked correctly, standing in a balanced pose with his tail up and his expression alert. There had been no reason for Mr. Vega to dismiss the pair out of hand . . . except perhaps for the fact that Davey was twelve years old.

I growled under my breath.

"Now what?" Aunt Peg demanded.

The Standard Poodles had finished their first circuit of the ring. Seven were being allowed to relax beneath the tent while the judge began his individual examinations with the first dog in line. If Mr. Vega had taken note of Augie's superior movement, I'd seen no sign of it.

"I thought you said he was a good judge," I muttered.

Exhibitors pick and choose carefully before making their dog show entries. Some judges were quick to reward the professional handler who brought them a large entry. Others favored a single attribute—like color, soundness, or a pretty face—and glossed over everything else. And some judges who raced through the approval system to gain additional breeds simply didn't have a clue what they were looking at.

Fortunately, we had Aunt Peg to sort things out for us. Since she'd been everywhere and knew everyone, she was our authority on which dog shows to enter and which judges to support. I was quite certain that she'd approved of Mr. Vega.

"No," Aunt Peg replied carefully. "I told you to make the entry."

"Because you liked the judge," I insisted. Why else would she have told us to do all the work required to get Augie ready, not to mention making the trip and standing around all day in the rain?

"No, because of basketball," Aunt Peg said. "And soccer season, and vacation, and final exams."

She'd lost me completely. "What about them?"

"It's always something with you and Davey. Look at that Poodle." She gestured toward Augie, who'd now moved up to the middle of the line. "That's a handsome dog. He needs to be finished. He deserves to be a champion. And Davey has barely shown him all year."

"Because dog shows aren't Davey's only interest. Nor should they be." Then, abruptly, I realized the implication of what she'd said. "You mean you told us to make the entry just so that Augie would get in the ring?"

Aunt Peg's gaze flicked my way. "The two of them needed the practice."

Seriously?

"They could have practiced at home," I said. "Please tell me you didn't make us come all this way just to show under a judge who isn't even going to give Augie a chance."

"We'll see," Aunt Peg replied. "He hasn't had his hands on him yet."

At this point, I doubted that would matter. Exhibitors quickly learned how to read judges' body language. So far I hadn't seen even a modicum of interest directed toward our entry.

"Have you even *seen* Mr. Vega judge before?" I asked.

She gave her head a small shake. "He's visiting from Brazil. They have lovely Standard Poodles there. I figured he was worth a try."

Worth a try. That was hardly high praise.

Aunt Peg went back to staring at the class. By now Mr. Vega had examined nearly all the dogs in the ring. He had yet to sink his hands deep into the coat of a single Poodle—an action necessary to inspect a dog's structure beneath what might be deceptive trimming. The judge had also paused for a friendly chat with two of the professional handlers while going over their dogs.

Aunt Peg had begun to frown. "I may have miscalculated," she admitted.

We watched as Davey set Augie up to be examined while the preceding Poodle gaited down and back. When Mr. Vega turned back to the line and saw Davey, his lips pursed in a frown. His inspection of Augie was cursory at best.

When Davey moved the Standard Poodle to the

end of the ring and back, Mr. Vega stared off into the distance. The pair had barely finished their pattern before being sent back around to stand at the end of the line. None of us were surprised when Augie wasn't included in the four class placements. He and Davey filed out of the ring with the other losers.

Shoulders slumped in disappointment, Davey made his way back to where we were waiting. "That was terrible," he said.

"Tell me about it," Terry agreed. Crawford's nice Standard dog had only placed fourth.

Handler and assistant exchanged Poodles beside us, with Crawford handing off his beaten dog and taking his Open Bitch entry from Terry. Crawford snapped the dog's armband out from beneath the rubber band at the top of his arm and tossed it in the trash. He didn't look any more pleased about the way things had turned out than we were.

The difference between us, however, was that while we were finished for the day, Crawford still had a good chance of getting "his piece" in either the bitch competition or Best of Variety.

"I thought Augie looked good," Davey said glumly. "He was trying really hard."

Though he hadn't mentioned his own efforts, Davey had been trying hard too. That made the day's outcome all the more disappointing.

"There will be another day," Aunt Peg said briskly. "That's only one judge's opinion."

"Yeah," Davey grumbled. "A stupid judge."

"Hey," I said sharply. "That's not nice."

"No, but it's true. He never even *looked* at Augie."

"Yes, and that's a shame after all the hard work you did. But different judges look for different things in a dog, and today just wasn't your day. You and Augie have done really well together, but you can't win every time."

"Why not?" Davey slid a glance my way. "My soccer team wins almost every game. I like winning all the time."

"Of course you do." Terry reached over and pretended to bop him on the head. "But then what would Crawford and I do? We have to have a chance too."

Davey ducked down to avoid the slap and came up grinning. "You guys can have all the wins in bitches. And sometimes Best of Variety."

Crawford joined the conversation. "Says the kid who's heading for early retirement. Give me a break." He stopped and shook his head. "Do you want to know the secret to winning at dog shows?"

We all fell silent. Crawford was one of the most successful handlers in New England and the Mid-Atlantic states. Over the course of his long career, he'd won more groups and Bests in Show than most exhibitors could even dream of. If he was willing to share his knowledge and insight with us, we all wanted to listen.

Crawford leaned down so that he and Davey were eye to eye and said, "Work hard. Learn from the most talented people you can find. Show up every day. And always do your best."

"What about when my best isn't good enough?"

The plaintive note in Davey's voice tugged at my heart.

"That's easy," Crawford told him. "Then you work at it until you get better." He straightened and gazed down at Augie. "Tell me something. Where does that Poodle sleep at night?"

My son looked relieved to be asked a question for which he knew the answer. "He sleeps next to my bed."

"So I guess he must be a pretty good dog?"

"Pretty good? He's the best!"

"Suppose you could trade him for the dog that just beat you and won today's major?" Crawford asked. "Would you do it?"

In the ring, the Winners Dog class had just ended. The Open dog had picked up the points. The Standard Poodle who'd been second in the Open class was awarded Reserve.

"No way." Davey curled an arm around Augie protectively.

Crawford smiled. "So it looks to me like you think you have the best dog at the show. Right?"

Davey nodded slowly.

"Even if he doesn't always win?"

My son nodded again.

"Then count yourself lucky." Crawford glanced over toward the ring. The Standard Puppy Bitch class was in. We still had a few more minutes before Open Bitches. "And if you want to complain about losing, you get back to me when you've lost as many times as I have. Let's see, I started when I was a teenager so let's call it forty-five years. With all the dogs I show, I bet I've lost ten thousand times by now, give or take. You don't see me moping around, do you?"

"No," Davey admitted. Then he flashed Crawford a cheeky grin. "But that's because your specials dog is going to win the Variety."

Caught by surprise, Crawford barked out a laugh. "Kids," he said to Sam and me. "You can have 'em. I give up."

I walked around to where the handler stood and gave him a quick hug. "You did great," I whispered in his ear. Then I stepped back and said out loud, "Ten thousand times? *Really*? That's just depressing."

"You think that's depressing, watch this." The Open Bitches were getting ready to enter the ring and Crawford moved to join the end of the line. "Here comes ten thousand and one."

Saturday's dog show had a lot in common with the one the day before. Both shows were hosted by the same kennel club, and both took place at the same location in Carmel. The weekend's second show also featured a major entry in Standard Poodles. Thankfully there were two major differences: better weather and a different Poodle judge.

Unfortunately neither of those changes resulted in a significantly better outcome for Davey and Augie. The trouble started as soon as the pair entered the ring for their class. Since the entries hadn't been called in catalog order, Davey took a position closer to the front of the line.

At most dog shows, Davey allowed Augie to free-bait during the judge's first look. That meant that rather than stacking the Poodle, he walked him naturally into a good position. Then, instead of standing behind Augie and holding up his head and tail, he stood out in front facing him while offering a piece of bait to draw his attention.

The maneuver had several benefits. In a long row of dogs—most of whom needed their handlers' support—Augie's different positioning made him stand out. Also, having Augie's eyes trained on Davey emphasized the Poodle's wonderful expression. Lastly, Augie's independent stance sent a clear message to the judge: *Nobody has to make me look the part. I'm that good all on my own.*

Today, however, Davey hustled Augie into the line, then quickly set him up, lifting each foot and placing it precisely where he thought it should be. When he was finished, Davey pulled back and had a look. Frowning at what he saw, he began the job all over again, hastily re-setting all four feet.

That much fiddling on Davey's part had the predictable result of making Augie fidgety. When the judge walked past them for the first time, the Poodle wasn't standing straight. Instead, his body was bowed in the middle as he cranked his head around to look at Davey. Augie's expression was one of obvious confusion.

From there, things went steadily downhill. At the previous dog show, Davey had tried to do well. Now he stepped his efforts up a notch. Rather than simply letting Augie be very good, Davey was aiming for perfection.

Only minutes into the class Davey was second-guessing everything he did. His usually fluid movements became choppy and rigid. Even worse, it wasn't long before the anxiety he was feeling worked its way down the leash to Augie. Suddenly unsure of what he was meant to do, the Poodle lost his confidence and his performance fell apart.

Even worse, in contrast to the judge from the day before, this one clearly liked Augie. He went out of his way to give the Poodle every chance to succeed. There's a reason it's called a dog *show*, however, and in the end there was only so much leeway the judge could give the pair. With other nice dogs in the class being shown flawlessly by their handlers, we counted ourselves lucky when Davey and Augie were awarded the white ribbon for fourth place.

Once again, Davey exited the ring looking dejected. "I thought the judge *liked* Augie."

"He did," Aunt Peg replied crisply. "You're the one who blew it."

Davey's head came up in surprise. "What do you mean?"

Aunt Peg opened her mouth to speak, but I quickly stepped between them. "I'll take it from here."

"But I have several useful things to say!"

"We're sure you do," Sam agreed. "But now is not the time. Why don't you come with Kevin and me? We'll watch the rest of the judging from the other side of the ring."

"I'm quite comfortable right here," Aunt Peg declared. "I can see perfectly well from where I'm standing."

"Standing *quietly*," I ordered.

When I turned back to Davey, he was staring away from us, his gaze focused on the ring where Crawford's Standard Poodle had just been named Winners Dog. I reached down and laid a hand on his shoulder.

"Remember a few years ago when you gave Junior Showmanship a try?" I asked.

"Sure."

"As I recall, you didn't like it much."

"No, not really. I thought it would be fun, but it wasn't."

"Because you felt like you were under a lot of pressure to win, right?"

I didn't have to name names. We all knew who had supplied that pressure.

"Yeah, I guess."

"Well, that's what you did to Augie today."

Davey turned and looked at me. I could see that he was puzzled.

"Showing Augie is also supposed to be fun. Finishing his championship is a project for you and Sam to enjoy together. There's no time limit on this. Nobody cares how long it takes."

Aunt Peg harrumphed under her breath. Davey and I both ignored her.

"You lost yesterday—" I began.

"I lost today too, in case you didn't notice," Davey said unhappily.

I stopped and sighed, then started over. "It looked like you felt the need to change some things."

"I guess." Davey shrugged. "Crawford told me to try and do better."

Oh. Right.

"Yes, but he didn't mean that you should change everything all at once."

Davey nodded. "I guess maybe Augie got a little confused."

"That's what it looked like," Sam told him. "And when Augie got confused, he stopped having fun."

"*Now* may I speak?" Aunt Peg said archly.

"If you can say something nice," I warned.

Aunt Peg ignored me and directed her question to Davey. "Do you know what the word 'Poodliness' means?"

"Umm . . . no?"

"Then I'll explain it to you. What sets a Poodle apart from other dogs is his intelligence combined with a sense of fun. A Poodle has *joie de vivre*. When he walks into the show ring, he should look like there's nowhere else he'd rather be. A good Poodle shows itself off. He exhibits a kind of gaiety that makes the judge smile—and want to take that dog home with him. *That*," Aunt Peg finished with satisfaction, "is Poodliness."

Davey glanced down at the dog by his side. "Augie can do that."

"Of course he can. Augie has Poodliness in spades. But not today." Aunt Peg gestured toward the ring. "The two of you were stiff as a board in there. No judge in his right mind could have rewarded that performance. You need to take a deep breath and learn to relax. Trust me, that will fix everything."

Sam and I exchanged a look. *Learn to relax* coming from Aunt Peg? The thought was mind boggling.

We watched the remainder of the Standard Poodle judging. Crawford won in dogs, lost in bitches, and won again in Best of Variety. After the final ribbons were awarded, the judge took a short break for pictures.

Sam, Davey, and Aunt Peg took Augie back to the handlers' tent. Kev and I lingered behind. Dalmatians were scheduled to be judged after Standard Poodles and they'd already begun to gather outside the gate. The day before, I hadn't had a chance to watch Libby Rothko show Troy. Now I decided to remedy that.

Kevin was entranced by the spotted dogs milling around us. "Just like Bud!" he crowed with delight.

I choked back a laugh. I had no desire to hurt my son's feelings, but this collection of handsome carriage dogs looked *nothing* like Bud.

"Do you want to watch?" I asked.

Kev nodded enthusiastically. Hand in hand, we moved closer to low slatted boards that marked the ring's boundary. Inside the enclosure, the show photographer was taking pictures of French Bulldogs. Crawford waited nearby with the Standard Poodle that had gone Winners Dog.

Terry was outside the ring, holding Crawford's Best of Variety winner. That dog wouldn't have his picture taken now in the hope that it would be necessary to take a photo later—after he had won or placed in the Non-Sporting group. Terry sidled over to stand beside Kevin and me.

"What do you make of that?" he asked, nodding toward the far side of the ring.

I gazed across to where Terry had indicated. Two women, one of them holding a liver-spotted Dalmatian, were engaged in a furious conversation. Their body language was so combative I was amazed that I hadn't noticed them sooner. Then abruptly, I realized that the woman with the Dal was Libby Rothko.

Beside me, Terry was bouncing up and down on his toes. "I love a good chick fight," he said, making no attempt to contain his glee. "And any minute now, those two are going to come to blows."

Chapter 13

"**I** know that woman," I said to Terry.

"Which one?" His gaze slid my way only briefly. He was loath to take his eyes off the action. "The one whose face is turning purple or the one whose hands are balled into fists?"

"Angry face," I said. "The one holding the Dalmatian. That's Libby Rothko."

"The name sounds familiar," Terry mused.

"Her father was Leo Brody."

That got his attention in a hurry. "*The* Leo Brody?"

"Yes. The man who died last week in Greenwich."

"Interesting," Terry said wryly. "There must be a major show in Dals. I hope the funeral isn't today."

Apparently I wasn't the only one who found it a little odd that Libby was competing in a dog show only days after her father had lost his life.

"No and shut *up*," I said fondly.

As if that would work. It didn't even slow Terry down.

"Who's the other babe?" he asked.

The second woman was older than Libby. Her round face and plain features were now sharpened into a furious scowl. Short frosted hair curled around her earlobes, accenting a pair of large gold earrings. Though the woman's attire was casual—slacks and a T-shirt with an embroidered neckline—her sandals were much too fussy for the grassy setting. A dog person would definitely have known better.

"I have no idea," I said. "I've never seen her before."

"Well, she's not one of us," Terry scoffed. "Look at those sandals."

Great minds, I thought.

I dug an elbow into Terry's side. "Go find out what they're fighting about."

"You mean *listen in?*" He tried to sound scandalized and failed utterly.

"Of course I mean listen in, you ninny. I can't go over there. Libby knows who I am. But if you wander past, she'll never even notice."

"I beg your pardon." Terry's eyebrows waggled. "I am a highly noticeable person."

Of course he was. That wasn't even up for debate.

"Go anyway," I said. "You know you want to. And hurry! Get there before the fight ends."

It turned out I didn't have to worry. In the time it took Terry to lead his Standard Poodle out from beneath the tent and make a circuit of the ring, matters had intensified between the two women. Neither one of them paid any attention to Terry's eye-catching looks. Libby and her companion probably wouldn't have noticed if I had driven by in a Sherman tank.

I was so busy watching Terry stake out a perfect spot near the still-battling women that I didn't see Crawford coming until he was right beside me.

"What are you two getting up to now?" he asked pleasantly. His gaze skimmed back and forth between Terry and me.

Before I could reply, Kevin stepped in. "There's a fight," he informed him. "We're listening in."

"That's what I was afraid of." Crawford turned and had a better look. "Seems like Libby's got a real bee up her butt."

"You know Libby Rothko?"

"Sure, she's had Dals for ages. Good ones too. Three, four years ago, she had a nice specials dog. We butted heads in quite a few groups."

"Who's the other woman?" I asked curiously.

"That I can't tell you. I'm pretty sure she's not a regular."

Probably the shoes again.

Crawford reached down, cupped the tall Poodle's muzzle in his palm and prepared to move away. "When you get done corrupting my assistant, send him back to the grooming tent. It might surprise you to know that we've got real work to do."

I'd have thought that Crawford was above the use of sarcasm. Apparently I would have been wrong.

Three minutes later, Terry was heading back.

The Dalmatians were in the ring by then. The Puppy Dog class had just ended. Libby's liver Dal was the only entrant in Bred-by. Terry followed her to the in-gate, then continued on around until he reached Kev and me.

The woman Libby had been arguing with cast one last angry glare at the ring, then turned her back and stalked away. Her dramatic exit was marred by the comical wobble in her walk caused by her heels sinking into the soft turf. If she'd stuck around longer, she probably would have been gratified to see that Libby still looked seriously rattled in the aftermath of their encounter. Her performance in the Bred-by class was so sloppy and inattentive that the only reason her Dalmatian received a blue ribbon was because they were a single entry.

"What?" I asked eagerly when Terry finally reached us.

"They were fighting over a dog."

I gave an exaggerated look around. Yup, we were still at a dog show.

"Well, duh," I said.

"Strappy Sandals seems to think that Libby owes her money. She's very upset that she hasn't been paid back."

"For what?" I wondered aloud.

"A dog!" Kev sang out happily. He was listening too. "Right, Mommy?"

"Right, sweetie. Aren't you supposed to be watching the nice Dalmatians?" I turned him back to face the dogs in the ring, then refocused on Terry. "What else did you hear?"

"Oh, you know," he said with a deliberately casual shrug. "Just the usual sorts of threats and ugly promises."

The usual sort. As if there were such a thing.

"Like what?" I asked.

"You'll be sorry. I'll make sure you're sorry. You think you can get away with this, but you can't."

"Wow," I said on an exhale. "And what did Libby have to say about that?"

"Not much. By the time I got over there, she was mostly seething in silence. You could tell she was wishing that the whole thing would just *stop happening.* Even her Dal looked upset."

We're dog people. We notice stuff like that.

"Did you find out the other woman's name?" I asked.

"Nope. Didn't come up. I wouldn't have known who Libby Rothko was if you hadn't told me. But speaking of which, wasn't Leo Brody famous for having major bucks?"

I nodded.

"Now that he's dead, you'd think there would be plenty to go around. So why would his daughter be fighting with someone—in public, no less— over money?"

"I have no idea," I admitted.

Terry left to return to the handlers' tent and I turned back to the ring. Dalmatian dogs were already finished, and Libby and Troy had disappeared. Given their performance, it came as no surprise that Libby's Dal had lost in the Winners class and therefore wasn't required for further judging.

Kev and I remained until the end of the breed. A kindly exhibitor with a friendly Dalmatian puppy let Kevin play with the dog while we watched. By the time we made our way back to the setup, we found that Augie's topknot and neck hair had been taken down, brushed out, and rewrapped. The Poodle had been watered and exercised and was sitting quietly on the grooming table. Davey and Aunt Peg were packing up, and Sam had gone to retrieve the car.

Another weekend. Another pair of unsuccessful dog shows. Sometimes I wondered why we even did this. Then I thought about Faith, who was waiting for me at home, and brightened. It had taken years of selective breeding to produce such a treasure. *That* was why we did it.

Start with my brother Graham, Libby Rothko had said.

As if it were just that easy. I didn't know where Graham Brody lived. I didn't have his phone number. And I had no idea whether or not he would consent to talk to me.

Since the next day was Sunday, I ignored those problems and took time off to go to the beach with Sam and the boys. I figured I'd start on Monday by getting back in touch with Libby. She was the one who wanted me to go snooping around her family. The least she could do was provide me with some introductions.

But late that morning my cell phone rang. "Fred Brody here," a voice snapped out. "What's this nonsense I hear about Libby sending you to sniff around the family like some stupid Bloodhound?"

"Excuse me?" I'd just put on my bathing suit, and my head was filled with visions of soft sand and gentle waves. It took a moment to clear it. "Who is this?"

"Fred Brody. I just told you that."

Oh, right. The man with the microphone. Fred was one of Leo Brody's sons. He'd been a bit pompous and certainly arrogant, but in the end he'd been reasonable enough to surrender his spot as announcer.

"Of course." I picked up a towel and shoved it into a beach tote. "We met last week at Puppy Fest."

"The day of my father's death," he said darkly. "Apparently we need to talk. I'm available this afternoon."

"Umm . . ."

I supposed there was no point in wondering how he'd gotten my cell phone number. It was easy to envision a clear trail leading straight through his sister to Aunt Peg.

"Don't bother hesitating," Fred told me. "I'm a busy man. If you're smart, you'll grab your chance when you can. You may not get another opportunity."

The statement was intended to put me in my place. *Duly noted.* On the other hand, if Fred Brody was willing to talk to me about his father's death, who was I to turn him away?

"This afternoon," I agreed. "When and where?"

Fred barked out his address in Old Greenwich, then repeated it a second time for good measure. "Two o'clock," he said before ringing off. "Don't be late. I despise tardiness."

"It sounds like you won't be coming to the beach with us." Sam was standing in the bedroom doorway with a pair of swimmies in his hand.

"Of course I'm coming," I told him. "I just can't stay all afternoon."

"Then you'd better bring your own car. Because I'm not bringing Kevin home until he's so worn out that he falls into bed and sleeps through the night."

"That sounds like an excellent plan," I said.

Promptly at two o'clock, I presented myself at the gleaming white front door to Fred Brody's two-story, weathered shingle home in Old Greenwich. Despite the house's modest size, spartan landscaping, and humble siding, I was well aware that its waterfront location was enough to make the dwelling a precious commodity in the Fairfield County housing market.

I shook what I hoped was the last of the sand out of my hair, straightened the dress-like cover-up that I'd pulled on over my bathing suit, and wished that I wasn't wearing flip-flops. Too late to worry about that now.

I rang the bell, and a minute later, Fred answered the door himself. Last time I'd seen him, he'd been wearing a suit and standing very much upon his dignity. Now, at home, he was dressed down in khakis, docksiders, and an open-neck linen shirt. The curl of his lip indicated that my very casual attire hadn't made the best first impression.

He was holding a highball glass half-filled with amber liquid in his left hand. He extended his right and said, "I'm Fred Brody."

"Melanie Travis." I reminded him again, "We met last week."

"So you said." He didn't look convinced. "At Puppy Fest?"

I wondered if I should mention the context of our prior meeting—one that had ended with him deprived of a performance he'd clearly coveted. Then it occurred to me that I was still standing on his front step. My outfit had already gotten me off to a bad start. One more wrong move and I might never find myself invited inside.

"I was there to help out with the puppies," I said instead.

"Ah, you came with Jane."

"Not exactly. But we did end up working together."

Fred stepped back and motioned me into the house. "I suppose you'd better come inside."

I walked into a center hallway that ran the width of the home, starting at the front door and ending in a bright sun porch. A row of tall windows formed that room's rear wall. From where I stood, I could see the sun sparkling on the bright blue water of Long Island Sound. A sailboat with multicolored sails went drifting by, its jib fluttering in the light breeze.

"Wow, what a gorgeous view," I said.

"Yes," Fred replied.

His tone conveyed a palpable lack of interest in discussing the vivid scenery outside his windows. That was enough to quell further comment from me. When Fred strode across the hall into a small room that looked as though it served as his office, I followed behind meekly.

The furniture inside the room was dark and austere. Two windows had their shades lowered to block the afternoon sun. A Persian rug in muted colors only added to the room's air of somber dignity.

Fred set his drink down on a table beside one of two straight-backed chairs. The narrowed look he aimed my way made me suspect he was wondering whether I was dry enough or clean enough to grace his dreary-looking furniture. Ignoring the implied insult, I sat down demurely and waited.

Since Fred thought this was his meeting, I would let him take the lead.

"I am Leo Brody's oldest son," he said when he'd lowered himself into a seat opposite me. "As such, it is my responsibility to speak for the family."

Interesting. I was pretty sure there were other family members—Libby among them—who would quibble with Fred's assessment. But I was more than happy to hear what he had to say.

"I am not entirely sure what my half sister told you. Or what services Libby has hired you to perform. But let me assure you that your efforts will be wholly unnecessary."

"I'm afraid your sister doesn't agree," I said affably.

"Of course not." Fred picked up his glass and

took a sip, then settled back in his chair. "How well do you know Libby?"

"We only met recently," I admitted.

"Then let me tell you about her. Libby can be rather . . . high-strung. She loves to surround herself with intrigue and drama. Her goal is to keep those around her off-balance and unclear about her true intentions. It's no wonder she behaves that way. Libby's mother was much the same."

I leaned forward in my seat. "Her mother?"

Fred didn't require any encouragement from me. He was delighted to hold the floor.

"My stepmother, Maria, was a fiery Latin virago who was never happier than when our entire household was in turmoil. She *had* to be the center of attention at all times. The rest of us were always either leaping to do her bidding or soothing her hurt feelings. My father didn't make many mistakes in life. Not in business or in his personal dealings. But I'm quite certain he would tell you that marrying Maria was one of them."

I wasn't sure I liked the fact that Fred was putting words in his father's mouth. Especially since Leo Brody wasn't here to dispute them.

"How old were you when Maria became your stepmother?" I asked.

"Eight." Fred's lips flattened in a thin smile. "An impressionable age, wouldn't you say?"

I nodded silently.

"My sister, Nancy, was two years older than me. My brother, Ron, one year younger. Until my mother broke the news to us that she and my father were divorcing so that he could marry his pregnant mistress, we thought that nothing bad could ever touch us."

"Your mother actually told you that?" I said, shocked.

"No, not precisely. At least not then." Fred waved away my concern. "I suppose we didn't hear *all* the details until we were a bit older. And some of it we had to figure out for ourselves. But once I knew what really happened, the story became a single, cohesive piece of history in my mind. The truth was, Maria seduced my father away from us when I was a young child. And after that, nothing was ever the same."

I pondered that. Fred's recollection of his childhood was light years away from the "one, big, happy family" story I'd been told by Libby. Especially with regard to their parents.

"Maria was Leo Brody's second wife," I said. "He married again after that, didn't he?"

"Well, you know how these things go." Fred's voice had a brittle edge. "It was perfectly obvious to all of us that Maria would never last. That she didn't *belong*. She and my father had two daughters before he got fed up. It cost him a great deal of money to make her go away, but he paid it. Three years later, he met and married Clarissa."

"How old were you then?"

"Fourteen. I served as my father's best man at the wedding. Quite happily, I might add. After Maria's fickleness and tantrums, Clarissa was a breath of fresh air. She was ten years younger than my father, and he adored her."

"Was she a good stepmother?" I asked.

"Much better than the alternative, certainly. Clarissa styled herself as a free spirit. She believed that too many rules and mandates would stifle a child's creativity."

It took effort not to laugh. "I can certainly see how that would make her a popular stepparent."

"Another thing Clarissa apparently didn't believe in was birth control." Fred's lips pursed in disapproval. "The first four years she and my father were together, she produced three children. Jane was her first. But you probably already know that since you work with her at Puppy Posse."

I thought about explaining my connection to Jane and Puppy Fest more fully, but then decided it didn't matter. Fred enjoyed listening to himself speak, but he didn't appear to be paying much attention to anything I said.

"You were present at Puppy Fest," I said, changing the subject.

"All day," Fred confirmed, nodding. "Wonderful event, my father's favorite. I never missed it."

"Did you see anything unusual?"

"You mean aside from my father's untimely death?" he asked drily.

I bit my lip. "Yes."

"No, not a thing. Nor was I looking. I was in the ballroom the entire time, doing my part to make Puppy Fest a success. I had no idea what was going on in other areas of the house. There was no reason to suspect that anything untoward might be. And let me make it clear that I resent your asking such a question."

"I'm sorry, but—"

"But nothing," Fred said firmly. "My sister Libby is an alarmist. Do yourself a favor and pay no attention to anything she says. My father was an important man. He was universally loved and respected. The authorities came to the correct conclusion. Leo Brody's death was an accident. It had to be, because it's simply not possible for it to have been anything else."

Chapter 14

Fred rose from his seat and stared down at me pointedly. It was clear he thought that our interview had come to an end. Reluctantly, I stood up as well.

It seemed to me that there was a lot of ground we'd left uncovered. But since I suspected that Fred wasn't going to answer the questions I really wanted to ask, I lobbed him a softball query about something that had been bugging me since I'd first become acquainted with the Brody family.

"Why do you refer to your father as Leo Brody?"

Fred was already walking toward the door. He paused, surprised by the question. "Because that's who he is . . . who he was. Leo Brody was not just our father—he was also a public figure. We were all raised to understand that. It was our duty not to distract him from his work with our petty family issues. We were honored to share him with the world."

Wow, I thought. *Hyperbole much?*

"You also shared him with Becca Montague," I pointed out.

This time Fred's stride didn't falter. "Why would you bring up that woman's name?"

"She was the one who found your father's body."

"Shortly before you arrived, I was told."

I nodded. "Are you aware that she tried to convince me not to call for help? That she forbade me to contact the authorities?"

"I don't see what difference that makes," Fred said as I joined him next to the door. "My father was already dead at the time. Is that correct?"

"Yes—"

"Beyond help then, wouldn't you say?"

"Even so—"

"What Becca Montague did or didn't do in that moment means nothing to me." Fred grasped the knob and drew the door open. "That woman is too dumb to be anything but insignificant. And that's all I have to say on the subject."

Bright sunlight filled the doorway. I stepped out onto the narrow porch. A light breeze blowing up off the Sound ruffled my hair.

"I understand that you don't agree with what Libby asked me to do," I said. "But since it's going to happen anyway, wouldn't you rather be able to exert some control over the process?"

Fred's silent, stony glare spoke volumes. It wasn't a stretch to imagine smoke coming out of his ears.

I didn't expect a reply, but I asked anyway. "Who should I talk to next?"

His voice was crisp with exasperation. "If you truly intend to continue with this ridiculous enterprise, it had better be Caroline. Obviously I have failed to make you see sense. Maybe she will be able to succeed where I have failed. Caroline will confirm every word I said."

Fred took a step back and the door clicked shut between us.

Sam wasn't kidding about staying at the beach all day. I not only beat the rest of my family home, I also had time to take the canine crew for an extended run around the neighborhood, shower and change, and prepare a picnic dinner to eat outside on the deck.

It was a good thing I hadn't wasted much time cooking. Kev arrived home half-asleep, and Sam and Davey had been munching on snacks all afternoon at the beach. We put the marinated chicken breasts on the grill, tossed a salad as a side dish, and called it a meal.

When we were finished eating, the Poodle pack lined up for leftovers. Bud's mealtime manners had been atrocious upon his arrival. Now I was glad to see he was beginning to learn that he didn't need to snatch food or run the risk of going hungry. The grateful look on the little dog's face as he politely accepted a piece of chicken from my outstretched fingers was enough to make me curse his previous owners yet again.

Kevin was too sleepy for a bath. I carried him upstairs and sat him on his bed to exchange his T-shirt and shorts for pajamas. Brushing his teeth woke him up enough for Kev to demand a story.

Dr. Seuss is a perennial favorite and *Horton Hears*

a Who! was on top of the stack of books beside his bed. Kevin scooted up the mattress toward his pillow, then snuggled beneath the covers and pulled the Mickey Mouse quilt all the way up to his chin. I perched at the foot of the bed and began to read. It wasn't long before we heard the sound of approaching footsteps. Sam and the dogs were coming upstairs to say good night.

Three black Poodle faces appeared in the doorway. Then there was a sudden scrabble of nails on the hardwood floor in the hall. Bud threaded his way through the Poodles' legs and came hurtling into the room.

The spotted dog barely spared me a glance. In his mind, I was only an impediment to where he wanted to be. To where he seemed to think he belonged.

Head cocked to one side, Bud looked for an opening between me and the low guardrail that ran along the side of Kevin's bed. Seeing his spot, the dog crouched down, then sprang up onto the mattress. As if this was a routine they'd performed before, Kev patted his pillow and Bud scampered up to join him. Child and dog burrowed under the covers together.

I was the only one in the room who looked nonplussed by this maneuver. Sam accepted Bud's presence in Kevin's bed without a quibble. Even the Poodles—whose standard of behavior was often higher than mine—remained unruffled. Apparently I was out of the loop.

"When did that start?" I asked Sam.

"A few days ago," he whispered. Snug beneath the quilt with Bud, Kevin's eyes were already closed.

"Right after we decided that Bud was housebroken enough not to have to sleep in a crate."

"How did I not notice?"

Sam beckoned silently. I lifted my weight off the mattress, put down the book, and turned off the bedside lamp. The Poodles followed us quietly out of the room.

Sam waited until we'd reached the other end of the hall before speaking again. "You've been a little preoccupied lately."

"I know."

Even before I'd met Libby Rothko at the dog show, Leo Brody's murder had been on my mind. I hadn't stumbled over a dead body in a very long time. Now I couldn't seem to banish the image from my thoughts. And I didn't even want to *look* at a box of cookies.

"I guess I've been neglecting you guys, huh?"

"Don't worry about us. It's summer and the boys and I have plenty of ways to keep busy. Faith might be feeling a little left out though." Sam knew just what to say to evoke a response. I felt an immediate rush of guilt.

Faith had come to me when she was barely ten weeks old. Now she was well into middle age. Though I couldn't bear to think about it, I knew I wouldn't have her steady, loving presence beside me forever. No matter how distracted I'd been, it was stupid of me to waste even a minute of our time together.

"You're right," I said.

Faith wagged her tail. She'd heard her name. She knew we were talking about her.

I squatted down, gathered her close, and spoke into her ear. "I promise I will do better."

Faith reached around and licked my cheek in forgiveness.

Dogs make it so easy on us. Easier than we deserve.

Monday morning was the start of a bright, shiny, new week. Davey was due at soccer camp at nine so I called Caroline Richland at eight. She picked up right away.

I introduced myself, reminded her that we'd met briefly at Puppy Fest, then asked if I was calling too early.

"Oh please," Caroline said breezily. "I have two teenage boys in the house and my husband takes the early train into the city. Nobody gets to sleep late around here. Anyway, I was expecting your call. Fred warned me that I'd hear from you."

I wondered what else Fred had felt the need to warn his half sister about. Not that I was about to complain. It probably helped that he'd smoothed the way for me.

"So Libby thinks we should talk," Caroline said. "Let's get it over with. I have time this morning. How about ten o'clock—does that suit?"

One thing you had to say for the Brody family. They didn't beat around the bush.

When I agreed and Caroline told me her address, I recognized the name of the road. Like Aunt Peg, the Richlands lived in backcountry Greenwich. I wouldn't have any trouble finding my way there.

I fed the kids, fed the dogs, and checked twice that Davey had everything he needed for camp crammed inside his backpack. Kevin was signed up for a Parent and Toddler Swim at the Y that morning. Sam, who swam like Aquaman, was planning to go with him.

That freed me up go see Caroline as soon as I'd dropped Davey off at camp. Actually, it left me with half an hour to spare. I spent the time lingering over a mocha latte at Starbucks and pondering what little I knew about the various relationships within the Brody family. If Caroline was more loquacious than Fred had been—and her comment about getting our chat "over with" did nothing to reassure me on that point—I'd ask her to outline which siblings belonged where and who was related to whom.

Caroline and Richard Richland's house was set deep in the woods at the end of a long, winding driveway. Really. His name was Richard Richland. I looked it up. I have no idea why parents do that to their kids.

Perched on the edge of a small lake, the house was a soaring masterpiece of contemporary architecture. It was constructed of glass and polished steel, and rose three stories into the air. The structure's glistening surface both reflected and blended into the trees that surrounded it. With entire walls made up of windows, I could understand why the Richlands had chosen such a private setting for their dramatically designed home.

I stared at the house as I made the final approach down the driveway. I was still looking as I parked my car and got out. Even so, by the time I'd crossed the macadam to reach a walkway whose crisscross pattern formed overlapping geometric designs, I still hadn't managed to locate the home's front door.

That was embarrassing.

Briefly I paused at the edge of the driveway, hoping for inspiration. None came. Instead I heard a grinding noise that sounded vaguely familiar. After a moment, I realized why.

Way down at the other end of the house, a garage door was opening. As it slid upward, a black Porsche 911 Carrera came backing out. The sports car executed a neat two-point turn, then straightened on the driveway and came zooming directly at me.

Zero to sixty in how many seconds?

For a moment I was too shocked to react. Then, thankfully, survival instinct kicked in. I leapt up in the air and landed, none too gracefully, in a flowerbed packed with colorful blossoms.

I'd jumped just in time. The Porsche sped by, passing so close to me that a draft of warm air raised the hairs on the back of my neck.

As quickly as the nimble car had accelerated, it now slammed to a stop. Its wide tires left a trail of scorched skid marks on the blacktop. The driver's-side window slid down and a teenage boy stuck out his head. He looked as though he might be tamping down a smirk.

"Hey, sorry about that," he said. "I didn't see you standing there."

I drew in a deep breath, then let it out slowly. All my working parts seemed to be accounted for. *No harm done*, I told myself.

"That's all right." I stepped carefully over a small cantilever ledge, back down onto the driveway. "My heart needed a good jolt. Nice car."

"Thanks. It was a birthday present. I turned seventeen last month."

Sure, I thought. *That's what a learner car ought to look like.*

The boy opened the door and got out of the Porsche. He had a slender torso and long, skinny legs. His brown hair was straight and badly in need of combing. Unruly bangs flopped down over his eyes. Black framed glasses gave his face a studious look.

We hadn't gotten off to the best start, but the teenager had a nice smile and I couldn't fault his manners when he held out his hand and said, "I'm Trace Richland. Are you here to see my mother?"

"Yes, she's expecting me." My heart was still thumping like a wild beast in my chest. I hoped he couldn't feel it when I took his hand and shook it. "I'm Melanie Travis. I was just . . . um . . ."

"Looking for the door?" Trace asked with a grin. "You wouldn't be the first. My father thinks that placing it flush in the wall like that was the architect's private joke. My mother says it cuts down on visits from people she doesn't want to see. When my parents hold parties, sometimes they send out diagrams with the invitations."

As he spoke, I found myself turning his name over in my mind. I knew it sounded familiar; I just couldn't think why. Then abruptly the brain cells clicked together and illumination surfaced. Will from Puppy Posse had mentioned Trace when we were in the salon at the Puppy Fest.

This was the guy Will had called *Without a Trace.*

"You and I nearly met last week," I told him. "I was helping out at Puppy Fest."

"Really?" The teen looked briefly startled. Considering what had transpired at the event, I wondered if it was a sore subject. "Yeah, I was there."

"I'm surprised I didn't see you. I was helping out with the puppies too."

"Oh, wait." Trace shook his head. "Sorry, I was thinking of something else. Man, that was a busy weekend. I meant to show up, but I never got there. Come on, let me take you to the door."

"I'm very sorry for your loss," I said, as Trace escorted me to the house. "Were you and your grandfather close?"

"Well, sure." He didn't sound entirely convinced. "Although we didn't really see him that much. He was the kind of guy who was always on the move. Leo had a lot of stuff going on. Sometimes family wasn't as important to him as other things, you know?"

I nodded.

"Now I wish I'd had the chance to get to know him better—"

Abruptly, a portion of the seemingly solid wall in front of us shifted.

A glass door drew open and another teenage boy came flying out. He was dressed in white shorts and sneakers and carrying a metal tennis racket with an oversized head. This teen was younger than Trace, and there was no doubt that the two of them were brothers.

In an instant, Trace forgot all about me. "Damn

it, Nelson, what took you so long? Hurry up and
get in the car. We're gonna be late."

The two boys ran to the Porsche, hopped in,
and slammed the doors. Tires squealed as the
sports car went careening down the driveway.

So there I was, standing by myself on the front
walk.

The younger boy had left the door partially
open. I stepped up next to it and looked in vain
for a doorbell. I supposed that was hidden too.
The door was composed of a substantial pane of
glass, so I reached up and knocked.

Nothing happened. I waited, then tried again.

"Coming!" a voice called.

A minute passed before I finally heard the sound
of approaching footsteps. If Caroline Richland was
trying to convey the impression that our meeting
wasn't particularly important to her, she was doing
an excellent job. Her brother, Fred, might have
been supercilious, but at least he was prompt.

Eventually she came gliding toward me across
an open expanse that looked like it might be the
living room. Then she saw the open door and
stopped in surprise. "Oh my. What happened?"

"Two teenage boys," I said. "They were in a hurry."

Caroline was dressed better for a morning at
home than I would have been for dinner at a fancy
French restaurant. Her bright pink silk blouse was
tucked into skinny white slacks and her sandals
had five-inch heels. Her sleek blond bob hung in a
shiny wave around her perfectly made-up face.

She lifted her arm and glanced down at a slim
watch. "Nelson has a tennis lesson at ten. They're
going to be late."

"That's what Trace said."

Caroline looked up. "You know Trace?"

"We met earlier."

I nearly added "when he almost ran me over with his car," but then I thought better of it. No mother likes to hear criticism of her child—no matter how badly he might deserve it.

"Sometimes I don't know what's the matter with that boy. He shouldn't have left you standing out there. Please, come inside."

Caroline gestured me into a house whose interior was every bit as spectacular as it had looked from outside. The open floor plan and stark décor—blond hardwood floors and minimalist modern furniture—did nothing to draw the eye away from the panorama visible through the glass walls. Stepping inside was like walking into the most amazing tree house ever.

I had to hand it to the Brody siblings. They sure knew how to create a great visual.

Caroline paused to let me take it all in. She seemed to be waiting for me to comment.

A different kind of welcome might have elicited some pretty effusive compliments. Now I just shifted my eyes downward and took a seat on a white couch whose straight lines and lack of padding didn't seem too likely to offer much in the way of comfort.

Caroline perched on the edge of a wooden armchair opposite me. She sat with her shoulders erect and her knees and ankles aligned. Her hands, with their perfectly manicured nails, curled into a tight ball in her lap. To my surprise, she looked nervous. For a woman who seemingly had it all, she was wound tighter than a spring.

"Thank you for taking the time to talk to me," I began. Hopefully easing into the conversation would help her to relax.

"It's not as if I had a choice."

All righty then. No relaxing.

"Sure, you had a choice," I said. "You could have told Fred no."

Caroline waved a hand in the air. "If you believe that, you don't know a thing about my brother. Besides, it wasn't Fred who told me I had to talk to you. That was Libby's doing. She's always thought the fact that she's two years older entitles her to boss me around. Do you have siblings?"

"One. A younger brother."

"Do you tell him what to do?"

"I used to try. But mostly Frank just ignored me."

"That doesn't work with Libby," Caroline said. "She just raises her voice and insists."

"That doesn't sound very pleasant."

She looked at me across the glass-topped table between us and sighed. "Believe me, it isn't."

It had never crossed my mind that I might sympathize with Caroline—a woman with a fancy house, a designer wardrobe, and a teenage son who drove too fast—but suddenly I did. "Would you like me to leave?" I asked.

"No. What would be the point? Libby would just be mad at me, and probably Fred too. We might as well just get this over with."

"You're not what I expected," I said.

Caroline glanced around the room, as if she somehow thought that the magnificent setting had let her down. She probably wasn't used to that.

Maybe I should have offered up those compliments.

"In what way?" she wanted to know.

"I guess I thought that you would want to cooperate with your sister's wishes."

A flicker of annoyance crossed Caroline's face. "Did Libby tell you that?"

"No."

"Fred?"

"Actually," I admitted, "he said much the opposite. Fred is certain that your father's death was an accident. He told me you would agree with him. Before coming here, I thought that was a little odd. Now maybe I get it."

"You figured I'd take Libby's side because she and I share the same mother while Fred and I are only half-siblings?"

"I thought it was a possibility."

"That doesn't give me much credit for independent thought."

I shrugged. I had seen her smudging lipstick all over puppies, after all.

When I remained silent, Caroline said, "Libby and I are sisters, but we don't have a lot in common. She takes after our mother. I'm much more like our father. I was the quiet child, the one who always thought carefully about things before jumping in. In a family as boisterous as ours, that often made me feel like the odd one out.

"Fred is ten years older. That seemed like a whole different generation to me then. Even when I was just a little kid, he noticed me when others didn't. I guess he felt sorry for me because he took me under his wing."

"So Fred must be used to having you following his lead."

"I suppose. In his eyes, I'm still the little sister who wanted to tag along everywhere he went. But the hero worship I felt back then is long gone. I love Fred dearly, but I'm not immune to his flaws. No matter how much he might wish it, I won't allow him to dictate what I say or do."

Chapter 15

"Flaws?" My ears perked up.

"How much do you know about my family?" Caroline asked.

She was side-stepping my question but I didn't mind. I needed a tutorial on the Brody family. I was pretty sure I could work my way back to Fred's faults later.

Even better, Caroline was finally beginning to relax. I watched as she settled back in her chair. Her shoulders still looked as though they'd been stiffened by a rod, but at least I no longer got the impression that she might spring up and dart away at any moment.

"Only the basics," I said. "I know that Leo Brody had three wives and quite a few children."

"There are nine of us." Caroline shook her head at the number. "And despite our obvious common ground, we're all very different from one another. Fred's mother, Wendy, married my father just after they graduated from college. Their first child is my oldest sister, Nancy. Nancy is like her mother, sweet and unassuming. So much so that people are apt to take advantage of her."

I wondered if that was an oblique reference to Fred.

"Nancy and her husband, Ike, have two children. They live on a farm in North Salem and lead a very quiet life. Truthfully, I don't see them very often."

I could easily imagine why not. Caroline didn't seem like the kind of woman who would want anything to do with a quiet life.

"Fred came next," she continued. "He's the oldest son."

"So he told me," I said.

"I'm not surprised. He never lets anyone forget it. It bugs the living daylights out of him that he's not the oldest child, period."

"Is he married?" I hadn't seen any sign of a female inhabitant at his home, but I figured I should ask anyway.

"No, never." Caroline looked perplexed. "And it's not like he hasn't had plenty of chances. But whenever a relationship started to get serious, he would find some reason to decide it wasn't working. Fred's approaching fifty now so I guess it's not going to happen. It seems like he never met someone who could live up to his standards."

I tried to feel sorry for Fred and failed utterly.

"He mentioned a brother?" I said.

"That would be Ron, Wendy's last child. Ron and Fred are only one year apart in age. You'd think that they would get along, but the two of them have always fought like cats and dogs. I'm not sure what started it, but they've been that way as long as I've known them. Ron is married to Karen and they have twin daughters."

"Ashley and Megan? I met them at the Puppy Fest."

"Those two." Caroline sighed. "Karen lets them run wild. She says it's a good thing to let them learn how to think for themselves and make their own decisions. At their age, I think it's bull hockey."

"How old are they?"

"Eighteen, one year older than Trace. Megan will be going to college in the fall. Ashley is taking a gap year. What that really means is that she didn't keep her grades high enough to get into a decent college. When the kids were younger, all four cousins were great friends. But I've put a stop to that. I want my boys to grow up knowing what's expected of them and taking responsibility for their actions."

Based on Will's comments at Puppy Fest and my own experience with Caroline's sons earlier, her efforts didn't appear to be entirely successful.

"So Wendy had three children," I said. "And your mother, Maria, had two. I'm beginning to think I need a scorecard to keep all this straight. Who comes next?"

"That would be Clarissa. I was six when my father married her. *He* was forty, which seemed ancient to me. I thought Leo was entirely too old to be thinking about getting married again." Caroline frowned briefly. "Up until then, I'd always been the youngest. I was Daddy's girl. It never even crossed my mind that he would start a new family and leave the rest of us behind."

"That must have been traumatic for you."

"It was. And the situation was exacerbated by my mother, who was outraged when my father asked her for a divorce. She responded by making everything incredibly difficult for everyone involved. I went from being a happy child with two parents and four siblings living on an estate in Greenwich, to getting dumped in a little house in Darien with just Libby and my mother. Libby coped with the change much better than I did. I was bereft."

"Did you see your father often after that?"

"When he wasn't busy." The careless shrug that accompanied the comment didn't succeed in mitigating its sting. "My parents had joint custody. So even though we had moved out of Leo's house, Libby and I still spent a lot of time there. But of course it wasn't the same. My father was totally wrapped up in Clarissa then. And in hardly any time at all, three more children came along."

Caroline paused. Her expression was wry. "I'm not good at sharing. Even all these years later, I still think of Clarissa's kids as interlopers."

"Jane was the oldest," I said. Fred had told me that.

"Right. Then Joe was born a year later. Graham followed two years after that."

"That's only eight," I pointed out. "Somebody's missing."

Caroline nodded. "That's Annette. There was a five-year gap between her and Graham. I was fifteen when she was born. Nothing could have interested me less than yet another baby. It was clear that my father and Clarissa were having problems by then. If I had to guess, I'd say that she was conceived to save their marriage."

"I assume it didn't work?"

"Maybe for a little while." Caroline sounded disinterested in her stepmother's marital difficulties. "But eventually Daddy and Clarissa divorced anyway. After that, he said he would never marry again."

"Now I have the family straight," I said. "Tell me more about Fred."

"You're probably wondering why I went off on such a tangent, but I wanted you to understand the context," Caroline said. "A family the size of mine generates lots of squabbling, and plenty of competition. All of us kids were constantly vying for Daddy's attention. We each tried to stake out our own little piece of turf—you know, come up with some individual thing that we were good at and that made us feel important."

Caroline's childhood was years in the past. Still, the mere thought of growing up in a household with that much rivalry and dissension made me want to reach over and give her a hug.

"What was your specialty?" I asked curiously.

Caroline's lips twisted. She spread her arms out wide, then ran her hands up and down, indicating the length of her body. "Can't you tell? I was the pretty one, the girly girl. The child who always looked perfect and never did anything that wasn't expected of her."

"That sounds stifling."

Caroline shook her head. "You don't have to feel sorry for me. I could have had it worse. At least, in my case, the raw material was there. All I had to do was make the most of it. Things were harder for Fred. As the oldest boy in the family, he thought of himself as Leo's heir. So it was only natural that he would try to copy everything Daddy did. Fred positioned himself as the smart one in the family."

"That was a problem?"

"Don't get me wrong—it's not like Fred is dumb or anything. In a normal family, he'd have stood out like a shining beacon of intelligence. But in Leo Brody's family, nothing was ever normal, you know?"

I nodded.

"The whole world saw my father from the outside. He was *Leo Brody, Noted Entrepreneur and Philanthropist.* Some people looked up to him. Others envied him. Plenty hoped to emulate his success. They all felt like they knew him—and that they knew what it meant to live in Leo Brody's world."

"I'm sure that world looked very different from the inside," I said.

"It's not like I'm going to complain about the way we grew up. Even with our ups and downs, we all knew we had a pretty cushy life. One thing the nine of us had in common—maybe the only thing aside from our father—was that we all knew he was a hard act to follow. Kids want to make their parents proud of their achievements, you know? But how could we do that when our father had not only already done everything, but also succeeded at all of it in a very public way?"

"It sounds as though you put a lot of pressure on yourselves."

"Wherever the pressure came from, all I know is that it was always there. It was like a constant drumbeat in the background of our lives pushing us to try harder, to do better, to excel at everything we did."

Caroline braced her hands on the arms of her chair and stood. Her seat probably wasn't any more comfortable than mine was. She stepped over to the nearest pane of glass and stared out at the trees.

"As you can probably guess, the three divorces didn't help. When you're a child, you think the fact that your father left must be your fault. That if you'd behaved better or gotten higher grades in school, maybe he wouldn't have gone off to start a new family. Because it's obvious that who you are wasn't good enough to make him want to stay."

"Now that you're an adult, you must know that isn't true," I said slowly.

"Yeah, sure." Caroline glanced at me over her shoulder. "But you can file that bit of learning under 'too little too late.' "

I pegged Caroline's age as being pretty close to mine. If my math was right, her parents had been divorced for more than thirty years. That seemed like an awfully long time to be carrying around so much resentment.

"Are you close to your mother now?" I asked.

"My mother is no longer alive." Caroline had turned away from me again and was once more facing the window. I wished I could see her expressions as we spoke. "She died when I was in college. Her death was very sudden. She was only in her late forties, but she had a massive stroke."

"I'm sorry," I said.

"It was a huge shock at the time. But that was years ago. I don't dwell on what happened."

It sounded as though she'd gotten over her mother's death more easily than her parents' divorce. Maybe it was just me, but I thought she had her priorities backwards.

"Enough about me," Caroline said briskly. "You asked about Fred. With each new wife and every new child that was added to the family, he saw the slice of Daddy's attention that was directed toward him diminish. That drove him even harder to excel, to make an impression. Fred was always good in school, but by the time he got to high school, he wouldn't settle for being anything but the best. Daddy went to Princeton."

"Good school," I commented.

Caroline turned around. Now that we were no longer talking about her, the conversation flowed more easily. She came back and perched on the arm of her chair, still managing to sit with her knees together and her legs primly crossed at the ankles. The position looked like a habit left over from a convent upbringing.

"Fred went to Lawrenceville. That's in New Jersey."

I nodded.

"The rest of us were happy going to school in Connecticut, but Fred wanted to do everything he could to follow in our father's footsteps."

"So he must have gone to Princeton, too."

"That was the plan, but it didn't happen. In fact, Fred didn't even graduate from Lawrenceville. During his junior year, he was accused of cheating on an exam. He denied it, of course, but the evidence against him was pretty damning. Fred was asked to leave the school. Even Leo Brody's influence—and believe me it was brought to bear—couldn't fix things. I'm sure that's why Fred wants so badly to believe that our father's death was an accident."

"I don't get it," I said. "What does one thing have to do with the other?"

"Nothing that takes place in Leo Brody's family happens under the radar. Being thrown out of school was a huge disgrace for Fred. The newspapers had a field day with the story. Imagine seeing stories with headlines like 'Brody's Son Falls Flat' and 'Even Daddy's Money Can't Save You' written about yourself."

I winced in sympathy and Caroline nodded.

"Everything about it was awful. No surprise, the episode left a lasting impression on Fred. I know for a fact that he would do anything to avoid being subjected to that kind of public embarrassment again. There's no way he'd allow there to be a scandal over Leo Brody's death if he could prevent it."

"But what if he's wrong?" I asked.

"I think Fred would find that easier to live with than the other alternative of seeing his family dragged through the mud."

"How do you feel about that?"

Caroline's tongue moistened her lips before she spoke. "Despite the impression he might have given you, my brother doesn't speak for me. To be perfectly honest, I don't know what to believe about my father's death. I'm sure you've been told that he wasn't a careless man. Daddy would never have eaten something unless he was sure about where it had come from." She paused, then added, "Or sure of the person who gave it to him."

"Like maybe someone inside your family."

Caroline didn't acknowledge my comment. Instead she said, "Do you remember that old TV show, *The Brady Bunch?*"

"Sure."

"Well, that wasn't my family. Not even close." Caroline snorted delicately. "The press sometimes thought it was clever to refer to us as The Brody Bunch, but we never blended that smoothly. Even so, it's nearly impossible for me to believe that somebody I grew up with might have wished our father harm."

I nodded. I could see that. "Do you have any other ideas?"

"Frankly, I try not to think about it."

"But if you did?"

Her eyes narrowed. "Have you met Becca Montague? That woman's a snake. I wouldn't believe a word she said about anything. I told the detective he should check her out and he said he would, but then nothing ever came of it." Her fingers twisted together in her lap. "It doesn't seem right that we're not going to get any answers."

"Libby feels the same way. That's why she enlisted my help," I said.

"On one level, I hate what Libby asked you to do. But on another . . ." Caroline shrugged helplessly. "If you think your poking around can help us figure out what happened, you have my blessing."

This time when she rose to her feet, she looked ready to escort me out.

"I know you were at Puppy Fest," I said as we walked to the door together. "I saw you kissing puppies in the salon. Where did you go after that?"

Caroline was no dope. She saw immediately where I was heading.

"You want to know where I was when my father died."

"Yes. I didn't see you in the ballroom during the game."

"That's because I was gone by then. I'd already done my bit. There was no reason for me to hang around any longer. I didn't even hear the news until an hour later. Nobody thought to call me."

She opened the glass door, and I passed through the doorway. I paused just outside. "So how did you find out about your father's death?"

"It was a reporter who reached me first. He was looking for a scoop. I thought he was lying and I hung up on him. But then I confirmed the news online."

Not The Brady Bunch indeed, I thought.

Chapter 16

My visit with Caroline had been relatively quick. When I arrived home, Sam and Kevin were still at the Y. In their absence the Poodle Posse—including its honorary new member, Bud—made a great welcoming committee.

As usual, Tar and Augie pushed their way to the front of the pack when I came through the door. The three bitches hung back in a more dignified manner. It was easy to read the expressions on the their faces. *Boys. Always in such a hurry when there's nowhere to go.*

I tossed my purse on the side table and squatted down to say hello. The Poodles crowded around me, tails wagging in unison. Smaller than the rest, Bud made a bid for attention by standing on his hind legs and jumping up and down like a demented ballet dancer. When I still didn't get to him fast enough, he began to bark with each leap.

That drew a reproachful glare from Faith. Chastened, Bud immediately dropped down to all fours. I reached over and scooped him up into my arms.

That did the trick. The little dog parted his lips in a doggy grin and his stubby tail began to wiggle back and forth.

"Into the kitchen," I said. "Biscuits for everyone."

All right, I admit it. I'm a soft touch. You would be too if you lived with the best dogs in the world.

I carried half a dozen peanut butter biscuits outside to the deck and passed them around. The dogs scattered to different corners of the patio, lay down, and began to chew. I sank into a wicker chair with a plump cushion on its seat. Compared to Caroline's furniture, this was bliss.

Ten days had passed since Davey and I had brought Bud home. To everybody's relief, the attempts we'd made to find his previous owners had brought no response. Over the weekend, Bud had had another bath. His nails were trimmed and his ears cleaned. The sores around his neck were healing nicely. He'd already put on a pound or two, and his coat was beginning to acquire a healthy sheen.

In every way, the little dog was doing his best to fit into our family seamlessly. With Davey teaching and Kevin supervising, Bud had also begun to acquire a repertoire of tricks. So far he could jump through a hoop, sit up on his haunches and beg, and balance a biscuit on his nose.

I didn't care what anybody said. Bud was here to stay.

On the drive back from Greenwich, it had occurred to me that I'd never asked Libby about the disposition of Leo Brody's will. I pulled out my phone and gave her a call.

After half a dozen rings, Libby picked up. "Who is this?" she snapped.

"Melanie Travis."

"Oh." Her tone softened slightly. "Okay."

"Who were you expecting?"

"Some vulture from the press or a celebrity news show. It's incredible how insensitive people are. Ever since word got out that my father died from eating cookies, comedians are making jokes and reporters are spinning cautionary tales about peanut allergies. Everyone wants to capitalize on the event."

"I'm sorry," I said. "That must be hard for you."

"I don't even bother to say 'no comment' anymore. I just hang up the phone. That gets rid of them. So . . . what have you found out?"

"Not a whole lot yet. I'm just getting started. You're going to have to be patient."

"Patience isn't my strong suit."

I could have guessed that. "In the meantime, I was wondering about your father's will."

"What about it?"

"Has it been read yet?"

"Of course. We met with the lawyers last week."

"*And?*"

Libby was supposed to be on my side, but she wasn't making this easy. Surely she could guess what I wanted to know.

"You expect me to give you specifics?" Her tone conveyed enough outrage to make me lift the phone away from my ear.

"Libby, I'm not a member of the press trying to pry into your secrets. You *asked* me to look into what happened."

"What does that have to do with Leo Brody's will?"

"Because if somebody gave your father those cookies on purpose, they had to have had a motive."

Silence. Crickets.

Faith padded over and pushed her muzzle into my free hand. I patted my lap, and she jumped the front half of her body onto my legs. I slipped my fingers under her throat and began to scratch her chin.

"You mean money," Libby said after a minute.

I would have thought that was assumed, but apparently not.

"Yes, money," I replied patiently. "Where did it go?"

"My father provided vital support for a number of important charities. He also served on the boards of several philanthropic foundations. He strongly believed that it was his duty to leave the world a better place than he'd found it."

Really? That was her answer? It sounded as though she was quoting from a press release. And not in a helpful way.

"Right." If I hadn't made myself clear previously, I had every intention of doing so now. "Do you think that a charitable foundation sent someone to kill your father for his money?"

"Of course not," Libby shot back. "Don't be ridiculous."

"So let's try looking a little closer to home, okay? What did the family members inherit? I don't need specific numbers, just a general idea."

"We got money too. I guess you could call it a lot of money."

That was what I'd figured. "You're talking about Leo Brody's children?"

"That's right," she confirmed.

"What about the grandchildren?"

"There are trusts set up for them. They'll come into their money later. Not a huge amount because they'll also inherit through their parents."

"And the ex-wives?"

"What about them?" Libby sounded surprised.

"Did they inherit anything?"

"Certainly not. They left the family. They're not part of Us anymore."

That's right. Us had a capital letter. Kind of like the Royal We.

"Anyone else?" I asked.

"Isn't that enough?" The snippy tone was back.

"If you say so," I told her. "I'm just trying to get things clear in my mind."

"Then let me clarify something else for you. I'm uncomfortable sharing private family business. And frankly I don't see how this discussion is helpful at all. If inheritance was a factor in my father's death, the entire family shared the same motive."

"Yes," I said. "But they don't all share the same needs."

We both thought about that for a bit before Libby broke the silence grudgingly. "I guess there's something else you should know. My father had been thinking about changing his will."

"In whose favor?"

"Not the family. His intention was to leave more of his assets to places where he felt they could do the most good. You know, like globally."

"Was that a recent change of heart on your father's part?" I asked.

"He'd been talking about it for a few months."

"Who else besides you knew about that?"

The question made Libby laugh. "*Everybody.* When Leo Brody got an idea, he shared it with the world. There were articles on the *Forbes* website and *Huff Post.* 'Noted philanthropist urges others to follow his lead . . .' That kind of thing."

"But he didn't actually change his will before he died?" I said.

"Apparently not. His death was unexpected. I'm sure he thought he'd have more time."

Thank you, Captain Obvious.

"That's all I know," Libby said. "Are we done here?"

"I guess so. Thank you for answering my questions."

"I told you to talk to my brother, Graham. Have you done that yet?"

"No, I—"

"If I were you, I'd get right on it." The line went dead.

I put the phone away and looked down at Faith. She tipped her face up toward mine. Her tail swished slowly from side to side.

"That family thinks they rule the world," I said.

Faith woofed in reply.

She ruled my world, and she knew it.

* * *

Graham Brody was expecting my call. I can't say
I was surprised. By now, I was becoming accustomed
to both Brody family dynamics and to Libby's powers
of persuasion when it came to bending others to her
will.

Graham told me that he and his brother, Joe,
would be available to see me after lunch and gave
me directions to his place in Cos Cob. Two birds
with one stone. I liked the sound of that

Sam and Kevin arrived home as I was mixing up
some egg salad for lunch. While we ate, Kev told
me all about swim class. He waved his hands in the
air with great enthusiasm to demonstrate the
stroke he'd practiced that morning. It looked suspiciously like a doggie paddle, but hey, whatever
kept his head above water was fine with me.

After lunch, Sam had work to do which meant
that the munchkin was coming with me. Hopefully
the Brody brothers wouldn't mind the unexpected
addition to our group. I'd already met Joe—he'd
directed me to the cache of bottled water in the
pantry during Puppy Fest—and he'd seemed like
an easygoing guy. With luck, his brother would be
the same.

Cos Cob is a small coastal community situated
just east of Greenwich. Not quite large enough to
qualify as a separate town, it does have its own post
office, fire station, and schools, as well as coveted
access to Long Island Sound.

Kev and I took the Post Road west from Stamford. He was bouncing up and down in his car seat
happily. "Going swimming!" he cried.

I glanced back at him over my shoulder. "No,

you already went swimming this morning. Now we're going somewhere else."

Kev loves going places. Despite the fact that I'd dashed his plans, his smile remained firmly in place. "Supermarket?" he guessed.

"No."

"Library? Dog food store?"

"No, we're going to visit some people I need to talk to."

"Talk to people," he agreed happily. "Friends."

I hoped he was right about that.

Graham's directions led me to a modest clapboard house on a residential street north of the village. The home was painted dove gray with white trim and had arched windows, a peaked roof, and a narrow front porch. A short driveway led to a detached single-car garage whose door was closed. The pavement in the driveway was cracked in several places, and the yard around the house needed mowing.

I couldn't help but be struck by the disparity between this house and the other Brody residences I'd visited. Graham and Joe were from Leo's most recent marriage. By my estimation, these brothers were nearly twenty years younger than Fred and almost a decade younger than Caroline. These younger siblings wouldn't have had as much time to establish themselves in careers as Leo Brody's older children had. I wondered whether that was the reason for the difference or if there was some other factor at play.

Kevin likes to ring doorbells so I picked him up and let him have at it. He managed to push the buzzer twice before I pulled him hastily away.

"Sorry about that," I said when the door opened only seconds later. I indicated Kev, now on the porch. "My son got a little carried away."

"I'm Kevin Driver," Kev announced. "Who are you?"

"Graham Brody." He reached down, took Kevin's hand, and gave it a gentle shake. "It's a pleasure to meet you."

"You too," Kev agreed.

Graham was shorter than his brother but not by much. Both men shared the same coffee-colored hair and gym-ready builds. And just like Joe, Graham had a great smile.

"I'm Melanie Travis," I said. "I hope it's okay if Kev joins us?"

"No problem." He waved us both inside. "Joe's pouring us a couple of beers. Can I get you something?"

"No thanks. I have a juice box and some Matchbox cars in my bag. Kevin can entertain himself while we talk."

Graham preceded me into a living room whose décor could best be described as "vintage bachelor pad." The focal point of the room was an enormous flat-screen TV. It was affixed to a wall opposite a charcoal suede couch that was flanked by a pair of matching recliners. Black metal accent tables and a dead plant in the corner completed the furnishings.

"Have a seat," said Graham.

Kev looked around at the choices and staked out a spot on the floor. I handed him a trio of model cars, then sat down on the couch. I'd barely gotten settled before Joe appeared through a doorway that led to the kitchen. He was holding two bottles of Heineken by their necks.

"Hey, good to see you again." He lifted his hand and tipped a bottle in my direction. "Want one?"

"No thanks."

"We've covered that already. She doesn't want a beer," Graham told him.

Joe shrugged. "Never hurts to ask."

Graham looked my way as he took a seat in one of the recliners. "Joe's two years older than me. For some reason, he thinks that makes him smarter."

"If the shoe fits . . ." Joe's brows waggled up and down. He nodded toward Kev, who was parking his cars in a row beneath the coffee table. "Cute kid. Yours?"

I hoped that wasn't a serious question.

"His name is Kevin," I said. "He's three."

Kev glanced up. "Three and a half," he corrected.

"That's a great age," Joe said. He sank down in the other recliner.

"You have children?" I asked, surprised.

"No, but I remember it well."

Graham stared at his brother. "You remember being three," he said skeptically.

"Of course. Don't you? We lived in a big house with a swimming pool that had a slide. Jane had a pony. It used to crap all over the lawn."

"Don't listen to a word he says," Graham told me. "He's making it up."

"Scout's honor." Joe raised his hand and formed a salute with his fingers. "I remember everything."

"Except maybe the fact that you were never a Boy Scout."

"A mere technicality." Joe lifted his bottle and took a long swallow of beer.

Graham followed suit. The two of them were like peas in a pod. Maybe that was why they couldn't resist taking jabs at one another.

"Do the two of you live here together?" I asked.

"Yes," said Joe. "He's the tenant. I'm the landlord."

"But not for long," Graham said.

"You'll be moving out?"

He nodded. "Libby filled us in on what you're doing so I'm sure you know that my circumstances . . . that all our circumstances . . . have changed recently."

"With your father's death," I said.

"That's right."

His matter-of-fact tone stopped me from offering condolences. I moved on instead. "Were you at the house that day for Puppy Fest?"

"Sure, I was there," Graham replied. "We were all there."

"I don't remember seeing you."

"It's a big house." He shrugged. "I didn't see you either. Puppy Fest is pretty much a command performance for us Brodys. That explains my presence. How come you were there?"

"Claire Travis, the woman who was running the event, asked me to come and help with the puppies."

A look passed between the two brothers. Before I could decipher what it meant, it was already gone.

"You were working with Jane," Joe said quickly, speaking up before Graham had a chance to reply.

I wondered if there was something he didn't want his brother to say.

"Yes, I was. She's your sister, right?"

Joe nodded. "We have five sisters. But yes, Jane is one of them."

"The bossy one." Graham looked pained.

"The closest to us in age," Joe added. "Jane's the oldest in our part of the family. I came along next, followed by Graham. Annette was last. She's spending the summer in Chile with a youth group. They're working with disadvantaged kids."

"That sounds like something your father would have approved of."

"He did," Joe told me. "Leo was determined that each of his children would have what he called 'real world experience.' I worked for Habitat for Humanity. Graham did a stint with AmeriCares."

"And what do you do now?" I asked.

"I guess you might say that I'm between opportunities. Right now, I'm bartending at a restaurant in Rye. But as Graham pointed out earlier, my prospects are about to improve."

Indeed.

I turned to Graham. "What do you do?"

"I'm a venture capitalist."

"Big words." Joe winked at me. "Small results."

"So far." Graham glared at his brother. "But I'm currently involved with several innovative tech startups. As soon as one of them hits, that will change."

"You've been singing that same tune for the last three years," Joe said with a smirk. "It's beginning to get old."

"Oh? And I suppose you think you're doing so much better, spending your nights behind a bar watching people get drunk?"

I wasn't aware that Kevin had been listening to our conversation, but now he raised his head. "I like bars," he said.

He was thinking of jungle gyms. At least I hoped he was.

"You do?" Joe sounded amused. "You must be very precocious."

"I am." Kevin nodded firmly. Lack of comprehension has never stopped him from agreeing with anything.

"In that case, you should bring your mother to my bar to visit me some time." Joe's gaze slid my way. When his eyes locked on mine, I wondered what in the world he was thinking. "Do you think she might like that?"

Kevin just looked confused. Which was pretty much the way I felt. Joe's husky-toned remark had sounded as though it was meant to be a come-on. But surely I had to be mistaken about that.

Graham cleared his throat loudly, drawing all eyes his way. He still appeared to be angry at his brother's repeated needling, and his next words only confirmed that impression.

"Enough beating around the bush," he said shortly. "Let's talk about why you're really here."

Chapter 17

"I'm sure Libby explained that to you," I said in the same kind of soothing tone I'd have used to calm an angry dog. "She has doubts about the way your father's death was handled. You were there that day. What do you think happened?"

Graham ignored my second question and zeroed in on the first. "Why are you asking me?" he demanded.

Joe spoke up before I could respond. "That's easy. Melanie wants to hear what you have to say about Leo's death because you're the one who always needs money."

Really? He had to go there?

Even though Libby had said much the same thing, I was still annoyed. Joe was fanning the flames of his brother's anger deliberately. And unnecessarily.

"What does that have to do with anything?" Graham shot back. "If you think that gives me some kind of motive, you're crazy. I loved my father. I would *never* have done anything to hurt him."

He reached for his beer bottle and chugged half of it down in one long gulp. Joe glanced at me and rolled his eyes. I focused on Graham and ignored him.

"That's a stupid idea anyway." Graham set the empty bottle back down on the tabletop with a sharp snap of his wrist. "I'm not the only one in this family who needs money."

"Who else?" I asked with interest.

"Caroline, for starters. She and her husband put up a good front but he's been living off her dough for years. And what about Nancy with her endless causes? Save the redwoods! Save the whales! Save the butterflies! Money flows through her fingers like water."

"Graham, that's enough," Joe said sharply. "Melanie doesn't want to hear about that stuff."

Joe couldn't have been more wrong. That was *exactly* what I wanted to hear about. And Joe had shut his brother down precisely when things started to get interesting.

"Then how about you?" I challenged him. "What do you think happened?"

Joe thought before answering. "Truthfully, I don't know. Obviously I was at the house that day too. I had seen my father earlier, just before I ran into you. He and I talked about Puppy Fest and how excited he was to be hosting the event again."

He stopped and sighed. "Leo Brody wasn't just our father. He was also a man who genuinely cared about making the world a better place. His passing isn't only our loss—it's a loss for everyone who would have benefitted from his good works in the future. I can't imagine anyone wanting to end his life."

"That's because our father's death was an accident," Graham snapped. "It was a stupid, senseless tragedy that should never have happened." He'd barely finished speaking before he pushed himself to his feet and left the room.

Joe and I watched him leave in silence. Then we resumed our conversation. I asked a few more questions and got a few more nebulous replies. Joe kept diverting the discussion away from Leo Brody's death by asking me questions about my life. Which wasn't useful at all.

Eventually I just gave up. Maybe that was his plan all along.

"I want to apologize for my brother's behavior," Joe said as he walked Kevin and me to the door. "Graham has a short fuse, but he never stays mad for long. After he blows up, he's always sorry later."

"I hope I didn't upset him too much. I know the questions I was asking weren't easy."

To my surprise, Joe lifted his arm and curled it around my shoulders, pulling me closer to his side. His fingers squeezed gently. "It's kind of you to look at it that way. You seem like a very understanding woman."

His gesture was not only unexpected, it also felt oddly possessive. And inappropriate. I took a deliberate step back and Joe's hand fell away. He appeared amused by my retreat.

We both reached for the doorknob at the same time. Our arms crossed, and his hand landed on top of mine. Joe looked at me and smiled.

"What are you doing?" I asked.

"Flirting with you."

"No, you're not."

"I am." His lips quirked upward in one corner. No doubt he was accustomed to using that lopsided grin to great effect.

"Why?"

"If you need to ask that, you've been spending your time with the wrong kind of men."

I slid my hand out from beneath his. "I haven't been spending my time with any men. I'm married."

Joe just shrugged. Somehow he made the motion look like an invitation. He turned the knob and drew the door open.

"Any time you want to continue our conversation, just give me a call," he said.

I should have come back with a snappy retort. Something that would put Joe in his place. Instead I was rendered speechless. Thankfully Kevin came to the rescue.

He gave my hand a sharp tug. "Mommy, let's *go*," he said.

We made it all the way to the car before I looked back. The door to the house was still open. Joe was standing in the doorway staring after us.

Kevin and I spent some time at the library, then picked up Davey at camp. When we arrived home, I found out that Sam had invited Aunt Peg to dinner.

"Are you cooking?" I asked hopefully.

Sam gestured toward the grill, his favorite go-to appliance.

"Is Aunt Peg bringing dessert?"

Aunt Peg has a sweet tooth of near-mythical proportion. Thanks to her influence, I now share her fondness—bordering on addiction—for cakes from the St. Moritz Bakery in Greenwich.

"I told her that was part of the deal," Sam said.

"What's the other part?" I asked, suddenly suspicious.

"I'd imagine she's going to want to hear all about the dastardly doings of Libby Rothko's relatives."

"Fine by me." That part was easy. "I'll try to come up with some before she gets here."

Before Aunt Peg's minivan had even turned in the driveway, the Poodle posse was already lined up at the front door waiting for her. I didn't know why that happened, but it wasn't the first time I'd seen the dogs respond that way. I guessed she must send out a vibe that's akin to the Bat Signal. I know she's fully capable of making the hair on the back of my neck stand up.

Davey raced outside as Aunt Peg's minivan was rolling to a stop. Kevin was hot on his heels. The Poodles—bless their hearts—paused to ask for permission before scrambling en masse out the door. At least somebody was well trained.

When I reached the front walk, Aunt Peg was wading through the Poodle pack milling around her legs. She stopped and peered down at Bud. "I see you're still here."

"Of course he's still here," Davey said stoutly.

"This is where he lives." His eyes went to the cardboard box tied with white string in Aunt Peg's hand. "Is that cake?"

She handed him the box. "I got a shadow cake. Black and white in honor of Bud. How's that for a good idea?"

"Perfect," I said.

"Bud and I are having cake," Kevin crowed.

I reached down and ruffled his hair. "*After* dinner. Now go and wash your hands. We're almost ready to eat."

Both my children followed directions and went inside the house. That was more like it. Who cared if their compliance was probably due to the promise of cake? I was choosing to look on the bright side.

"I spoke with Libby before coming here tonight," Aunt Peg said.

"Oh? How is she?"

"Quite cross, if you must know."

"I wonder why," I said innocently.

She looked at me askance. "Libby wants answers."

"She and I met for the first time on Friday," I pointed out. "Now it's Monday. I hope you told her that I'm not the Energizer Bunny."

"I told her you're doing your best," Aunt Peg said on a long exhale.

"That would sound more impressive if you said it without the sigh."

"What would *be* more impressive is results."

Sam stuck his head out the door. He had a grilling fork in one hand and an oven mitt on the other. "Hey, we're hungry in here. If you two don't hurry up, we're going to eat without you."

We both hurried to comply. Whatever Sam was cooking smelled great. Aunt Peg lifted her head and sniffed the air like a dog on the scent of a rabbit.

"Trout," she said with satisfaction. "Good for my diet."

And then there would be cake. Good for our taste buds.

While we ate, Aunt Peg grilled me about what I'd learned so far. I started by outlining the various relationships within Leo Brody's extended family. She listened for less than five minutes, then waved me on impatiently.

"Enough about the siblings. What about Leo's will? Where did all that money go? And which of his relatives couldn't wait to get his or her grubby hands on it?"

"That's the problem," I said. "They *all* inherited. The children each received a share of Leo Brody's money and the grandchildren's bequests were put in trust for them."

"Now things are starting to get interesting," Aunt Peg said with satisfaction. "Which of the siblings was in dire need of cash?"

"According to Libby, it's Graham," I said. "But according to Graham, he's not the only one."

"Libby seems to be rather well situated," Aunt Peg mused.

"So does her sister Caroline. She and her family live in a showplace of a house in Greenwich. But Graham says that she and her husband are strapped for cash. He also told me that Nancy, the oldest, goes through money like water."

"This Graham character sounds like he had a

lot to say." Aunt Peg sounded pleased. "What does he do?"

"He calls himself a venture capitalist. But his brother, Joe, implied that he's not very successful."

"That's one way to lose a lot of cash fast," Sam commented.

We all nodded in agreement. Even Kevin, who was busy eating his peas. He doesn't love the taste but he enjoys the challenge of trying to keep them on his fork long enough to get them to his mouth.

"Don't forget," Aunt Peg interjected, "according to what Libby told us, none of Leo's adult children were being supported by him and they were bitter about that. It appears they all felt their relationship with their father entitled them to a higher standard of living."

"If they were looking for financial gain, most of the siblings haven't made the best career choices," I said. "Joe is currently bartending. Jane manages the Puppy Posse. Nancy, whom I haven't met yet, lives on a farm in North Salem."

"So they all stood to benefit from their father's death," Sam summed up.

"Right. And there's something else. Earlier today, Libby told me that her father was thinking about changing his will. He'd decided to allocate more of his assets for the global good."

Aunt Peg shook her head. "Leo's children can't have been happy about that."

"No, indeed," Sam agreed. "And then along came Puppy Fest."

"The timing could hardly have been more convenient," I said. "Because of the event, most of the family was present at the house that day. And of course Mr. Brody was guaranteed to be there too. Not only that, but the place is huge. The siblings grew up in that house and I'm sure they're all well aware of how to slip in and out of places without being seen."

"This is all very interesting," Aunt Peg said. "You've certainly been dealt a full house of suspects."

Davey groaned. Sam bit back a smile. I just sighed.

"So far, they've all either tried to convince me that Brody's death was an accident, or they've pointed a finger at somebody else," I said. "To hear them tell it, each of the siblings adored their father and would *never* have done anything to harm him."

"Of course they would say that to you," Aunt Peg replied skeptically. "What you need is an outsider's opinion of that family."

"I hate to break it to you, but even with the access Libby has provided, I *am* an outsider. I'm quite certain that I'm being told only what the Brody family wants me to hear."

"Precisely. That's why you should talk to Claire."

"Claire?" Sam and I exchanged a startled look. "What would she know about Leo Brody's family?"

Aunt Peg set down her fork. The only way her plate could have gotten any cleaner was if she'd picked it up and licked it. Come to think of it, I wouldn't put that past her. Rather than replying to my question, she veered toward a new topic. It was a perennial favorite: dogs.

"Claire and I have been getting together to work on Thor and Jojo's training. Have you met them?"

Only Aunt Peg would phrase the question that way—as if Thor and Jojo were acquaintances of Claire's whom she might have introduced me to at some point. In reality, they were dogs. Thor was a powerful Rottweiler mix and Jojo was a little tan terrier with a wiry coat. Both had been adopted from the pound by Claire's late brother, the talented dog whisperer Nick Walden.

Nothing was known about the dogs' lives before Nick took them in, and both still carried emotional scars from their previous situations. Thor's insecurities manifested themselves in a pugnacious and sometimes aggressive attitude. Jojo was timid and afraid of strangers. Nick had been in the process of re-socializing the pair when he'd died the previous year.

Claire was doing the best she could for Thor and Jojo, but she didn't share her brother's intuitive touch. Now that she and Aunt Peg had gotten to know one another, it didn't surprise me that Claire had turned to Peg for help.

"I've met them both and I'm glad you've stepped in to work with them. They can be a handful for Claire, especially Thor."

"I can't help but feel sorry for that poor dog," Aunt Peg said. "He doesn't want to be bad. But early on, someone must have gotten in his face and taught him that fighting back and bullying his way through life was the only way to get what he needed. Claire's slowly getting him turned around. What she lacks in knowledge she makes up in patience and willingness to learn. I hope your ex-husband realizes what a gem he got when he married that woman."

Bob had never been one of Aunt Peg's favorite people. Not that I could blame her for that. For years, he hadn't been one of mine either. It had taken us a long time to become friends again, with Davey being the catalyst for our rapprochement. For my son's sake, I'd forgiven a lot. Aunt Peg was coming around more slowly.

"You were going to tell us something about Claire and the Brody family?" Sam prompted.

Aunt Peg nodded. "As you might imagine, Claire and I have had several opportunities to chat recently."

"And yet somehow she neglected to tell you about Puppy Fest," I said under my breath.

Aunt Peg heard me anyway. Her gaze sharpened. "We've moved past that. Just this past week, she and I had an interesting chat about her participation in the event. Stop and think about it. Leo was a man with endless resources and connections. So how do you suppose Claire landed a job like that? Why would *she* have been hired to manage Puppy Fest?"

It had never occurred to me to question how Claire had gotten the assignment. She was an event planner. Puppy Fest was an event. That seemed logical enough to me.

"Claire's brother, Nick, did volunteer work at Puppy Posse, right?" I said. "So he and Jane knew one another. I figured that was the connection that brought Claire to Leo Brody's attention."

"That was one connection." Aunt Peg paused until all eyes around the table were trained on her.

She loves a dramatic flourish. "But it wasn't the only link between them. Nor the most important one."

Sam and I both perked up. Davey stopped eating and paid attention. Even Kevin, who probably hadn't a clue what we were talking about, looked interested.

"So there you have it." She braced her hands on the edge of the table and rose from her seat. "That's why you need to talk to Claire. Now, who's ready to give that shadow cake a try?"

"Wait . . . what?" I sputtered. "You mean you're not going to tell us?"

"No. It's not my story to tell."

"But you can't just leave us hanging."

Aunt Peg favored me with a sly smile. This was payback for that crack about Puppy Fest. It had to be.

"You may hang all you like," she said. "Meanwhile, Sam and the boys and I will be eating cake."

"Aww, Mom." Davey laughed. "You deserved that."

Chapter 18

Claire and I met for lunch at The Bean Counter the next day.

Opened half a dozen years earlier by my younger brother, Frank, the quaint café in North Stamford had originally been a coffee bar. Well-situated just outside the city's commercial zone, it also drew traffic from surrounding towns. The historic clapboard building had quickly become a popular lunch spot for shoppers, suburbanites, and nearby office workers.

As The Bean Counter's popularity had grown, so had its menu. The country bistro now offered a variety of sandwiches and pastries in addition to its signature gourmet coffees. The expanding business had also added a partner: Claire's husband, my ex-husband, Bob.

Frank's outgoing personality meant that he was at his best in the front of the house. He made sandwiches, kissed babies, and greeted returning customers by name. Bob ran the back office. Trained as an accountant, he did the books, managed payroll, and kept a sharp eye on inventory. Bob also reined in my brother's more outrageous impulses. We were all grateful for that.

Frank was behind the counter, bantering with customers, when I arrived. He sketched a quick wave and pointed toward a booth in the back of the room where Claire was already seated.

My brother and I shared the same light brown hair and slender build, but beyond that, we didn't have a lot in common. I was the shy child who worried about everything. Frank was the goof-off who made friends easily, cared deeply about nothing, and skated through life in the fast lane.

I'd spent much of my childhood making excuses for Frank and covering up for his misdeeds. All these years later, there were still times when I looked at the responsible adult he'd become and saw only the mischievous little boy who had driven me crazy.

Claire looked up from her phone as I slid into the booth opposite her. She quickly tucked the device away. "I ordered for us already. It was busy when I got here, and the line was growing quickly. I figured that would be more efficient. I hope you don't mind."

"Nope, that's fine," I said. "What am I having?"

It would be a treat to eat something that actually appeared on the blackboard for a change. Frank had a tendency to treat me like his own personal crash dummy. He served me all sorts of innovative concoctions—food combinations he'd dreamed up but hadn't yet deemed menu-worthy. Some were actually tasty. Others left me with heartburn and a sour taste in the back of my mouth.

"Caribbean chicken salad. It looked really good so I ordered one for each of us. And iced tea. How does that sound?"

"Perfect." I plucked my napkin off the table and settled it on my lap. "Even Frank can't screw that up."

Claire's lips thinned. "*Even* Frank? Really Melanie, look around you. Frank built The Bean Counter from scratch and this place is thriving. It's a random mid-week afternoon, and I could barely find a place for us to sit down. People are clamoring for what Frank does. Bob is amazed with how well things are going here. I don't think you give your brother enough credit."

Claire tells it like it is. It's one of the things I love about her. And I'd deserved that.

"You're right," I said. "I have to stop thinking of Frank as my annoying little brother and accept him for who he is now."

"Don't beat yourself up too badly." Claire grinned. "At times Frank can still be pretty annoying. Just ask Bertie."

I'd only been half-joking when I had warned Bertie not to marry my feckless brother. Fortunately for all concerned, she'd gone ahead and done it anyway. The union had turned both their lives around. And as a bonus, I'd gained the sister I'd always wanted.

"I talked to her this morning," I said. "Now that she's taking things easy, she's feeling pretty good. But she's still counting down the days—"

"Days?" Claire looked amused. "Bertie still has weeks to go."

"Don't try telling her that. She's ready for that kid to make an appearance right now."

The waitress appeared with our order. She placed our drinks to one side, then set a large wooden bowl down in front of each of us.

Claire and I paused to have a look. Grilled chicken, pineapple, avocado, and mango rested on a bed of leafy greens. Blue cheese crumbles and shredded coconut were sprinkled on top. There was a ramekin of tart vinaigrette on the side.

"Wow," I said. "I take back those mean things I ever said about Frank. This looks great."

"I told you." Claire sounded smug.

I stirred some sugar into my tea, then popped a piece of mango in my mouth. A burst of flavor lit up my mouth and I nearly moaned with pleasure. Claire poured a small amount of vinaigrette onto her salad, then took a bite of chicken. I waited until she'd swallowed before broaching the topic that had brought us together.

"I hear that Aunt Peg has been working with Thor and Jojo."

"Yes, she's been stopping by a couple times a week. As I'm sure you can imagine, her input is invaluable. Jojo's finally starting to come out of her shell, and even Thor is beginning to settle down." She glanced up. "But that's not really what we're here to talk about, is it?"

"No," I admitted. "I was trying to be subtle."

"You, subtle? I don't think so." Claire was too polite to laugh but I could see she was thinking about it. "I'm guessing that you want to hear about me and Joe."

"Joe?" I swallowed wrong and came up coughing. Whatever I'd expected her to say, it certainly wasn't that. I got my breath back and said, "*You and Joe Brody?*"

"Yes, me and Joe Brody. Didn't Peg tell you? I just assumed it was why we were here."

"No, she didn't tell me." And now that seemed odd. It wasn't like Aunt Peg to exercise discretion. Especially when she was in possession of a bombshell of this magnitude. "She made a cryptic comment about some secret connection that had brought you in contact with Leo Brody. But then she refused to give any details."

"Peg refusing to spill all? That has to be a first."

"It came as a shock to me too," I agreed. "So what are we talking about? Clandestine business dealings? Kindergarten memories? Some great unrequited love? I hope it's something juicy."

Abruptly Claire's amusement vanished. "No, no, and *no*. Most especially to the last."

Shakespeare, had he been lunching with us, would have said that the lady protested too much.

"You sound pretty adamant about that," I said. Her denial had also been loud enough to draw attention from surrounding tables. I didn't bother to mention that part.

"Sorry." Claire's voice dropped. "It's nothing really. Joe Brody and I are old news. Very old news. He plays no part in my life at all anymore."

"But he did at one time?"

She gazed at me across the table. Claire's usually

lively expression was grave. "Look, the main thing you need to know is that this all happened a long time ago. *Before* I met Bob."

"I never suspected any differently." That concern was easy to dismiss. "What, precisely, went on between you and Joe Brody?"

"He and I dated . . . no, that's a stupid word to describe it." She frowned and started over. "He and I were involved in a relationship for six months."

Holy moley. That was news.

I found myself leaning closer across the table. "Was it serious?"

"I thought so. Joe apparently felt differently."

"How did you guys meet?"

"Through Nick. He did some work for Jane at Puppy Posse. You know that, right?"

I nodded.

"One day Joe stopped by and he and Nick got to talking. They became friends and Nick introduced us. When I first met Joe, I had no idea who his family was. It's not like Brody is an unusual name. He was just some cute guy sitting on Nick's couch drinking a beer."

"And then what happened?"

Claire raised her eyebrows. "I assume you're not asking for a complete accounting of what came next?"

"No, heaven forbid. Just the general idea."

"You probably don't even need that," she said. "How about if I skip ahead to the moral of the story?"

"That sounds ominous."

"Let's just say that my time with Joe was a learning experience." Claire's gaze dropped. She'd been using her fork to push the food around her bowl rather than to eat it. "Did you meet Joe at Puppy Fest?"

"We crossed paths in the kitchen." I lifted a hand to forestall the inevitable question. "Jane sent me there to get bottled water for the puppies."

Claire opened her mouth to speak. After a moment, she reconsidered and shut it again.

That was pretty much how I felt about Jane.

"I talked to Joe again yesterday," I said. "His older sister, Libby, is convinced that their father's death wasn't an accident. She suspects that one of the family members might have had something to do with it."

Claire didn't look surprised. "Peg mentioned that."

"You were there," I said. "And apparently you know the Brodys better than most people. What's your take on the situation?"

"Off the top of my head?"

"Sure."

"I wouldn't put anything past that family."

Oh. I swallowed heavily.

"Let's get back to you and Joe for a minute," I said.

"There is no 'me and Joe.'" Very deliberately, Claire corrected me. "Not anymore."

"It sounds like that's a good thing," I told her. "How did it end?"

"Badly. Are you looking for details?"

"If you wouldn't mind."

"I don't mind talking about it. What I *do* mind is the way Joe treated me. That's why I asked a minute ago if you'd met him. Since you have, I'd be curious to hear what you think of him."

Bearing in mind that Claire had devoted six months of her life to Joe Brody, I said, "He seemed like a nice guy. Friendly, trying to be helpful. Joe was with his brother, Graham, when I saw him yesterday. For two people who live together, they don't appear to get along very well."

"Yeah, sparring has always been their thing," Claire said. "When they started picking at each other, I'll bet Joe was the one who stayed calm and unruffled. Graham probably lost it and Joe came off looking like the reasonable one, didn't he?"

I nodded slowly.

"That's what Joe does. He always seems so agreeable. Mr. Nice Guy who gets along with everybody. But after a while you begin to wonder why Joe gets so many opportunities to be the guy who remains calm in the midst of chaos. How come everybody else is always losing their temper when he's around?"

"Interesting," I said. "Go on."

"That amiable facade is what Joe wants the world to see. But the truth is, he's the kind of guy who gets his kicks from watching other people squirm. He loves to manipulate people's feelings and poke at their sore spots. Don't fall for Joe's act, Melanie. He is not the person he wants you to think he is."

I sat back in my seat, feeling hollow inside. I was shocked by Claire's confession. "Why didn't you ever tell me any of this before?"

"I don't tell anyone. The time I spent with Joe is

not something I'm proud of." She paused to suck in a deep breath. "I should have seen Joe for what he was a whole lot sooner and gotten *out*. I feel stupid for staying with him as long as I did."

"But if your relationship is over now—"

"It *is*," she said firmly.

"Then why do you suspect he had something to do with you being put in charge of Puppy Fest?"

"I don't know for sure, but it's the only thing that makes sense. The call about the job came out of the blue. Think about it. Leo Brody's office calling me? A tiny one-person party-planning company? That's crazy. If not for Joe, how else would they have even known my name?"

"I get that there's a possible connection there," I said slowly. "But why would Joe do something like that now, after so much time has passed?"

"I have no idea. I couldn't even begin to tell you how Joe Brody's devious mind works. For all I know, he was annoyed that I'm married and happy, and he couldn't resist sticking his nose back into my business to see if he could stir up trouble."

I returned to my salad, picking through the greens with my fork to spear a piece of chicken. "Under those circumstances . . . why would you accept the job?"

Claire looked surprised that I even had to ask.

"Are you kidding me? Puppy Fest was a *huge* opportunity for me. Since I left the corporate world, mostly what I get hired to do is arrange children's birthday parties. I'm not complaining, mind you. It's great to have steady work. But I'm capable of doing a lot more, you know?"

I nodded. I could see that.

"Puppy Fest was a challenge and a chance to use *all* my skills for a change. Even more important, just having my name associated with that event could make a big difference in who approaches me to do business in the future. I hoped Puppy Fest would be my big break. There was no way I was going to pass that up."

"But feeling as you do about Joe Brody, didn't it bother you that he was once again pulling strings behind the scenes?"

"No, because I refused to even think about it," Claire said with a clear sense of resolve. "I was wrong to ever let Joe push me around. Or to let him believe that he could dictate my life choices. I'm never going to give him that kind of power over me again."

"Good for you," I said roundly. "You must have seen Joe at the house during the event, though. Did the two of you talk?"

"No, not even once." Claire frowned as she thought back. "I thought that was a little odd. A couple of times, I saw him across the ballroom. Joe was just standing there, observing the activity from afar. But he never came to say hello to me, and it's not like I was going to make the first move."

We took a break from talking and devoted ourselves to our salads. The chicken was delicious, moist and slightly spicy, the perfect counterpoint to the sweet fruits that accompanied it. *Maybe I ought to ask Frank for the recipe,* I thought. That would probably make him laugh.

Five minutes later, Claire's meal was still mostly

untouched. Since she wasn't eating anyway, I figured I might as well go back to asking questions. "I know it's none of my business, but just how acrimonious was your breakup with Joe?"

"On a scale of 'we're still friends' to 'I hate your guts'?" Claire smiled grimly. "Probably a whole lot closer to the latter. Joe likes to be the one who decides when the relationship is over. He wasn't happy that I broke things off with him. Why?"

"What if he had an ulterior motive for getting you that job?" I asked. "What if he *knew* that something bad was going to happen at the house that day? You hoped that Puppy Fest would enhance your career. What if Joe hoped that your being associated with Leo Brody's death would have the opposite effect?"

Both of us stopped and considered that. For a long minute, there was only silence. Finally Claire looked up and spoke.

"I'm going to tell you something important," she said. "So listen and pay attention. You should watch your step around Joe, especially if he thinks you suspect him of something. When things get ugly with him, they get ugly fast."

"I'll definitely bear that in mind."

My thoughts went back to the previous afternoon, and the odd interlude Joe and I had shared as I was leaving. In light of the other things Claire had told me, I wondered if it was worth mentioning.

I must have been frowning because she reached across the table and poked me. "What?"

"It's probably no big deal. Just something that

happened yesterday with Joe that seemed a little . . . off."

"Tell me."

"There's not much to tell. He was just . . . flirt-ing . . . with me in a rather heavy-handed way. Which was stupid on a couple of levels but especially be-cause Kevin was standing right there beside me. I mean, seriously, what did he think I was going to do?"

"What did you do?" Claire asked.

"I left."

"Good answer. Even better if you stay away from him altogether."

The waitress brought our check. I'd not only in-vited Claire, I'd spent the meal pumping her for information. I nabbed the ticket before she even had a chance to look at it, added a credit card, and handed it back. Claire started to protest, but I overrode her objections.

"Lunch is on me," I said. "You earned it."

"All we did was talk."

"That's all I wanted. One more question while we wait for her to come back?"

Claire settled back in her seat. "Shoot."

"Becca Montague."

"Like I said before, I never met her. The only thing I know about her is that the rest of the family hated her."

"Who told you that?" I asked curiously.

"Jane talked about her once when we were going over some details for Puppy Fest. The siblings thought she was only after Leo for his money."

"That's the impression I got too. I've called Becca a couple of times, but she's never called me back."

"Now that Leo's gone, maybe she doesn't see the point."

"Becca's the one who found his body," I reminded her. "She was in the office with him when I got there."

"Then you'd better keep trying," she said.

Chapter 19

I watched Claire drive away, then sat in my car in The Bean Counter's tiny parking lot and tapped out Becca Montague's phone number. Again. I was about to hang up after the fifth ring when the call connected.

"This is Becca Montague," the woman trilled. She sounded unexpectedly cheerful for someone who'd lost a very dear friend just ten days earlier.

I introduced myself, then paused briefly, wondering if she would recognize my name. When she didn't comment, I took that as a no. Considering the circumstances of our initial encounter, I didn't see any reason to jog her memory.

Instead I said, "I'm hoping I can ask you a few questions about your relationship with Leo Brody?"

I half-expected Becca to disconnect the call—or to demand what right I had to ask anything of her. But once again, she surprised me.

"It's your lucky day," she said in a coy tone. "I guess I have a few minutes to talk. Which news outlet did you say you were from?"

Obviously, I hadn't. And now, caught red-handed, I didn't have a decent answer. Luckily, Becca forged ahead without waiting for my reply.

"Oh, never mind, it doesn't matter. I'm just glad you want to hear my story. I'd be delighted to tell you all about my exciting life with noted philanthropist Leo Brody. And I'd especially like to let you in on the plans that he and I were making for our wedding."

"Wedding?" I sputtered. This call was turning out to be one surprise after another. "You and Mr. Brody were planning to get married?"

"Yes, we were *madly* in love. It was all wonderfully romantic."

"I had no idea," I said. I was quite certain I wasn't the only one. "When was the wedding going to take place?"

"We didn't have a firm date yet," Becca said airily. "Leo and I were still ironing out the details. As I'm sure you know, he was a *very* important man. So it took a great deal of planning to clear enough time in his schedule for a proper honeymoon."

"Of course," I murmured.

"Leo offered to take me anywhere in the world. Isn't that fabulous? So naturally I chose Paris. He and I were going to explore the City of Light as husband and wife." She hammered her point home yet again.

"That sounds wonderful. I'm sure the rest of the

Brody family must have been thrilled that their father had found true love at last."

I was laying it on a little thick. But not only did Becca not mind, she loved it.

"You're exactly right," she enthused. "What Leo and I shared *was* true love. He and I were soul mates."

"And his family?" I prodded gently.

"If you must know, Leo hadn't yet told his children about our impending nuptials. Children, indeed!" She snorted under her breath. "They are all fully grown adults. But Leo said he was waiting for just the right moment to tell them about our plans. In the meantime, the engagement was *our secret*. That made things even more delicious, don't you think?"

"Absolutely."

Agreeing with Becca was the easiest way to keep her talking, even if I didn't believe much of what she was saying. A secret engagement sounded highly unlikely to me. But with Leo no longer able to set the record straight, Becca appeared to be rewriting her own story.

"Under the circumstances, Mr. Brody's sudden death must have come as a huge shock to you," I said.

"*Huge*," Becca echoed the word back to me. "I felt like my whole world ended right then and there. I'm not over it yet."

I should hope not. It had barely been more than a week.

"I understand you were there when it happened. How did Mr. Brody die?"

"From eating a cookie, of all things. Leo was severely allergic to peanuts. Only his closest confidants were privy to that weakness of his. Of course *I* was well aware."

She obviously hoped that nugget of information would depict her as a member of Leo's inner circle, but the ploy was lost on me. Everyone I'd spoken to—all of them more credible than Becca was turning out to be—had told me that Leo Brody's peanut allergy was widely known.

Unfortunately this conversation wasn't getting me anywhere. Though Becca was turning out to be wonderfully loquacious, I hadn't learned a single thing I didn't already know. I crossed my fingers and took a flyer.

"Tell me about those cookies," I said. "Where did they come from? Did you bring them with you as a present for your fiancé?"

I heard a gasp and knew I'd pushed my luck too far.

"Certainly not!" Becca snapped. "What are you implying? Those blasted cookies were just sitting there in Leo's office. I had nothing to do with them."

"But you must have seen him pick one up—"

When Becca broke in, her voice had hardened. "What did you say your name was again?"

"Melanie Travis."

"I've heard that name before."

I bet she was wishing she'd been paying more attention when I'd identified myself earlier. It wasn't my fault that Becca had been so eager to air her story to the press, she hadn't stopped to check my credentials.

"You're that woman," she said suddenly. "The one who called the police."

"That's right. I'm the one who happened upon the scene and found you leaning over Leo Brody's body." I hoped that disclosure might provoke her to say something imprudent, but Becca wasn't listening to me anymore.

"Where did you get my phone number?" she demanded. "How dare you call and harass me like this? Are you stalking me now? I'm going to get an order of protection. I'll see you in court—"

She probably kept yelling, but I'd already disconnected.

It appeared the Brody siblings had been right to be concerned about Becca's determined pursuit of their father. I wondered how solid her relationship with Leo had actually been. While he was alive, Becca had a chance to make her dream of becoming Leo's fourth wife come true. But maybe he'd had other ideas.

Caroline had said that her father had no intention of ever marrying again. It wasn't a stretch to imagine that Becca wouldn't have been happy to find that out. She'd already admitted that she was aware of Leo's peanut allergy. Not only that, but I'd just seen for myself that it didn't take much to spark her temper.

Several of the siblings had told me that Becca Montague wasn't important. But suddenly I wasn't so sure about that.

* * *

The day was turning out to be full of surprises. When I arrived home, there were visitors waiting for me.

Sam doesn't usually run to meet me as soon as I come in the door—that's the Poodles' job—but he must have hightailed it out to the hallway when he heard the garage door closing. I was barely inside the house before he accosted me.

"Thank God you're back," he said.

"Is something wrong?"

I glanced around and counted Poodle noses. My welcoming committee was unusually sparse. Only Faith and Eve were in evidence. That left a lot of dogs unaccounted for. And my younger son, of course.

"Where's Kevin?" I asked quickly.

"He's in my office. We're playing Chutes and Ladders. He's probably rearranging the board while I'm gone."

"Kevin *cheats*?" Relief made the question bubble out on a laugh.

"He doesn't seem to think of it as cheating. More like he's clearing his path to a win."

I stared at my husband. Frankly, I did not see the distinction. I was pretty sure he didn't either.

"Anyway," Sam continued, "Kev's not the problem."

"Who is?"

"Teenage girls, apparently. They're very different than teenage boys."

That wasn't news. I hoped Sam intended to get to the point soon.

"I had no idea that two girls could talk so incessantly. Or that anyone could for that matter. I think their mouths are moving faster than their brains. Actually it's amazing to watch. But then occasionally they squeal too." Sam grimaced as if reliving a burst of ear pain. "Kevin seemed entertained by it, though."

"Two teenage girls," I summed up. There'd been a car parked on the road as I'd come in, but I hadn't given it much thought. Since I'm a pretty good sleuth, however, I was almost certain that I knew the answer to the next question. "Do they have names?"

"Ashley and Megan . . . Brody." Sam frowned. "Were you expecting them?"

"Of course not. Otherwise I'd have been here." I peered around him into the living room. It was empty. "What did you do with them?"

"When they found out you were expected back shortly, they informed me that they would wait for your return. I offered them something to drink. They declined. I attempted to make conversation. They were not impressed. Apparently whatever was scrolling across the screens of their phones was more interesting than I was." Sam sounded pained by the realization.

I had to bite my lip not to smile at his wounded expression. "Don't worry, honey. You haven't lost your touch. Those two are just too young to appreciate your charms. Megan and Ashley are eighteen. Barely past jail bait."

Sam shook his head. "At that age, they should be old enough to know that when you're a guest in someone else's house, you don't get to dictate what happens next."

"Don't take it personally. The whole Brody family acts like that. As if they're the stars of every occasion and we're just bit players hovering in the background. So . . ." I was still curious. "What *did* happen next?"

"They parked themselves out on the deck to wait. Feet up, phones out, they looked perfectly happy so I left them to their own devices."

"Excellent pun," I said with a grin.

Sam acknowledged my smile with one of his own. "Bud's in my office with Kevin, but the Poodles elected to keep the girls company outside. It's been twenty minutes and I haven't heard a peep, so I assume they're still doing okay."

I looked down at Faith, who wagged her tail happily. "You would know. Is everything all right out there?"

I fully expected Faith to answer in the affirmative. Instead her tail abruptly stopped moving. All at once, she looked concerned. That wasn't good.

Sam went back to his office. The two Poodles and I hurried out to the deck to see what was up. Faith had warned me. Even so, the sight that greeted me when I walked outside was unexpected. And not in a good way.

Both twins had their backs to me as I came through the door. Dressed in a midriff-baring top and a miniscule pair of denim cut-offs, Megan Brody was lying stretched out on a chaise. She'd kicked off her shoes and her long, slender legs were extended out in front of her for maximum exposure to the sun. Since she was busy with her phone, it took her a minute to register my arrival.

Her sister, Ashley, sat beside her on a matching chaise. She'd obviously encouraged Augie to jump up beside her—something he knew better than to do without an invitation—because the big black Poodle lay draped across her lap. For some reason, Ashley had taken it upon herself to dig her fingers into the dog's coat and pop out the rows of tiny rubber bands that held his long topknot hair in place. Even worse, she was now in the process of replacing the neat, ordered ponytails with what appeared to be cornrows.

Raven and Tar were sitting nearby, observing this unprecedented event with matching expressions of misgiving. Faith and Eve looked plainly horrified. No wonder they'd come to get me as soon as I returned home.

"What the hell do you think you're doing?" I said. As greetings went, it wasn't my best moment.

Ashley looked up. So did Augie. His tail began to wave slowly back and forth. He was delighted to see me. And why not? He wasn't the one in trouble.

"Good, you're back," Megan said. "It's about time."

"I can see that." I nailed Ashley with a glare. "What are you doing to my dog?"

"Making improvements." The little twit smiled as if she actually believed what she was saying. "Ponytails are so *unoriginal*. Braids look much better, especially for a black dog. Don't you think?"

"No, I do not."

I looked at Augie and patted my thigh sharply. Immediately the Poodle pulled away from Ashley, hopped down from his perch, and trotted to my side. As soon as he began to move, a huge hank of loose hair fell forward over his face. The long strands covered his eyes and tangled in his mouth.

I smoothed the topknot hair back the moment he reached me, but without proper banding it wouldn't stay that way for long. The sheer audacity of what Ashley had done was astounding. I had to struggle to control my temper. Luckily I didn't see any black hair lying on the deck. Because if her antics had cost Augie any of his precious topknot hair, I was going to kick her boney little butt.

"I don't know why you're mad." Ashley's voice edged toward a whine. "You weren't here and I got bored."

"I wasn't here," I said between gritted teeth, "because I didn't know you were coming."

The two sisters traded a glance. "It was, like, a spur-of-the-moment decision."

"Hold on one minute," I told them. "I'll be right back." I cupped my hand around Augie's muzzle and led him across the deck to the kitchen door. "Sam? Can I have a little help?"

Sam came around the corner from his office and took in the situation in a glance. He strode over, and his hand replaced mine around Augie's muzzle. He was shaking his head as he led the Standard Poodle toward the small room off the kitchen where we did our grooming.

When I turned back to the twins, Megan had swung her legs to the ground and sat up. "Sorry about that." The words were offered so readily I figured she probably made a habit of apologizing for her twin. "Ash didn't mean to do anything wrong. Besides, it's only *dog* hair."

"Yeah," Ashley chimed in. "And considering how crazy the rest of him looks, I figured you probably needed my help. It's not as if I could have made that dog look any worse."

I thought about explaining the origin of the Poodle's highly styled continental clip. I could tell them that it had been developed in Germany more than a century earlier to serve as a practical hunting trim. Its design was meant to keep Standard Poodles comfortable when they did the work they'd originally been bred to do—retrieving game in cold water. But then I realized two things. The twins probably wouldn't care. And I really had no desire to try and educate them.

Instead I said, "Why are you girls here?"

"We heard that you were talking to everyone in the family," Megan replied. "Trace said you'd been by his house, and Graham told us the same thing. So we figured we'd save you a trip."

It was true that I'd been making the rounds—but of Leo Brody's children, not his grandchildren. Libby had directed me toward her siblings and I'd followed her lead. The only reason I'd met Trace and Nelson was because I'd been there to talk to their mother.

But if fate was going to hand me lemons, I might as well make lemonade.

"Excellent." I pulled a chair over beside the two chaise longues and sat down. "What do you want to tell me?"

"Um . . . about that." Ashley paused and looked at her sister.

"The thing is, we heard that you're asking questions about Leo's death," Megan said. "So we came to tell you that we don't know anything because, you know . . . why would we?"

"Maybe because you were there when it happened?" I said.

"That's a lie!" Ashley's shoulders stiffened in outrage. "Megan and I were *not* there. What a horrible thing to say. Isn't that, like, libel or something?"

Or something, I thought. Maybe she should talk to Becca. The two of them could discuss legal technicalities. Or maybe just their mutual dislike for me.

"But I saw you," I pointed out. "I was at Puppy Fest too. We were all together in the salon for a while. Don't you remember?"

"Oh." Ashley slumped back. "At Puppy Fest. Yeah, we went to that."

"That's what I said."

"I thought you meant"—the girl waved a hand vaguely—"you know, *there* there."

Megan just looked at her sister and sighed. I felt the same way.

"If you want to talk to people who were at Puppy Fest," she said. "You should go see Aunt Jane."

"How come?"

"Well, you know. She was there too."

"In the salon," I clarified.

The two girls exchanged another look. Silent twin-speak.

"She was in the salon sometimes," Megan said.

Okay, that was interesting. "Where was Jane the rest of the time?"

Ashley shrugged. "How would we know? It's not like we followed her around."

"But there's something else." Megan's voice dropped to just above a whisper. "I don't know if I should tell you this or not."

"Sure you should." *As if there were any doubt.*

"Aunt Jane likes to bake. She brought cookies to Puppy Fest."

"She did?"

Both twins nodded together. They looked like a matching set of bobblehead dolls.

"How do you know that?" I asked.

"Aunt Jane *always* brings cookies whenever the family gets together." Ashley rolled her eyes. "It's like her thing. There was a plate of cookies in the ballroom. She had to be the one that brought them. Because she always does."

I hadn't even noticed. I wondered whether Detective Young had been informed of Jane's "thing." Most likely he had—and then dismissed its relevance along with the other bits of information he'd gathered.

"What kind of cookies were they?" I asked.

The question made Megan laugh. "Do we *look* like we would know? I haven't had a cookie since I was, like, ten."

"The last time anything with sugar crossed my lips, I was eight." Ashley looked smug. As if abstinence were a competition and she'd won.

Megan stood up. Her sister followed suit. "So anyway, we just thought you should know."

I waited until Megan had slipped on her shoes

and Ashley had tugged her tiny shorts down into place, then led the two sisters around the house. There was a gate in the fence near the driveway. As we walked through it, I said, "Thanks for stopping by. Is there anything else you want to tell me?"

"No, but we were happy to save you a trip," Ashley said brightly.

That was the second time one of the twins had used that particular phrase. I wondered why. Color me skeptical, but the Brody sisters didn't strike me as the helpful sort.

"So now that you've seen us, you don't have to bother talking to our dad," Megan told me. "He's out of town anyway. And besides, he told us that you guys already met."

I knew that their father was Fred's younger brother, Ron. One of the three children born to Leo Brody's first wife. But if he and I had already met, I wasn't aware of it.

"We did?"

Ashley nodded. She looked at her sister and the two of them began to giggle as if they were sharing a private joke. Arm in arm, the pair sauntered down the driveway. They'd gone halfway when Ashley looked back over her shoulder and snickered.

"It was at Puppy Fest. Dad said he told you where to go."

Then I got it. Ron was the man who'd directed me to the ballroom when I'd first arrived.

"Hey!" I waited until they'd paused and turned, then said, "It's not the first time someone's done that."

The twins didn't look impressed. I couldn't

blame them. That had sounded a lot cleverer in my head.

So Megan and Ashley didn't want me to talk to their father, I mused. That was interesting. I wondered where Ron had gone so soon after Leo Brody's death. And how long it would be until he returned.

Chapter 20

Tuesday felt like a long day. Wednesday didn't start out a whole lot better.

For starters, Sam left very early that morning on a two-day business trip. It was just after 6 A.M. when I kissed him on the lips and pushed him out the door. The boys were still asleep upstairs. Even the three Poodles who'd come down with me to say good-bye looked groggy.

By seven, everyone was awake and I had breakfast on the table. By eight, the boys were dressed and fed, the dogs had been exercised, and I had Davey's camp supplies lined up next to the door. At eight-thirty, Kevin and I were on our way to drop Davey off at camp. After that, we were going to Westchester County to meet with Leo Brody's oldest child, Nancy, at her farm in North Salem. I felt as though I'd already put in an entire day's work.

That brought back memories. For most of

Davey's early life, I had been a single mom. Now I found myself remembering how hard that was and wondering how I'd ever managed.

Not easily, that's for sure.

Davey, two months away from his thirteenth birthday and almost as tall as I was, was sitting beside me in the front of the car. Kev sat behind us in his car seat. He leaned over, unzipped the backpack Davey had tossed on the seat beside him, and pulled out a shin guard.

Kevin had seen his brother's shin guards numerous times. He'd even tried them on. But now he held the piece of equipment up to the light and examined it as if it was a rare and precious artifact.

"I want to go to camp too," he announced.

"You can't," Davey said flatly. "You're too little."

In the mirror, I saw Kev's lower lip begin to quiver. I shot Davey a look. *Was that really necessary?*

"What?" Davey protested. "He *is*."

"I don't want to be little!" Kevin's voice broke on a wail.

I looked across the front seat. "Now look what you've done."

"Sheesh," Davey muttered. "How did this get to be my fault?" He turned around and addressed Kev. "The good thing about being your age is that you get to stay home all day."

"Don't wanna stay home." The wailing had stopped, but Kevin had managed to push out his lower lip in an impressive pout.

"If you're away all day and I'm away all day, who's going to play with Bud?"

Kevin thought about that. He didn't appear to have an answer.

"Having your own dog is a big responsibility," Davey said seriously.

I was impressed. Davey was taking a page from Aunt Peg's playbook. Who knew he'd even been listening to all those lectures we'd given him over the years?

"What if Bud gets hungry or he needs to go outside? Who's going to take care of him if you're not there?"

It was a good thing Kevin was only three. Any older and he'd be able to figure out the answers to those questions pretty easily. Now, however, he was nodding solemnly. Then all at once, he brightened.

"Faith will help Bud," Kev said happily. "She knows *everything.*"

Davey spun back around in his seat. "I tried. Now he's all yours."

I'd turned in the camp driveway a minute earlier and we were reaching the head of the drop-off line. Without thinking, I leaned over to give Davey a kiss. He shrank back in horror.

"Mom!"

"Oh yeah. Right." I straightened in my seat. A display of affection in front of the other kids was nothing short of mortifying. "Don't forget your shin guard!" I called as he scrambled hastily out of the car.

The back door opened. Davey swept up his gear. Then the door slammed again and he was gone.

I pulled out of line and headed out.

"Having a dog is a big 'sponsibility," Kev told me happily from the back seat.

I loved this age. That kid learned something new every day.

Despite being in a different state, North Salem wasn't far from North Stamford as the crow flies. Of course, Kev and I were making the trip by car. That took a bit longer.

Though situated only fifty miles from New York City, North Salem still retains aspects of its rural roots. The town is small and picturesque. Acres of open land create a quiet, pastoral atmosphere. On the way to our destination, Kevin and I meandered down several winding country roads, passing by fields populated by horses and cows.

When we came to the final turn Nancy had instructed me to take, there was no street sign on the corner. Instead, the single-lane road was simply marked PRIVATE. I nudged the Volvo between the two low stone walls that bordered either side of the narrow lane. As I slowed my speed, I turned in my seat to look at Kevin.

"We're almost there," I told him.

"Almost there," he parroted back. "Going to camp."

"Not camp," I said firmly. "We're visiting friends again."

"Yay!" Kev pumped a fist in the air.

Graham had made a point of telling me that his older sister, Nancy, was in need of money. But I never would have guessed that by looking at where she lived. On approach, I could see the farm was lovely.

I made another turn—this time between two

stone gateposts—and followed the driveway down a gentle incline that led to a wide green valley. Spacious, white fenced, pastures spread out on either side of a trim, two-story farmhouse. A big, red, center-aisle barn, whose doors were standing open in the summer heat, was visible behind the house.

Several elderly-looking ponies were grazing in one of the fields. The other contained a flock of sheep. A pair of spotted goats were housed inside a tall wire pen, and half a dozen chickens were scratching in the dirt in front of the barn.

As I parked beside the house, my gaze was still swiveling from side to side. Bemused, slightly astonished, I took it all in. I'd known that Nancy lived on a farm, but somehow I'd envisioned a residence that was more *Town and Country* and less Old MacDonald.

"Look Mommy, chickens!" Kev said with delight.

"I know." I hurried around to free him from his car seat. "This place is great, isn't it?"

As soon as Kevin's feet touched the ground, he took off at a run. *Damn.* I should have seen that coming.

That child moved with surprising speed for someone with such short legs. He was already halfway to the barn before I'd closed the car door and caught up. The chickens lifted their heads. They watched our precipitous approach with beady-eyed curiosity. Just in the nick of time, I grabbed Kevin and swung him up into my arms.

Arms outstretched, hands flailing in the direction of the flock, Kev let out a yelp. "Put me down! Want to play!"

"I'm sure you do. But the chickens probably don't feel the same way about you," I said.

"Actually they're very friendly."

I'd been so focused on nabbing Kev before he did something we'd both regret that I hadn't even noticed the girl who was standing in the doorway to the barn. She had fair, freckled skin and was dressed in a grubby T-shirt and cargo shorts. Her wheat-colored hair was gathered into a ponytail that reached to the middle of her back. The Brody family's pale blue eyes were visible above a friendly smile. The girl looked to be a couple of years older than Davey.

"I'm Miranda." She extended her hand. "Can I help you?"

I juggled Kevin into my other arm, then grasped her hand with my own. "I'm Melanie Travis. And this is Kevin. We're here to see your mother."

"Oh, sure." She waved back toward the barn's shaded interior. "Mom will be with you in a minute. She's just milking the cow."

Milking the cow? My startled thoughts must have shown on my face because Miranda began to laugh.

"That was a joke," she said between giggles. "It's just that you were standing there looking around like you thought you'd landed on *Green Acres*. And then for some reason . . ." She paused for another fit of giggles. ". . . you seemed to think that you had to rescue your son from *chickens.*"

Miranda reached down and scooped up a bird. I was surprised to see her scratch beneath the hen's chin, much as I might have done with one of my dogs. "Like I said, they're very sociable. Although for best results, you probably don't want to approach them at a dead run."

"Yes, sorry about that. Kevin loves animals. And he's sure they all want to be his best friend."

Miranda leaned in close. She gently picked up my son's hand and placed it on the chicken's back. "Hey Kevin, I agree with you. I've never met an animal I didn't like. How about you?"

Kev shook his head. Eyes wide, he ran his hand slowly down the feathered back. For once my son was speechless. This would make his day. Actually, it would probably make his month.

"Mom's inside," Miranda said after a minute. Reluctantly, she returned the chicken to the ground. The bird flapped its wings and trotted away. "Come on, I'll show you."

"This is a beautiful place," I said as we walked back toward the house.

Miranda nodded. "I love living on a farm. But it's a lot of work too. When you arrived, I was mucking stalls." She reached up and brushed sweaty bangs up off her forehead. "It's not my favorite way to spend the morning."

I seemed to recall that Nancy had two children. "Don't you have a brother to help out with that?"

"Bates is away at sailing camp on Nantucket. He's gone for the whole month. My brother thinks he's going to win the America's Cup someday." Miranda considered for a moment. "Who knows? He's pretty good. Maybe he will."

"I've met your other cousins," I told her. "You guys are all around the same age. I guess you must be pretty close?"

"No, not really," she said with a shrug. "Mostly I

only see them at family functions and stuff like
that. Mom doesn't like us hanging out with them."

I kept a firm hold of Kevin's hand and set him
down so he could walk beside us. "How come?"

"Trace and Nelson, they're kind of wild. And
Ashley and Megan are pretty spoiled. They get
everything they want just handed to them. My
mom hates that. She wants us to live a simpler kind
of life. More real, you know?"

"I do," I agreed. I wondered whether Trace's
wildness referred to his driving or whether there
was something more. "It sounds like you're the responsible one. What do your cousins get up to
when they're misbehaving?"

"I'm not really supposed to talk about that."

"Okay, sure." My tone was deliberately casual. "I
guess it's just typical teenage high jinks. I'm a
teacher. I see all sorts of stuff."

"Not like what they do." Miranda slid a look my
way. As I'd hoped, my indifference stung just
enough to goad her into replying. "Ashley? She
once started a fire in a school Dumpster to get out
of taking a test she hadn't studied for."

Okay, Miranda was right. That kind of behavior
went *way* beyond typical teenage high jinks.

"For real?" I asked.

"I'm telling the truth." Her shoulders stiffened.
"Those guys act crazy sometimes. That's why Bates
and I don't hang out with them. Besides, it's not
like we have anything in common. Trace and Nelson don't even like animals. Who would want to
spend time with people like that?"

Not me, I thought.

"Trace must like dogs a little because he volunteered to help Jane at Puppy Fest," I pointed out.

Miranda shaded her eyes from the sun and looked up at me. "Did he show up?"

"No."

"See? That's what I mean. The only way Trace would agree to work with puppies was if he was planning to pull their tails and pinch their ears when no one was looking."

"That's a pretty harsh assessment."

Miranda shrugged again. "That's not my fault. Mom says we always have to tell the truth, even if a lie would make people feel better."

"It's obvious that you love animals," I said. "How come I didn't see you at Puppy Fest?"

"Mom didn't want us to go this year. I have no idea why. If you want to know, you'll have to ask her yourself."

"Ask her what?"

Miranda had steered us toward the rear of the house. As we'd approached, the back door had opened and a woman had come out. Waiting for us on the stoop, she'd caught the tail end of our conversation.

"This is Melanie Travis," Miranda announced. "She said she came to see you. Her son, Kevin, likes chickens."

Nancy smiled down at her daughter. "Of course he likes chickens. Who doesn't?"

Knowing that Nancy was Leo Brody's eldest child and that she lived on a farm, I had pictured a woman who was matronly and makeup free. And maybe wearing her hair in a bun. I couldn't have been more wrong.

Nancy was tall and willowy. Her jeans, worn with wedge-heeled espadrilles, were tighter than mine. Blond frosted hair was cut to just above her jawline and the summer heat had turned the hairstyle into a becoming mop of curls. She had a chunky gold necklace around her neck and a tennis bracelet around one wrist.

But that was only the first surprise. The second was that I recognized Nancy. She was the woman whom I'd seen arguing with Libby at the dog show. The one who—according to Terry—had been threatening her sister with dire consequences if Libby didn't pay up.

Well, then. I supposed I knew what my first question was going to be.

"It's a pleasure to meet you," Nancy said graciously. Her manners appeared to be a cut above the rest of the family's. "Let's go inside."

"I have an idea," said Miranda.

We all turned to look at her.

"While you guys are talking, why don't I take Kevin with me? He and I can go pet the ponies."

I heard a squeal. I was pretty sure it came from Kev. He tipped his head back and looked up at me pleadingly.

"Are you finished with those stalls yet?" Nancy asked.

"Umm . . . not exactly," Miranda admitted. "But I could use a break. I can finish up after they leave."

"Then I guess it's all right with me." Nancy glanced my way, seeking my permission.

"Kevin's only three," I told Miranda. "If you

don't pay attention to him, he'll find a way to get into trouble."

"I'm good at keeping an eye on things," the teen replied seriously. "He and I'll have fun together."

"Mommy, pleeease!"

It would take a mother made of sterner stuff than I to resist a plea like that. Besides, who wouldn't want to pet a pony?

Nancy and I watched the two kids head back to the barn. Then I followed her inside the house.

"Don't worry, they'll be fine," she said. "Miranda's great with kids. She always wanted a little brother or sister." Nancy glanced back at me over her shoulder. "We'll sit in the kitchen, if you don't mind. Are you okay with cats?"

"Sort of." With a houseful of dogs, I hadn't been near a cat in a long time. Maybe I've outgrown my allergy, I thought hopefully.

"No problem. If they bother you, I'll just shoo them out of the room. These three think they own the place. It will do them good to have to listen to me for a change."

The kitchen was small and sunny. The focal point of the room was a round wooden table in the middle of the floor whose surface was scarred by years of use. A ceiling fan rotated lazily overhead. The countertops were cluttered with an eclectic selection of junk. I saw everything from empty flowerpots to dog-eared books, to a pair of sneakers that were missing their laces.

Across the room, an orange tabby cat was stretched out on a windowsill. It opened one eye and looked at us as we entered, then lowered its head and went back to sleep. A second cat, black with a white patch on its chest, was on the floor batting a small ball between its front paws. I wondered where number three was hiding.

"Have a seat." Nancy waved me to a chair at the table. "I'm on my third cup of coffee and I just brewed a fresh pot. Can I pour you a cup?"

"Absolutely." As I sat down, I felt my eyes slit to a half-squint. My nose began to twitch. Deliberately I chose a chair as far from the felines as possible. Maybe that would help.

Nancy delivered two steaming mugs to the table. Milk and sugar followed. Then Nancy sat down opposite me.

"Let's get straight to business," she said. "Libby told me to talk to you so here you are. I get that she's pissed. But here's something you can tell that sister of mine—I'm pissed too. And let me say up front that I have every right to be. By the way, you didn't introduce yourself as such but I assume you're Libby's attorney?"

I'd just finished adding milk to my mug and was taking a first cautious sip. When my head shot up in surprise, scalding liquid burned my throat.

"What? No . . ." I sputtered. "I have no idea what you're talking about. I'm not Libby's attorney. I'm not *anybody's* attorney."

We were off to a good start, weren't we?

"All right." Nancy's eyes narrowed. "Then what's your stake in all this?"

I put my mug down on the table. It seemed safer that way. "All *what*?" I asked slowly.

"This stupid business with Cavalier. Which, by the way, I am totally ready to be done with."

I was feeling dumber by the minute. I hate when that happens.

"Who's Cavalier?" I asked.

"Libby's Dalmatian. Her stud dog."

My face must have looked every bit as blank as my brain felt because Nancy's frown was growing even more ferocious.

"The one that I supposedly own half of?" she snapped.

"Oh." *Oh.* I finally got a clue. It was about time.

"That's what you and Libby were arguing about at the dog show," I said. "Cavalier."

Nancy gave a clipped nod. "Libby owes me money, and I'm tired of waiting for it. She's been putting me off for two years. As long as I was out of sight, she could pretend there wasn't a problem. That's why I went to the dog show. My sweet, conniving sister couldn't ignore me there, could she?"

Chapter 21

"Apparently not." Suddenly things were making more sense. "I guess the plan was to embarrass Libby in front of her friends so that she would pay you to go away?"

"Something like that," Nancy admitted. "I figured it must have worked, too, since you were here. Libby never does her own dirty work. I thought she was sending an attorney to negotiate a settlement."

"That seems a little extreme for a disagreement between sisters."

Nancy lifted her mug and took a healthy swallow. "Not in my family."

Wow, this was one tough crowd.

"Tell me about Cavalier," I said. "How did he become a source of contention between you?"

"How much do you know about show dogs?"

"More than most people. I breed and show Standard Poodles, and my aunt is a dog show judge."

"Of course you do." A small laugh escaped her. "Considering that you're friends with Libby, I guess I should have seen that coming. *Poodles . . . really?*"

"Yes, really," I confirmed. There was no point in taking offense. "Now talk to me about Cavalier."

"He's the best Dalmatian Libby has ever owned. Or so she says. It's not like I would know the difference. Four years ago, she could hardly talk about anything else. He'd won some important title that dog show people care about, and she wanted him to be a special dog."

"You mean she wanted to special him," I corrected automatically.

"Sure. Whatever. Apparently that's an expensive undertaking. Libby needed money to make it happen. She came to me and convinced me to invest in him."

People show dogs for all kinds of reasons. Some enjoy the competition, or the camaraderie between exhibitors. Others want to prove the merits of their line. Some just like to win. Investment potential is definitely *not* one of those reasons.

"That's an unusual request," I said mildly.

"Not according to what Libby told me at the time. I was supposed to put up the money to give Cavalier a career. Then after he'd done a lot of winning at big dog shows, she would retire him to stud. Libby said his stud fees would generate a lot of income. She and I would be partners, and I was supposed to earn my money back in no time."

Good luck with that, I thought.

"I'm assuming that's not how things worked out?"

"Oh, the first part of Libby's plan came off brilliantly," Nancy said with a grimace. "Cavalier won all sorts of awards. I even got to watch him run around a dog show ring on television. Originally Libby had said she would show him for one year. Instead they kept going for two. Libby told me Cavalier was doing so well that she couldn't stop."

"And you kept footing the bill?" I asked.

"I'd already made the commitment. It wasn't like I could back out after the fact."

"Plenty of people would have done just that," I pointed out. "Especially since the arrangement ended up costing you a lot more money than you'd bargained for."

"Libby is my sister," Nancy said coolly. "I thought I could trust her. I thought that she was looking out for both our interests."

"Then what happened?"

"I imagine you can guess the rest. Cavalier retired from the show ring two years ago. I'm sure Libby's making money off of him now. Probably a lot of money. But I haven't seen a single cent."

"That hardly sounds fair," I said over the rim of my mug.

"Tell me about it."

"Did you talk to Libby about paying you back?"

Nancy looked at me as though I was daft. "Of course I talked to her. Probably a dozen times. She admitted that Cavalier was doing well at stud, but she always had some excuse to explain why she didn't owe me any money yet."

"Yet?" I said curiously. "What does that mean?"

"According to Libby, she'd invested in Cavalier's

show career too. She said her time and expertise were worth every bit as much as the money I'd provided. Libby intends to pay herself back first. After that, she told me I'd be next in line."

With family like that, I thought, who needs enemies?

"That's really low," I said out loud. "I don't suppose the two of you put anything in writing about your arrangement?"

"*She's my sister—*"

"I know. And you trusted her. Which was apparently a mistake."

"You don't have to tell me that now," Nancy grumbled. "If I had it to do over, I'd change all sorts of things. Starting with showing Libby the door when she first came up with this crazy scheme."

She took another long drink of coffee and settled back in her chair. The gaze she trained in my direction was edged with hostility. "So in case you're wondering, I'm not likely to be enthused about whatever new bright idea my sister has that's brought you to my doorstep."

"I don't blame you one bit," I said. Under the circumstances, I figured I might as well lead with the headline. "Libby doesn't think your father's death was an accident."

Nancy's eyes widened. It took her a minute to come up with a reply. "That's rich," she said finally. "And she sent you here because she thinks *I* might have had something to do with it?"

"Libby asked me to talk to everyone in your family."

"The whole family?" Suddenly she sounded interested. "Who else have you seen?"

"I've been making the rounds of all your siblings."

"Then I'm surprised it took you so long to get around to me."

"Why is that?"

"Because when you're the oldest of nine children, everybody brings you their problems and their grievances. I was both the negotiator in the family and the keeper of secrets. So I'm used to being consulted when things go south. Old habits die hard, I guess."

"Is that why Libby approached you when she needed a loan?"

"It's one reason," Nancy said. "I guess the other is because everybody thinks I'm a soft touch. Fred's always telling me that I need to grow a backbone. Which is ironic because I've told him the same thing more than once."

The cat on the windowsill gave a languid stretch, then dropped to the floor. It cocked its head to one side and eyed me curiously. Any minute now, that tabby would be wrapping itself around my legs and meowing for attention. And then I would start to sneeze.

"I'm surprised to hear that. Fred seemed pretty forceful to me when I talked to him." I pushed my chair away from the table, adding an extra foot between me and the friendly feline.

"That's what he wanted you to think. That's what he wants *everybody* to think. Fred Brody: brainiac, investment banker, the man with nerves of steel and a heart to match. I suppose he told you that he's never married."

"No." I thought back. Caroline had mentioned

that. But not Fred. "He did talk quite a bit about your parents' divorce though. He sounded like he was still bitter about it. Is that why he never married anyone himself?"

Nancy laughed gently. "No, that whole mess is *old* news. Fred wants people to think that he never found a woman who could live up to his exacting standards. But the truth is he's been secretly in love with someone for years . . . the one woman in the world that he can't have."

"Fred confided in you about that?"

"Worse," she replied. "He came to me for advice. I've told him time and again that there's nothing I can do. Fred had his chance with Cynthia twenty years ago and he blew it."

"Blew it how?" I asked curiously. "Where is Cynthia now?"

"She's married to our younger brother, Ron."

"Yikes," I said, and Nancy laughed again.

"I know, right? It seems like nothing's ever easy in our family. Fred met Cynthia first, and they dated for nearly a year. When they broke up, Ron wasted no time in moving in on his brother's ex."

I shook my head. "You make it sound as though it was a competition, with Cynthia as the prize."

"Back then, maybe it was. Ron and Fred are only a year apart in age, but that small difference meant that Fred got to do everything first. Ron spent our entire childhood trying to keep up with his older brother. Whatever Fred had, Ron always wanted too."

Sibling rivalry. I knew how that worked.

"So Ron and Cynthia got married," I said.

Nancy nodded. "To hear Fred tell it, he'd already realized his mistake by then. But of course it was too late."

"Are Ron and Cynthia happily married?"

"In the beginning, they certainly appeared to be a happy couple. And the twins came along pretty quickly. But over time—if you were looking—you could see cracks beginning to form. Now, all these years later, the marriage is pretty much over. Ron and Cynthia are leading separate lives, and their girls behave like wild things. I don't even know who's in charge in that house anymore. Maybe no one is."

The more I learned about the Brody family, the saner my own relatives began to appear. I savored that pleasant thought for a moment before moving on.

"So Fred's been pining over Cynthia for years," I said. "Is the feeling mutual?"

Nancy picked up a napkin that was lying on the table. Her fingers began to shred the delicate paper. "I gather there's some reciprocal pining on her part. If I were to hazard a guess as to why her marriage stopped working."

"So?" I prompted.

Nancy looked up. "So what?"

"Am I the only one who thinks that a divorce might be in order?"

"No, Fred would be in perfect agreement with you. And according to what he tells me, so would Cynthia."

"So what's holding them back?"

"Ron won't give Cynthia a divorce. He won't even discuss it."

"Even though he's married to a woman who doesn't love him anymore?"

"That's not the part Ron cares about."

It's what I would care about, I thought.

"Don't tell me he's still trying to thwart his older brother," I said.

"Thankfully, no. The problem was Leo Brody."

"Your father?"

Nancy nodded. "Believe it or not, later in life he became vehemently opposed to the idea of divorce. Especially in a marriage where children would be affected."

I snorted incredulously. "That sounds like an epiphany that arrived conveniently after the fact."

"Doesn't it? But my father had a way of turning things around in his own mind so that they made sense to him even if nobody else agreed. With regard to divorce, he told Ron that his children should be smart enough to learn from his mistakes. And when Leo Brody decided something, it was *done.* Nobody ever dared to contradict him or go against his wishes."

"Not even within the family?" I asked.

"Especially not inside the family. We all knew how important it was to stay in his good graces. There was too much at stake to do otherwise."

I assumed we were talking about money. Then I gave myself a mental kick. *Of course* we were talking about the money.

As we'd been speaking, the two cats had joined forces on the floor. A spirited game for possession of the ball had ensued. Then the toy had rolled beneath the refrigerator. There'd been some futile poking, followed by plaintive meowing, before the pair gave up. Now both cats were heading my way.

Maybe I could just hold my breath for the next few minutes, I thought hopefully.

But of course that didn't work. I still had too many questions. "So Leo Brody's death released Fred, Ron, and Cynthia from the hold he had over them. Now they're free to do whatever they want."

"You got it. I expect we'll see a shake-up in the family dynamics shortly."

The cats came slinking closer. I stood up and backed away. The thought of them winding their way around my legs made my neck itch.

"I don't get it," I said to Nancy. "Why would you tell me all this stuff? Why betray your brothers' confidence?"

"Because I'm tired of being in the middle between the two of them. I never asked for that. In fact, I wish I didn't even know about the whole sorry business. And besides . . ."

Nancy stood up as well. We placed our mugs in the sink, then walked to the door. We were almost there when I sneezed violently. Once, and then a second time.

"Sorry." I gave her a bleary-eyed look. "Cats. And besides . . . ?"

"Anything that points my dear sister Libby in a direction away from me is a plus. You'll take this information back to her and she can put it to use in whatever manner she chooses." Nancy pushed open the door and I walked out onto the stoop. "Were you paying attention, Melanie?"

I was puzzled by the question. "Yes, of course—"

"Then maybe you noticed something. We Brodys

grew up knowing the importance of protecting ourselves. We learned early how to look out for number one. I shared my brothers' secrets with you.
But I didn't divulge a single one of my own."

Well, crap. Before I could say another thing, Nancy
stepped back. The door snicked shut between us.

Across the yard, Kevin and Miranda were in the
goat pen playing with the goats. I collected my son
and buckled him into the car. Together we sang
"Old MacDonald Had a Farm" all the way home.

The song's repetitive verses had one beneficial
effect. They kept me from thinking about how
neatly I'd been outmaneuvered.

Libby called while Kevin and I were waiting in
the pick-up line at Davey's camp that afternoon.

Just the person I wanted to talk to, I thought as I
lifted the phone to my ear. Faith was in the back
seat with Kev. The two of them could entertain
each other while Libby and I chatted.

The woman barely gave me a chance to say hello.
"I hear you're shaking things up," she blared. "Good
for you! That's just what my family needs."

"Some of them wouldn't agree with you," I said.

"That's their problem."

Apparently empathy was not Libby's strong suit.

"I spent the morning with your sister, Nancy," I
told her. "Did you really convince her that a specials career was a good investment?"

"Is that what she told you?"

The answer to that was obvious to both of us.

"Nancy thought you'd sent me to negotiate a
settlement for the money you owe her," I said.

"That's ridiculous. Nancy is delusional."

"She seemed pretty levelheaded to me." Libby was using me for her own purposes. I didn't see any reason why I couldn't do the same. "Nancy told me a story about a Dalmatian named Cavalier. Is he your current stud dog?"

"So what if he is? That spat you're referring to is private business between Nancy and me. It has nothing to do with my father's death."

"Unless one or the other of you was desperate for money," I pointed out.

"Well, that's certainly not true."

"Is it?"

"Of course," Libby snapped. "How dare you insinuate anything else?"

"Because that's what you asked me to do," I said mildly. "It's not my fault if the trail you placed me on doubled back in your direction."

I inched the car forward and glanced over my shoulder to check on things in the back seat. Faith was sitting up. One of her front paws was resting in Kevin's lap. He was playing "This Little Piggy" with her toes. Both appeared to be enjoying themselves.

"Look," Libby said. "My family isn't like other families, okay? There are elements in our relationships that you don't understand."

"Like what?"

"Not that it's something you need to know, but my mother didn't get together with Leo Brody under the best of circumstances."

That was hardly news. And since I'd spent the last four days interviewing Libby's siblings—some of whom had been seriously annoyed about her mandate to talk to me—you'd think it would have occurred to her that somebody had already spilled those beans.

"Nancy resents me. She always has." Libby's voice quavered. "My mother took the place of hers and she's never forgiven me for that. Imagine how it feels to be a child whose brothers and sister blame you for something that was totally beyond your control."

The explanation was clearly a plea for sympathy. I might have been more receptive if Libby hadn't described her childhood to me as idyllic just last week at the dog show. *Seriously.* This wasn't rocket science. Could nobody in the Brody family keep their stories straight for longer than the time it took to tell them?

When I didn't come back with the expected platitudes, Libby quickly changed tactics. "I'll tell you who probably needed money. Becca Montague. What does that awful woman have to say for herself?"

"That she and your father were in love." I paused to let that sink in, then added, "And that they were engaged to be married."

Libby's denial was swift and angry. "That's absurd! Becca Montague is a liar. I bet she's a murderer too."

"If you have proof of that, I'd love to hear it." I moved the car forward again. We were finally nearing the front of the line.

"Of course I don't have any proof," Libby snapped. "That's supposed to be your job."

Right.

"You told me that your father and Becca had been together for several months. Had you seen any recent signs that things weren't going smoothly between them?"

"You've got to be kidding. I didn't need signs to know that Leo and Becca never should have gotten together in the first place. And what about Jane?" Libby demanded. "She was at Puppy Fest all day. Why haven't you talked to her yet?"

Because I have two kids, six dogs, and a husband and there are only twenty-four hours in a day, I thought.

Aloud, I said, "Jane doesn't like me."

Libby blew off my objection. "That doesn't mean anything, Jane doesn't like anybody. You can find her at Puppy Posse every day between eight and six."

As I put the phone away, the passenger door was yanked open. Davey came flying in. His backpack landed with a thud on the floor. A half-empty water bottle came loose and rolled beneath the seat. Davey's clothes were dirty, his hair was disheveled, but he was grinning.

"Daaaavey!" Kev squealed from the back seat.

"Hey, squirt." Davey twisted around as he did up his seat belt. "Did you have a good day?"

"Great day," Kev replied. "I played with goats."

Davey looked at me. "Do I want to know?"

"Probably not." I eased the car out of line and headed for the exit. "Pizza for dinner. How does that sound?"

"Even better than goats," Davey said.

Chapter 22

The pizza was a big hit. So was the fact that I let Kevin stay up past his bedtime playing games with Davey. There was an ulterior motive behind that benevolence. I'd be taking Kev with me when I headed down to Puppy Posse the following morning. It would help if he wasn't his usual bundle of energy.

The Poodles and Bud were eager to join in the games. Bud upset the checkerboard twice. The first time it ended up on the floor, we shooed Bud off the tabletop, restored the board, and secured it more carefully. Then the little dog returned with a rawhide bone that he'd found beneath the couch.

Augie and Tar had their eyes on that enticing toy as soon as it appeared. They followed Bud across the room. When he dropped the bone in Davey's lap, both male Poodles dove for it at the same time. So technically, the second time the checkerboard went flying, it was Davey's fault.

Not surprisingly, mayhem ensued. Eve and Raven had been lying quietly on the floor. Now they jumped up to join the fray. Tar grabbed the bone and bounced up onto the back of the couch. As he dared Augie to come and get it, Bud began to race in excited circles around the room.

Faith and I watched the commotion from the sidelines. I don't know about her, but I was too old for those kinds of shenanigans. She and I could pick up the pieces when everyone else was finished carrying on.

My plan would have worked to perfection if only my still-drowsy son hadn't fallen asleep in the car after we dropped Davey off at camp the next morning. He woke up from his catnap, cheerful and raring to go, when I pulled into the Puppy Posse parking lot.

The rescue was housed in a nondescript brick building in a semi-industrial zone in south Stamford. Its lot was surrounded by a chain-link fence whose gate was held open by a piece of twisted wire. The drab edifice looked as though it might have belonged to a converted factory. The only cheerful aspect was colorful block lettering above the double glass doors, spelling out the Puppy Posse name.

"Ugh," Kevin pronounced from his car seat.

Fortunately, our impressions changed as soon as we entered the building. The front door opened directly into a spacious, well-lit lobby whose walls were decorated with whimsical life-size murals of puppies and dogs. One side of the room offered comfortable seating. The other had a low counter, behind which a young woman with a cheerful smile was waiting to greet us.

I recognized her right away. It was Lucy, who'd been assisting Jane at Puppy Fest. "May I help you?" she asked politely.

"Yes, I'm here to see Jane Brody. I'm Melanie Travis. We met at Puppy Fest, remember?"

"Sure, I guess."

Lucy and I had spent a day working together amicably, so I wasn't expecting such a lukewarm welcome. I wondered whether she'd observed the interactions between me and her boss and absorbed some of Jane's hostility.

"Do you have an appointment?" she asked.

I loosened my grip on Kev's hand. He trotted over to the nearest mural and examined it in fascination. "No, I don't. Do I need one?"

"Let me check. Please wait here."

Lucy exited through a door in the back wall. Before it closed, I caught a glimpse into the next room. A row of wire pens lined each wall, with a center aisle between them. Most of the pens appeared to be full, and more than a few of their occupants were barking.

Then the door clicked shut and the din quieted once more. I went and joined Kevin beside a giant painting of a Saint Bernard. Everything about the portrait was lifelike, right down to the long skein of drool that hung from the dog's mouth.

Jane kept us waiting fifteen minutes before putting in an appearance. I suspected she was hoping that I would give up and leave, which only made me more determined to wait her out. In the meantime, I got Kevin settled in a chair with a Richard Scarry picture book. He loved the one about cars and trucks. With luck it would hold his attention until my business at Puppy Posse was finished.

Kevin didn't even look up when the door opened and Jane entered the room. To my surprise her brother, Joe, was with her.

"Great place you have here," I said.

"Yes, it is," Jane replied. "We all work hard to make it that way."

Joe stepped out from behind his sister. He strode across the room and placed his hands on my shoulders. His lips brushed my cheek. "Nice to see you again, Melanie. Don't mind Jane. She's feeling a little prickly today."

As soon as Joe's fingers loosened their grasp, I moved away. I hadn't been expecting that level of familiarity. Suddenly I was feeling a little prickly myself.

Jane looked at us in surprise. "You two know each other?"

"We met at Puppy Fest," I told her.

"And then again a couple of days ago," Joe added. "Melanie stopped by to talk to me and Graham."

"Really?" She lifted a brow. "About what?"

"The old man . . . Haven't you heard? Libby's on the warpath about his death."

"Libby and I don't speak." Jane turned to me. "What does that have to do with you?"

"Libby asked me to make some inquiries—"

"Melanie is a *sleuuuth*." Joe drew out the last

word for several extra beats. "You know, like Nancy Drew? She's investigating us."

"Not me she isn't," Jane told her brother. Then she frowned at me. "If that's why you're here, you can show yourself out. *Now.*"

Joe held up a restraining hand. "No, Melanie, don't leave. Jane's just being a spoilsport. I want to hear what you've learned. I bet it's fascinating. How many of the obnoxious nine have you spoken to?"

"The obnoxious nine?"

"That was Dad's nickname for us," Joe said. "Funny, huh? He claimed it was a joke."

"Except that none of us were stupid enough to believe that." Jane wasn't amused. "Is Joe telling the truth? Have you really made the rounds of the entire family?"

"Just about," I said. "Aside from Annette, the only one I haven't spoken to is Ron. Ashley told me he was out of town."

A look passed between Jane and Joe. I wished I knew what it meant.

"Ron's around," Joe said after a moment. "Ashley doesn't know what she's talking about."

"As usual," Jane muttered. "If that girl's the one who's feeding you information we're all in trouble. What else did she tell you?"

"That you like to bake," I told her. "And that you always bring cookies to family gatherings."

Joe hooted so loudly that I winced and Kev looked up from his book. Only Jane showed no visible reaction.

"Good one, Ashley!" Joe laughed. "I'm amazed I missed that connection myself. You better be nice to me, Jane, otherwise I'll put it to good use. The tabloids would have a field day with that tidbit of information."

"Quit fooling around." Jane reached over and smacked her brother.

Joe dodged away, hopped two steps, and ended up standing entirely too close to me. The counter was at my back. I sidled sideways to give myself some extra room. Judging by the smug expression on Joe's face, he knew exactly what I was doing.

Damn. I'd really wanted to talk to Jane. And it would have been so much easier if I didn't have to navigate around her brother.

"Puppy Fest wasn't a family gathering. It was a semi-public event," Jane said. She uttered the words slowly and distinctly so no one could mistake their import. "And in case you didn't notice, I already had a job to do. Even if I had wanted to bring cookies, I wouldn't have had time. I was too busy."

I saw a flash of color and movement out of the corner of my eye. Briefly visible through the glass doors, another vehicle had turned into the Puppy Posse parking lot.

"Now what?" Jane followed the direction of my gaze.

"You might want to rearrange your attitude," I said. "Maybe that's someone who wants to adopt a cute puppy."

"We don't have any cute puppies, Puppy Fest took care of that. All we have now are older dogs, hard-luck cases, and dogs with special needs. And nobody ever wants those. That's why our pens are always full."

"You can climb down off your high horse," Joe

told his sister. "If someone just arrived, I'd imagine it was Trace. I told him to meet me here."

"Why?" she asked.

"He and I are going sailing in Darien. We both had other things to take care of this morning. This made a good halfway point to meet up when we were done."

"Sailing." Jane's voice dripped with disdain.

"Why not?" Joe refused to be baited. "It's a perfect day for it."

"Pity that *some* of us have to work," she said. "Even on beautiful summer days."

"I work too. But lucky for me, bartending is a night job." Joe looked my way. "Trace is Caroline's son. You probably met him at Puppy Fest."

"Nope. Didn't happen." Jane shook her head. "Trace never bothered to show up."

"Are you sure? I could have sworn I saw him driving in that morning."

"And you think Ashley doesn't have a clue," Jane scoffed. "You're no better. Maybe you ought to get your eyes checked. Or better yet, your brain."

It wasn't hard to envision the siblings as a pair of squabbling seven-year-olds. It didn't appear that their relationship had matured much in the meantime.

"Good morning!" Aunt Peg sang out cheerfully.

I swiveled around in surprise. Apparently the new arrival wasn't Trace after all.

"What are you doing here?" I blurted.

"Looking for you. Libby told me where you'd be."

Her gaze slid past me and kept going. That didn't come as a surprise. In Aunt Peg's world, I'm seldom the main attraction.

"You must be Jane Brody." She marched across the lobby. "I'm Peg Turnbull. I've heard a great deal about your establishment and the wonderful work you're doing here. Libby speaks very highly of your efforts."

"Libby does *what*?" Jane sputtered.

Aunt Peg glanced sideways at Joe. He was still standing almost on top of me. But when her beady gaze fastened on him, he finally shifted his weight away. Now at least there was breathing room between us.

Score one for the home team.

"You're performing a valuable service here." Aunt Peg turned back to Jane. "Kudos to you for rescuing dogs in need of a helping hand. Libby tells me that you have a wonderful way with animals. Is that true?"

"It is." Jane's habitual snarl softened. She was almost glowing in response to Aunt Peg's praise.

"Excellent. I was sorry to have missed out on Puppy Fest, but I assume you're still accepting donations?"

"Yes, of course."

"Very good. I'll see to that before I leave." Aunt Peg tipped her head my way. But once again, I realized, she wasn't looking at me. "And who is this young man?"

"Joe Brody." He straightened his shoulders, stepped across the space between them, and offered his hand.

Aunt Peg gave it a hearty shake. "Another one of Leo's offspring, I take it. My, that man was busy. I was a friend of your father's, did you know that?"

Considering that they'd only met a minute earlier, I was guessing the answer was no. But this was clearly Aunt Peg's show. Far be it from me to intervene.

"Terrible thing, Leo's death. You have my condolences, both of you. Your father was a fine man. He would have been the first to tell you that he still had a lot more to do in this world. Peanuts." She snorted derisively. "A cowardly method for murder, wouldn't you say?"

"Murder?" Jane's voice squeaked.

The door to the building opened again and Trace slipped into the lobby. The greeting he'd been about to offer to the room died on his lips when Aunt Peg spoke again.

"Yes, murder," she said firmly. "Leo was too careful for it to have been anything else. I never knew him to take a single bite that wasn't from a trusted source. So where did those cookies come from? Who brought them into his office? Libby asked Melanie to look into that. But if you ask me, she's too slow at figuring things out. I decided I should step in and lend a hand."

Trace caught Joe's eye and his brows rose. Joe shrugged in response. Still silent, Trace sidled over to stand beside his uncle. It was then that Aunt Peg noticed the teenager's presence.

"I see we have the arrival of yet another Brody." She sounded pleased. The more the merrier where Aunt Peg is concerned. "You have the family look."

"Trace is Libby's sister's son—" I started to explain.

"My name is Trace Richland," he interrupted me. "And you're wrong about what happened to my grandfather."

"Am I?" Aunt Peg was immediately interested. "Why do you say that?"

"Because nobody would have wanted Leo Brody to die."

"And yet he did," she said softly.

"It was an accident."

"You sound very sure of yourself."

"I *am* sure." Trace's shoulders stiffened. "Despite my last name, I'm a Brody too. And that means I know what I'm talking about. Whoever you are, your opinion doesn't matter."

"*Trace.*" There was a warning in Joe's tone. He set a hand down heavily on his nephew's shoulder. "Enough."

Trace shrugged his uncle's hand away. But his gaze dropped and his eyes began to blink rapidly as if he was holding back tears. His belligerence melted away. All at once, he looked very young.

"We'd better be going," Joe said. "Time and tide wait for no man." He hustled Trace out the door.

"Time and tide?" Aunt Peg looked puzzled. "He didn't strike me as the Chaucer type."

"They're on their way to go sailing," I told her as we watched them leave through the glass.

"Joe's probably never even heard of Chaucer," said Jane. "He just likes to say things he thinks make him sound intelligent."

"Goodness." Aunt Peg was still staring after them. "Does it work?"

Jane shrugged. "Joe's a bartender. In that milieu, it doesn't take much. I believe you mentioned something about a donation?"

"I did indeed. But first I think you might offer me a tour of your kennel while we get better acquainted."

As Jane and Aunt Peg disappeared into the next room, I went to get Kevin. He'd just finished perusing his picture book. He slapped it shut and slid down out of the chair.

"Time to go?" he asked.

"In a few minutes." I bent down and retied his sneakers. "As soon as Aunt Peg is ready."

When the two women emerged from the kennel, Jane was smiling and Aunt Peg was pulling out her checkbook. The two of them looked quite pleased with themselves. Jane even managed to be polite to me as we said good-bye.

Out in the parking lot, Aunt Peg's minivan was right beside my Volvo. "How did you manage that?" I asked incredulously as I put Kevin in the car.

"Manage what?"

"Jane has barely said a single civil word to me since we met. Now suddenly you and she look like best friends."

"Why not? I'm a very friendly person."

"Because the reason she didn't like me was because of my association with you."

"*Me?*" Aunt Peg was all innocence. "What have I done?"

I waved a hand to encompass the rescue facility behind us. "Apparently you're part of the problem."

"Don't be silly. There isn't a single Poodle in that building. Nor one in all of Fairfield County waiting to be re-homed. The local Poodle club takes care of that, and I'm a dab hand at rescue myself." Aunt Peg nailed me with a look. "Did you know we have a waiting list for the Poodles we take in?"

I shook my head guiltily.

"Jane and I both want what's best for our canine companions," Aunt Peg informed me. "We're on the same side. Pity I can't say the same for the young man I just met in there."

"Trace?"

"No, not him. He was just being a teenager. The other one. The Brody son."

"Joe."

The beady gaze I'd seen earlier was now trained my way. "If you ask me, that one's up to no good."

Kev was buckled in. He began to bounce up and down in his seat impatiently. It was time to go.

I closed the car door and said, "You never told me why you were looking for me."

"I should think that was obvious. Time's passing, Melanie. Things needed to be shaken up. I figured I was just the person for the job."

Nobody, least of all me, could argue with that.

Chapter 23

Sam arrived home late Thursday afternoon. While he was away, I'd helped Davey clip Augie and grind his nails. All that remained to be done was the Standard Poodle's pre-show bath and blow dry. On Friday Augie was entered in a small dog show in southern Massachusetts. This time there wouldn't be any majors at stake. An easier entry might be just what Davey needed to rebuild his confidence.

Sam came in the door, hugged me and Kevin, and tossed his overnight bag at the foot of the stairs. Then he grabbed Davey and Augie. The three of them disappeared into the grooming room and went to work.

Kev and I were in the kitchen having a snack when I heard Sam's cell phone ring. Judging by the sounds coming from the next room, he and Davey had just finished giving Augie a bath. They were ready to transfer the wet dog onto the grooming table.

Under the circumstances, I'd have expected Sam to let the call go to voice mail. Instead he picked up.

Aunt Peg isn't the only one in the family who inherited the nosy gene. I tried to eavesdrop, but unfortunately Sam's conversation was obscured by the loud whine of the big blow dryer. *Rats.*

Five minutes later he emerged from the grooming room. Kev and I were sitting at the kitchen table finishing our yogurt. Sam took in the scene in a glance.

"Hey Kev, why don't you go keep Davey company while he's working on Augie?"

"Okay."

That kid's easy. He didn't even ask why. He just slipped down out of his chair and went padding away.

Sam motioned toward the back door. It was propped half-open so the dogs could go in and out at will. "Let's take a spin around the backyard."

"Sure." I gathered up the empty yogurt containers and dumped them in the garbage. Together we walked out onto the deck.

The remaining four Poodles were outside snoozing in the shade. Faith and Eve lifted their heads to check us out when we came through the door. Then they quickly settled back down. I shaded my eyes against the sun and looked around for Bud.

It didn't take long to spot him. The small dog was way out at the far end of the yard. That little stinker appeared to be digging a hole under the fence.

Sam must have seen the same thing I did. He

immediately struck out in Bud's direction. I fell in beside him.

"What's up?" I asked as we left the deck.

"Tell me about Joe Brody."

I glanced over in surprise. I hadn't expected that.

"He's the second youngest of the Brody sons," I said. "His mother was Leo's third wife. He and his brother, Graham, share an apartment in Cos Cob. He works as a bartender in Rye."

"What else?" Sam asked.

"I don't know." I shrugged. "I guess that's about it."

"That's not what Claire said."

"*Claire?* When did you . . . ?" Oh. The penny dropped. "That was Claire on the phone."

"It was. She called me because she's worried about you."

"That's silly. There's nothing to worry about."

"On the contrary, where you're concerned there's *always* something to worry about. Claire seems to think that this Joe character is someone you don't want to be involved with."

"That's perfect," I said. "Because I'm not involved with him."

Sam didn't look convinced. "Why would Claire think otherwise?"

"Joe is a former boyfriend of hers," I told him. "She doesn't remember him fondly."

"What does that have to do with you?"

"I guess I told her that he was acting a little . . . weird . . . when I met him." And then again yesterday, I thought silently.

"Weird how?"

"Stupid," I said. "Pushier than he should have been."

"He pushed you around?"

"I think he thought he was flirting with me."

Sam stopped walking. The expression on his face was almost comical. "*Joe Brody was flirting with you?*"

"You don't have to look so surprised." My hands propped themselves on my hips. "Which, by the way, is a little insulting."

"But . . ." Sam sputtered. "You're Davey and Kev's *mother.*"

"Still insulting," I said.

We were three-quarters of the way across the yard. Bud must have seen us coming because his frantic activity suddenly stopped. The little dog's front feet were standing in a hole six inches deep. When he lifted his head and turned our way, I saw that his muzzle and chest were covered with dirt.

It looked like there was a bath in his future too.

I sighed and started walking again. I'd taken a dozen steps before Sam realized I was gone. Then he hurried to catch up.

Bud, meanwhile, was backing casually away from his handiwork. *Hole? What hole? I don't see any hole.* He lifted his leg and peed on the fence. Then he looked at us and wagged his tail.

"You." I pointed my finger at his nose. "Come with me." Looping a finger through Bud's collar, I led him back to the scene of the crime. "Who did that?" I asked him.

The little dog looked down. His body cringed away from me like he was afraid he was going to be hit. Or worse.

"Dammit," I chastised myself. I'd forgotten about Bud's background and treated him like he was one of the Poodles. *Idiot.*

Quickly I released Bud's collar and sank down into the grass beside him. Crossing my legs to create an inviting lap, I patted my knees and said, "Come here."

Bud didn't need to be asked twice. He spun around and hopped in. I wrapped my arms around the spotted dog and gave him a hug. Then I turned him and pointed him toward the hole once again.

"Who did that?" I asked.

Safe and secure in my lap, Bud wagged his tail happily. *Not me! Not me! It must have been some other dog.*

Standing above me, Sam cleared his throat. I think he was trying to keep from laughing. "Maybe I'll just go fill that in," he said.

"Good idea."

I set Bud down on the ground and he went scampering back to the house. Sam and I kicked the loose dirt back into the hole and tamped it down into place. Sam found a heavy rock and we stuck it on top of the small depression. Bud wouldn't be digging here again.

"Claire told me Joe Brody isn't a nice guy," he said as we headed back in together. I figured that was pretty brave of him, considering that he'd already come to grief on this topic once. "I don't like the fact that he thinks he can push you around."

"He can't," I said firmly.

"Do you want me to punch him?"

I choked on a laugh. "No."

"I'm serious."

"So am I." I reached out and looped my arm through Sam's. "You don't have to go all caveman on me. I handled it."

"It would be better if you didn't have to handle anything. Maybe you should just stay away from him."

Usually I bristle when Sam tries to tell me what to do. This time, however, we were in complete agreement.

Aunt Peg called early the next morning to say that her minivan had a flat tire. So we swung by and picked her up on the way to the dog show. I told her we were only giving her a ride on one condition. She wasn't allowed to discuss the upcoming competition with Davey.

Aunt Peg got back at me for that. She treated us to a running commentary on every piece of scenery we drove past. Since the show was ninety miles away, that encompassed quite a bit of landscape. After the first hour, I was more than ready to cry uncle. Either that or pull over and leave her by the side of the road.

Sam, as usual, took everything in stride. He and Peg had one discussion about historic covered bridges and another about the merits of dry stone walls versus wet. Every so often, Kevin broke into song and Davey joined in. Their lack of musical ability made Augie press his wrapped ears tight against the sides of his head. I knew just how he felt.

The show site was a spacious campground nestled in the shadow of a small mountain. By the time we arrived, I think we were all relieved to leave the SUV's cramped quarters behind. We quickly unpacked and set up under the grooming tent.

This single dog show, located in the middle of nowhere, always drew a small entry. Most Poodle exhibitors, including our friends Crawford and Terry, had bypassed the event in favor of a three-show weekend in New Jersey. It seemed strange to look around the tent and see very few Poodles out on the tabletops.

Aunt Peg consulted her catalog. "There are five Standard dogs and two bitches. I hope they all show up."

"How many in Davey's class?" Sam asked.

"There are three in Open. The other two are puppies." She squinted at the fine print, then added, "Very young puppies at that. Possibly just here for the experience."

"I still have to beat them," Davey said philosophically. Augie was lying on the table. Davey was line-brushing his off side first.

"You will—" Aunt Peg began.

My glare stopped her in her tracks. Just as it was meant to.

Even so, her resulting change of subject was so abrupt that it caught me by surprise. "If the Brody family members I met yesterday are indicative of the rest of the group," she said, "Leo was not to be commended on his child-rearing skills."

Sam shot me a quizzical look.

"Kevin and I went to Puppy Posse. Aunt Peg decided to join us there."

"I met Jane and her brother, Joe," Aunt Peg told him. "And an argumentative youngster who came slinking in at the end."

"That was Trace, their nephew," I said.

Aunt Peg dismissed the teenager with a wave of her hand. The gesture should have made me move the conversation along. Instead it had the opposite effect. Suddenly it occurred to me that I'd been doing the same thing.

I'd been concentrating my inquiries on the second generation of Leo Brody's family—his children—and giving the grandchildren a pass. Maybe that was a mistake. It might even be a big mistake. There'd been something niggling in the back of my mind for several days and now, all at once, I realized what it was.

"Trace," I said thoughtfully.

"What about him?" Sam asked.

"He was supposed to be at Puppy Fest helping Jane with the puppies. But he never showed up. Later when I asked him about it, Trace told me he *was* there. I mentioned I hadn't seen him and he backpedalled and said he was thinking about something else."

"He sounds like a typical teenage boy to me," Sam said. "I bet he told his parents he was going to Puppy Fest, then skipped out and went somewhere else. He was probably afraid you'd bust him if you knew the truth."

"Possibly." I wasn't convinced. "But the subject came up again yesterday. Jane and Joe were talking about it."

"I don't remember that," said Aunt Peg.

"It was before you got there. Jane and Joe got

into a spat about it. Jane denied that Trace was ever there, while Joe maintained that he'd seen him arriving at Leo Brody's house that morning."

"Maybe Joe was mistaken," Sam said.

"I doubt it. The kid drives a black Porsche Carrera. It's kind of hard to mistake that."

"A Porsche Carrera?" That got Davey's attention. "Cool."

"Not really." I suddenly remembered something else. "The first time I met Trace, he nearly ran me over with it."

"He did what?" All eyes turned my way.

"Trace said it was an accident, that he hadn't seen me standing there," I told them. "At the time, I believed him. At worst, I thought he was just showing off. But now . . ."

Aunt Peg knew immediately what I was thinking. "If Trace didn't go to his grandfather's house to work on Puppy Fest like he was supposed to, why *was* he there? And why did he lie about it later?"

"I hope he wasn't there to deliver a plate of cookies," I said darkly.

"Cookies?" Kevin looked up. He was playing in the grass at out feet. "Time for cookies?"

"Not now, sweetie. Maybe after Davey and Augie go in the ring."

"Chocolate chip." Kev placed his order. "They're my favorite." Like we didn't already know that.

"Maybe Detective Young would like to hear about this," I said.

"I should say so," Aunt Peg agreed.

Even Sam nodded. "You should go talk to him tomorrow."

A consensus was a rare occurrence in my family.

"I will," I said. "I'll tell him everything and see what he makes of it."

"Now that that's settled," said Davey, "is anybody going to help me with Augie's topknot?"

"Me!" Kevin jumped to his feet.

"I don't think so." I leaned down and lifted him up. "But you and I can go pick up Davey's armband."

I held out my hand, but Kevin ignored it. Instead he wriggled between two sets of stacked crates and dodged handily through the next row of setups. He spurted out of the tent and took off toward the show rings.

"Apparently we're on our way," I said. "Be back in a few minutes."

To nobody's surprise, Kevin and I got sidetracked several times. We stopped to watch a class of Great Danes gait around their ring. Then we saw a black Labrador Retriever who was splashing around in a wading pool to cool off. Luckily maternal instinct kicked in just in time, and a quick move on my part prevented Kevin from hopping in to join him.

The Poodle ring was running on time and we picked up Davey's number from the steward. I squatted down and ran two rubber bands up to the top of Kevin's slender arm. When they were firmly in place, I slipped the cardboard square beneath them. Kev cocked his elbow outward and admired my handiwork. He began to swing his arm from side to side.

"Don't lose that," I told him. "Augie needs it to go in the ring."

"Augie's going to win," Kevin informed me. He must have been talking to Aunt Peg.

Back at the handlers' tent, Sam and Davey had Augie's topknot in and they were beginning to spray up his neck hair. Since he'd been shown the week before, the big dog would only need a cursory scissoring. He was almost ready to go.

Aunt Peg was standing at the edge of the setup. "I've had a discreet look around," she said in a low tone. "There isn't another Standard here today that can touch this dog."

"If I said something like that," I mentioned, "you would yell at me for jinxing them."

"Don't be a spoilsport," Aunt Peg sniffed. "I'm merely stating a fact."

"Yeah, Mom." Davey grinned. "Do as I say, not as I do."

"You are a fresh kid," I told him. The half-hearted rebuke was softened by a laugh. "And you're not even a teenager yet."

"Six weeks 'til my birthday," Davey said. "Then watch out."

"What's going on in the ring?" Sam asked. Luckily one of us was keeping his mind on business.

"The judge is right on time." I turned back to Davey. "And he's not taking his dogs in catalog order. So you probably want to go to the head of the line."

Most judges can find a good dog anywhere. But it never hurts to give them a subliminal nudge by placing your dog where you intend for it to be when the judging is finished.

"That'll give Stan an eyeful right off the bat," Aunt Peg said with satisfaction.

"Who's Stan?" I asked.

"Stan Harvey. The judge."

"We're on a first-name basis with the judge?" Somehow that seemed almost indecent to me.

Not to Aunt Peg. She stopped just short of rolling her eyes. "In case you've forgotten, Melanie, I'm a judge too."

There was that.

"And when other judges have questions about the Poodle breed, who do you think they turn to?"

There was that too.

Feeling suitably chastened, I said, "Is Stan a good judge?"

"He'd better be," Aunt Peg muttered. "I taught him everything he knows."

That tidbit of information took us up to the ring in good spirits.

We waited near the in-gate and observed the Standard Poodle Puppy Dog class. Mr. Harvey sorted out the small entry with a capable eye and a kind hand. He was smiling as he watched the pair of playful puppies make their last circuit of the ring.

Kevin was standing on the ground in front of me. As Davey prepared to enter the ring, Kev reached up and tugged on the hem of my shirt. I wondered if he couldn't see from where he was.

"Do you want me to pick you up?" I asked.

Kev didn't answer. Instead he simply pointed to the top of his arm.

"Oh crap!" I snatched the numbered armband out from beneath the rubber bands that were holding it in place. "Davey, wait!"

Luckily the switch only took a moment and Davey and Augie still managed to be the first pair into the ring when the Open Dog class was called. A big white dog with a coarse head and flat feet fell into line behind them. A weedy silver with a conspicuously low tail set followed.

"What did I tell you?" Aunt Peg whispered out of the side of her mouth.

I shushed her and kept my eyes trained on the ring. I was happy to see that in contrast to their performance the previous weekend, Davey and Augie were now working as a team. This time, the two of them were having fun. Augie showed like a dream and managed to make it look effortless.

I wasn't surprised but I was relieved when Augie won the Open class. Then I held my breath until the judge had picked him over the Puppy winner and awarded Augie the purple ribbon for Winners Dog.

While I was busy congratulating my son on a job well done, Mr. Harvey made short work of his small bitch entry. No specials were entered in Standard Poodles so when the Best of Variety class was called to the ring, Davey and Augie found themselves once again at the head of the line. It was a position they never relinquished.

When the breed judging was over, Davey emerged from the ring with a huge smile on his face and Augie dancing at his side. Davey was clutching both the blue-and-white Best of Winners ribbon and the purple-and-gold rosette for Best of Variety.

"Holy cow," I said. "You won the whole thing."

Augie wouldn't gain any extra points for the BOV win. But the honor of having him chosen as the best Standard Poodle at the dog show was enough to make us all giddy.

"You know what this means," Aunt Peg said.

Our ringside celebration paused briefly. We were hav-ing such a wonderful moment that none of us had given a thought to anything beyond it. Except of course, for Aunt Peg.

"Now we have to stay for the group," she announced.

Chapter 24

The Non-Sporting group was scheduled to be judged last. That gave us several hours to kill. We ate lunch, then wandered around the show ground, stopping to peruse the activity at various rings. Davey was particularly interested in the obedience dogs competing in the Utility class.

He watched a Border Collie lie down, then sit up in response to its handler's silent signals from across the ring. "Maybe Augie and I will try that next," he said.

"Not agility?" Sam was surprised.

"Nope." Davey cast a telling glance in Aunt Peg's direction. Between judging assignments, she competed in agility with Eve's littermate, Zeke.

"Utility is the PhD of obedience," I told him. "You and Augie will have to begin with the basics and work your way up."

"That's okay. It makes sense to start with easy stuff. And speaking of which . . ." Davey let the sentence dangle until both Sam and I had turned to face him. "I think Sam should show Augie in the group."

"No way," I said quickly.

"Think about it, Mom. No group judge is going to look at a dog with a kid on the end of the lead."

"That's not true," said Aunt Peg.

"Maybe not when you're judging," Davey allowed. "But you're different."

She cleared her throat. "I shall endeavor to take that as a compliment."

Davey looked at the three of us. "Sam's won plenty of groups. Augie deserves to be shown by someone who can do a better job with him than I can."

"You and Augie are a team," Aunt Peg said firmly. "What that dog deserves is to walk into the big, scary group ring with his best friend at his side."

If I had expressed that sentiment, Davey would have brushed it off. But coming from Aunt Peg, it made his face glow. All right, I'll admit it. It made mine glow a little too.

"I'm glad that's settled," said Sam.

An English Setter won the Sporting Group. A Scottish Deerhound triumphed in Hounds. One by one, the groups went by. It was almost five o'clock by the time a Briard was sent to the first place marker in the penultimate Working group. Non-Sporting was next and last.

Sam stayed by Davey's side until he and Augie were ready to enter the ring. Then he hurried around to join us on the other side.

In group judging, the breeds line up in size

order. The larger, faster dogs are at the head of the line and the slower, smaller ones bring up the rear. Though Standard Poodles often lead the Non-Sporting dogs, Sam had advised Davey to fall in behind the Dalmatian so he and Augie could follow someone with more experience.

Davey started out a little stiff, but by the time the group of dogs had made their first circuit around the ring, he began to relax and enjoy himself. Augie was a big moving Poodle, and the dimensions of the larger arena worked to his advantage. I knew I wasn't the only one who'd noticed how long the judge's gaze had lingered on him during the first go-round.

Davey and Augie completed their individual examination and went to the back of the line. Eighteen breeds had shown up for the group. The judge was working his way through them quickly and efficiently.

"This isn't the best group of Non-Sporting dogs I've ever seen," Aunt Peg said under her breath. "Augie looks rather good in there."

"Don't," I shushed her quickly. "Don't even say it."

I was thrilled for Davey's sake when he and Augie made the cut. Sam had the good grace not to wince when I grabbed his arm and held on tight. Fortunately the competition was almost over and he didn't have to suffer long.

The judge swiftly rearranged his remaining dogs, then sent them around the ring one last time before pointing at his winners. "I'll have the Bichon, the Löwchen, the Shar-Pei, and the Standard Poodle."

The last words were barely out of his mouth before Davey's cheering section began to jump up and down and scream like crazy people. Okay, maybe that was just me. Inside the ring, my son ducked his head in momentary embarrassment, but there was no mistaking the huge grin on his face when the judge handed him the big white rosette for fourth place.

"Davey's winning!" Kevin shrieked.

"He is indeed," Aunt Peg agreed. "That was well done."

Sam grabbed a comb and made minor repairs to Augie's ears and neck hair while the photographer set up to take pictures. Davey was still smiling when it was Augie's turn in front of the camera. My son's euphoria must have been contagious because the judge and the photographer ended up grinning with him. I was sure the resulting picture would end up hanging on his bedroom wall.

We remained at ringside to watch Best in Show. The Bichon that had beaten Davey was a contender, but in the end the judge went with the Old English Sheepdog from the Herding group.

"I would have put up the English Setter," Davey said as we headed back to the handlers' tent.

"Why?" Aunt Peg wanted to know.

"I don't know. I just liked him best."

"I did too," Peg concurred. "It'll be a shame when you decide to move on. The obedience ring's gain will be conformation's loss."

"Maybe," Davey said under his breath. "We'll see."

We were a quieter group on the long drive home from the dog show, but it was a contented silence. Davey and Augie had turned in the winning performance, but we all shared in their sense of accomplishment. Drifting along in our happy bubble, none of us paid any attention to the first sign that something might be amiss.

As Sam exited the Merritt Parkway at North Street and turned away from town toward Aunt Peg's house, I dimly registered the sound of sirens in the distance. A minute later, flashing lights came flying up behind us. Quickly Sam pulled over to the side of the road. Two fire engines went speeding past.

"I wonder where they're going," Aunt Peg said. "I hope it's nothing serious."

We'd spent so long at the dog show that the sun was dropping on the horizon. When Sam pulled back onto the otherwise empty road, the emergency lights were clearly visible ahead of us. We were all heading in the same direction.

"Look!" Davey sat up suddenly and pointed out the front window. "That's smoke."

In the gathering dusk, I could barely see anything above the tops of the surrounding trees. As I squinted into the distance, Aunt Peg abruptly leaned forward in her seat. She poked Sam hard in the shoulder.

"Drive faster!" she commanded.

Sam pushed his foot to the floor. We'd almost caught up to the fire engines when they slowed fractionally to make a sharp right-hand turn. I was familiar with the narrow lane the trucks went careening into. It led to only four widely spaced homes. Sam and I exchanged a look.

"Uh oh," Davey said under his breath.

Aunt Peg lives in an early-twentieth-century farmhouse that was once the hub of a working farm. Over the years, the farm's acreage had been sold off and developed into a group of stately homes on spacious, private lots. Aunt Peg's property consists of the original house and five acres of land around it. The parcel is large enough, and secluded enough, to provide the perfect setting for her Cedar Crest Kennels.

Years earlier when Aunt Peg's husband was still alive, the kennel building behind the house had been home to more than a dozen Standard Poodles. In more recent times, she had scaled back her breeding program. Now the pens in the kennel building sat empty and Aunt Peg's four remaining Poodles lived inside the house.

The first fire engine charged down the lane and swept into Aunt Peg's driveway. The second one quickly followed. Several people were clustered together in the road. One man held a cell phone. Another waved the emergency vehicles toward the right location.

The smoke was much thicker here. It formed a wide plume that billowed into the darkening sky. Even with the car windows closed, its acrid scent filled my nose.

Sam steered the SUV to the side of the road out of the way. Briefly his headlights glinted off of something farther down the lane. It looked like a bicycle propped against a tree. There was no time to look again, however. As soon as the car stopped, I unsnapped my seat belt and twisted in my seat.

Reaching back, I grabbed Davey's hand. "You and Kevin stay here. You're in charge and you'll have to watch out for Augie too. Nobody gets out

of the car until we come back for you. Understand?"

"But Mom—!"

"No arguments." Sam backed me up. He and
Aunt Peg were already scrambling out of the SUV.

"But I can help," Davey protested.

"You *are* helping," I told him. "You're keeping
your little brother safe. That's the most important
job. Promise me the three of you will stay right
here."

"I promise," Davey said grudgingly.

Sam and Aunt Peg were already halfway down
the driveway by the time I caught up with them. As
we drew closer, I could see that the house itself appeared to be unscathed. The thick black smoke
seemed to be coming from the kennel building,
nestled in a stand of trees thirty feet farther away.

Both gates to Aunt Peg's fenced backyard stood
open. At the head of the driveway, a dozen firemen were working quickly and efficiently. Some
were donning equipment. Others unspooled thick
hoses and dragged them around the house. One
stood ready to turn on the water.

As we dodged around the fire trucks, the kennel
finally came into view. Lit by the raging fire, the
compact wooden structure stood out vividly against
the dark sky. I was shocked to see that it was already
nearly consumed. The building's clapboard siding
had curled and buckled. Two front windows were
broken. Flames shot out through the roof and a
host of bright sparks floated upward, hissing and
popping in the dry air.

For a moment we just stood there, transfixed by
the horrifying sight. Then I heard the sudden

squeal of another siren behind us. The three of us jumped to one side as a patrol car came racing in the driveway. Two policemen hopped out, assessed the situation briefly, then approached us.

"You'll have to step back out to the road," the first one said. He and his partner held out their arms as if they intended to herd us away. "It isn't safe for you to be here."

"This is my house," Aunt Peg said stoutly. "I'm not going anywhere."

The fire chief had been busy issuing directions. Now he came hurrying our way. "Ma'am, did I hear you say this is your house?"

"Yes, that's right."

"Is there anyone inside that building?"

"No, it's empty."

I heard Aunt Peg's voice crack and knew what she was thinking.

Technically the kennel was empty, but it still held decades worth of memories. Though the dogs had left, the building remained home to Aunt Peg's elaborate trophy room. There, rosettes from Westminster and Morris & Essex hung beside win-photos of generations of Cedar Crest Standard Poodles. Not to mention the silverware that had accompanied those wins. In the space of an instant, all of that was gone.

"What is that building?" the fire chief asked. "A guest house?"

"It's a kennel."

"A kennel?" He sounded surprised. "Like with dogs?" At Aunt Peg's nod, he said, "Any in there now?"

Only someone unfamiliar with my aunt could have asked that question. If her Poodles had been locked inside the kennel, she wouldn't have been standing here watching it burn. Nor would Sam and I.

"No," Aunt Peg said softly. "They're in the house."

We all looked that way. Between all the noise and commotion, I hadn't heard her Poodles barking. Now I could see that the four big, black dogs had run into the room over the garage. Clearly agitated, they were leaping against the windows above us.

"Are they safe where they are?" Aunt Peg asked with sudden concern. "Should I bring them out here?"

"No, don't do that." The chief held up a hand. "They're much better off contained and out of the way."

"But the house . . . ?" I asked.

"Don't worry, it's not in jeopardy. You'll lose your kennel and probably a tree or two, but we'll have the fire under control before it goes any farther. We'll wet down the roof as a precaution and we'll stay right here until we're sure everything is fine."

"Thank you." Aunt Peg's shoulders sagged in relief. "Thank you for everything."

Sam slipped his arm around her and pulled her close to his body for support. For the first time I noticed that Aunt Peg was shaking. The shock of watching her kennel burn was too much for her to bear. Sam intercepted my glance and nodded.

"We're going to go sit down," he said.

As he led Aunt Peg to the low stone wall that bordered her front yard, I turned back to the fire chief. "Do you know how the fire started?"

"Not yet. Although for a building to burn this hot and this quickly . . ." He shook his head. "I'm guessing there must have been multiple sources."

"Multiple sources?" It took me a few seconds to process the information. "You mean, it was set deliberately?"

"We'll know more after we complete our investigation, but as of right now, that would be my theory. If you'll excuse me, I need to get back to work."

"Of course. Thank you for your help."

I turned to check on Sam and Aunt Peg and saw that an ambulance was now parked at the end of the driveway. A pair of EMTs had made their way to Aunt Peg and were offering aid. She was shaking her head vehemently.

Good luck with that, I thought.

Out on the road, the crowd of onlookers had grown. More than a dozen people were milling around, pointing and staring, and sharing eagerly in the excitement. Avid spectators to someone else's misfortune, they all looked like ghouls to me.

Several people had their phones out and were videoing the proceedings. I wondered unhappily if Aunt Peg would have to watch a replay of her own personal tragedy on tomorrow's evening news.

I jumped at the sound of a loud crash behind me. The kennel roof had collapsed. A cloud of sparks burst upward from the flaming debris, lighting the night sky like a host of twinkling stars. The audience gasped with delight at the show.

A new car came coasting slowly down the narrow lane. Its headlights swept through the crowd, and I felt a jolt of recognition as the beams illuminated the shadows and briefly revealed two familiar figures. Two heads—one blond, one brunette—were tipped toward each other in whispered conversation. Megan and Ashley Brody.

What were they doing here?

Chapter 25

Quick, angry strides carried me down the length of the driveway to the road. I was still ten feet away when the twins looked up and saw me coming. Both sets of eyes widened simultaneously. Both girls looked around as if tempted to flee— but there was nowhere they could go that I wouldn't follow.

I saw the moment Megan and Ashley realized that. By unspoken accord, the pair decided to stand their ground.

"What a surprise!" Megan's voice sounded unnaturally high. "We didn't expect to see you here."

"This is my aunt's house." My tone was sharp. "That's her kennel that's burning."

"It *is*?" Ashley's head whipped around in an exaggerated show of surprise. "We had no idea. Megan and I were just in the neighborhood—"

"—on our way to visit our cousin, Trace," Megan said. "He lives nearby."

"We saw the commotion and came to find out what was happening," Ashley finished.

Once again it came back to Trace, I thought bitterly.

Ashley peered around me for a better view of the flames. Thanks to the efforts of the firemen, the blaze was finally beginning to subside. "This is tragic. I hope your aunt didn't lose anything *too* valuable."

The teenager sounded sympathetic. But there was just enough light for me to see that her blue eyes were glittering with suppressed excitement. And something else. Something worse.

It took me a moment to define that second emotion. Then all at once I remembered Miranda's stories about her cousins' wild antics. With that came the realization that what I was seeing was satisfaction. Ashley was delighted by the sight of the roaring fire—and it wasn't the first time she'd created a blaze to further her own ends.

I took a step toward the blond twin. Deliberately I stood too close. "You did this," I hissed.

A look of surprise flashed across Ashley's face. After a telling pause, she shook her head vehemently. "You're crazy! I had nothing to do with it."

"I don't believe you," I snapped. "You knew this was Aunt Peg's house. You set that fire on purpose."

"You're wrong. You must be imagining things." Ashley looked to her twin for support. "Tell her, Megan."

Even in the half-light, I could see that Megan's face was ashen. Rather than answering, she began to back away.

I grabbed Ashley's arm, closing my fingers around it firmly. "The police are here," I told her. "They're going to want to talk to you."

"No. I won't! You can't make me. I didn't do anything!"

"You can tell that to the officer in charge." I started across the road, pulling the reluctant girl with me. "You can tell the fire chief too. There's going to be an investigation into the cause of the blaze. I'm betting they'll find proof—"

"Stop it!" Suddenly Megan was beside us too. She grabbed at my hand, trying to pry my fingers loose. "Leave her alone. Ashley's not lying. She didn't set the fire."

Abruptly I stopped walking. I looked back and forth between the two girls. "Then who did?"

For a moment, neither one said a thing. Then Ashley blurted out, "It was Trace. He's the one who started it."

She'd given me the name I expected to hear. But even so, I wasn't sure I believed her. Was Ashley telling the truth, or was she throwing her cousin under the bus in an attempt to save herself?

"Why?" My tone let them know that the answer had better be good. "Why would Trace burn down my aunt's kennel?"

"It was your fault," Ashley spat.

Right. I wasn't about to let them get away with that. "What did I do?"

"You're so stupid. You don't know anything," said Megan.

"Tell me."

"You had no right to get involved with the Brody

family. Poking around and meddling in things that were none of your concern. If you'd stayed away, everything would have been fine."

"Everybody knows better than to make Trace mad," Ashley said with a sneer. "Except *you*. Trace said you and your aunt needed a warning. Something to make you back off."

"So you knew what he intended to do," I said. "Did you come here tonight to help?"

"No," Megan denied furiously. "That's not what happened at all. We came to try and stop him."

"*That is such bullshit.*"

Trace stepped out of the surrounding darkness to join us. I'd wondered how long it would take for him to appear. Radiating anger, the teenage boy glared at the three of us.

"You can't blame this on me, Ash. Don't even try, or I'll make you so sorry you'll wish you'd never been born. I am *not* taking the fall for your stupidity."

"Don't listen to him, Melanie." Deliberately Ashley drew my gaze away from her cousin and back to her. "He doesn't know what he's talking about."

"I know *exactly* what I'm talking about." Trace inserted himself between us. "In fact, you wouldn't believe what I know."

"Shut up!" Megan cried. "Just shut up, all right? Everybody stop talking."

Trace glanced at her and his expression softened. "I did it to help you."

"No, you didn't," she said. "You never listen. You just took over and did what you wanted. As usual."

"Hey, I didn't start any of this." Trace held up his hands in a protest of innocence. "That was all on you."

"Not me." Megan looked around wildly as though seeking someone to blame. "It was Ashley's idea. She's the one who made it happen."

"Don't be ridiculous," Ashley scoffed. "Nobody would believe that. I don't even know how to bake cookies."

A minute earlier, Megan had called for quiet. Now she suddenly got her wish.

"Cookies?" I said into the yawning silence that followed.

Then everyone was talking at once. Ashley rounded on her sister. "You're the one who said it would work like it does on TV."

"You got the idea *from a TV show*?" Trace looked every bit as shocked as I felt. "You two are idiots. I can't believe I ever thought a pair of dimwits would know what they were doing."

"I'm not an idiot," Megan said angrily. "It was a good plan. It should have worked. Leo's whole life was about giving money to worthy causes. Who's more worthy than his own relatives?"

"And we would have paid him back," Ashley added. "Just as soon as we were raking in money ourselves."

"Yeah, because that's easy . . . starting your own fashion company in New York. With no experience, no training"—Trace leveled a look at Ashley—"and not even a college degree."

"That didn't stop the Olsen twins—"

He stared at the girls incredulously. "You've got to be kidding me. The Olsen twins are your role models? They didn't need college. They were already famous."

"We could have been famous too." Megan thrust out her chin. "Our name would have opened plenty of doors. All we needed was a little help getting started. It's not like Leo didn't have the money. It was his fault for refusing to share it with us."

Ashley's eyes welled with tears. "We just wanted to give him a little nudge. Make him realize that he wasn't going to be around forever and he should be nicer to his family while he had the chance."

"Yeah, well your plan sucked," Trace said. "Big time."

"It should have worked," Megan repeated plaintively. "There's a character on *The Big Bang Theory* who's allergic to nuts. When he eats them his face swells up and it's funny—"

"—then they take him to the emergency room and the doctors fix him and he's *fine*," Ashley chimed in. "Just like Leo was supposed to be."

I could scarcely believe what I was hearing. The scope of the twins' naiveté, not to mention their sense of entitlement, was absolutely staggering.

"Are you *serious*?" I asked. "You truly believed that a near-death experience would make your grandfather change his mind about giving you money?"

The three cousins seemed startled by the sound of my voice. In their haste to dodge responsibility for what had happened, it appeared they'd forgotten I was even there.

"You don't understand," said Megan. "It was supposed to be a prank."

"You're the ones who don't get it," I shot back. "Your *prank* resulted in someone's death."

"That wasn't our fault," Ashley whined.

The twins seemed to think that if they repeated the statement often enough, that would make it true.

I ignored her and turned to Trace. "I know you were at Leo's house that day. Joe saw you there. What was your part in all this?"

"Nothing," he replied quickly. "It was all them. I had nothing to do with any of it."

Megan shot him an angry look. "That's not true. Trace had the idea to take the EpiPen from Leo's desk. Ash and I never would have thought of that on our own. Maybe our plan did suck, but he was just as much a part of it as we were."

"Shut *up*, Megan." The teenager's tone was filled with menace.

"Try and make me," she snapped back. "I know you enjoyed sneaking into Leo's office and poking around in his things. You can't deny it now."

"I don't have to deny anything. I'm done here." Trace spun around and stalked away. He was quickly swallowed by the surrounding darkness.

I stared at the two remaining Brodys. "So you expect me to believe that the fire is all Trace's fault and that you tried to stop him?"

Both girls nodded sullenly.

"But apparently he didn't try to stop you two from baking those cookies and delivering them to your grandfather's office."

Ashley started to reply. Megan quickly forestalled that by speaking up herself. In the time we'd spent focusing on Trace's role in this debacle, she'd regained much of her composure.

"You're not nearly as clever as you think you are.

We're not going to let you trick us into admitting something we didn't do."

"It's too late to worry about that now. You two have already owned up to what you did." Strictly speaking, that wasn't entirely true but I figured it was close enough.

"If you're angry when you say something, it doesn't count," Ashley informed me in a superior tone.

"You can try using that excuse with the police," I said. "I doubt that they'll be any more impressed by it than I am."

"We're not talking to anyone and you can't make us." Megan looked at her sister. "This is a waste of time. Let's get out of here."

"Whether you come with me or not, I'm going to tell the police everything that happened here," I said before they could turn away. "It would be better for both of you if we talked to them to-gether."

Megan spread her lips in a feral grin. "You should stop and think very carefully about those lies you're planning to tell. I'm sure you wouldn't want to find yourself defending a lawsuit for slan-der and harassment. The Brody legal team knows exactly how to squash people like you. You'll be lucky to own the shoes on your feet by the time they get done."

Okay, I'll admit it. This time, that threat sounded like it had real teeth. Enough to cause a flutter of alarm in the pit of my stomach.

I nudged the feeling aside and said, "It's not slander if I'm telling the truth."

Megan stopped in her tracks. "The truth according to whom, *you*? What you think doesn't matter. Nobody's going to confirm your version of events. You know what that means? It didn't happen."

"You still don't get it," Ashley said. "We're the Brody family. Nobody takes us on and wins."

The two girls linked arms and strolled away. Unlike their cousin, Megan and Ashley took their time making an exit. The unhurried departure served to reinforce their previous message. The twins weren't even slightly intimidated by me. Or by what I might know.

Frowning in frustration, I watched the pair walk away. I still intended to get in touch with Detective Young, but the girls' parting words had had their desired effect. All at once I was swamped with doubt. My word against that of the Brody family and their legal machine? It wasn't difficult to guess how that might end.

I drew in a deep breath and flooded my body with oxygen. What I really needed right then was for my inner avenging angel to awaken, rise up in outrage, and propel me onward with a demand for justice. That seemed like a lot to ask at the end of such a long stressful day, but I waited a hopeful minute anyway.

Nothing happened. Not even a spark. Right now, my life felt more like a fizzle. It figured.

"Excuse me, miss?"

I spun around as someone tapped my shoulder from behind. The older man was pudgy and unshaven. Dressed in blue jeans and a rumpled shirt, he looked as though he'd recently woken up.

Then a second look revealed the shrewd gleam in his eyes and the small notepad in his hand.

Oh joy. The press had arrived. Now my day was complete.

"My name is Harley Jones. I'm a reporter with *The Stamford Advocate.* Maybe you've seen my by-line?"

Maybe I had. I couldn't remember and I didn't much care.

"What do you want?" I asked.

"I heard about the fire on my scanner. This part of Greenwich, pretty much everything that happens is news so I came right over. I couldn't help overhearing your conversation. One of those girls mentioned the name Brody. Would that be *Leo* Brody she was talking about?"

My first thought was to send him on his way. Then I stopped and reconsidered. "How much did you hear?"

"Just about everything they said." His gaze was speculative. "I took good notes too. I left the house in a hurry and forgot my recorder, but don't worry, I'm old school. I got it done."

The pad in his hand was flipped open. The pages were covered with neat dark script.

A spark of hope flickered inside me. The avenging angel unfolded her wings. Suddenly I felt reenergized.

"How long have you worked for the *Advocate*?" I asked.

"Twenty years. Before that, the *New York Times.* I'll be coming up on retirement soon, but I still hate to miss a story." Harley looked at me and smiled. "Especially one as interesting as this sounds like it might be."

I couldn't help it. I smiled right back at him.

"There's someone I'd like you to talk to," I said. "His name is Detective Young, and he's going to want to hear what we have to say."

Chapter 26

Aunt Peg's kennel was a total loss.

Several hours passed before the blaze was finally extinguished. By then even the diehard gawkers had moved on. When the emergency crews left, Aunt Peg brought out her Standard Poodles and loaded them in Sam's SUV. They all came home with us to spend the night. The next morning, we returned to survey the damage.

A portion of Aunt Peg's fence had been dismantled. Her previously lovely lawn was trampled and muddy. In the field behind the house where the tidy kennel building had stood for forty years, there now remained only a smoldering heap of rubble and ash.

Wire pens, half-melted by the intense heat, had twisted into grotesque shapes. A wink of silver amid the debris identified the former location of the trophy room. An improbable flash of red turned out to be a piece of a Best in Show streamer that had somehow survived the fiery destruction. The acrid aroma of the remains made me want to pinch my nose shut.

For a long time nobody spoke. We simply stood and stared at the wreckage.

Sam, holding Kevin in his arms, was the first to offer an opinion. "You were lucky," he said.

"Lucky?" Aunt Peg's head reared back. There might have been tears in her eyes. Either that or the stench was making them water. "I'd like to know how."

"It could have been much worse. You're safe and so are your dogs. Imagine what might have happened if you had been here alone when Trace arrived to do his dirty work."

The previous evening after Davey and Kevin had gone to bed, I'd told Sam and Aunt Peg everything that had transpired while they were busy elsewhere. Sam was relieved that we finally had answers. Predictably, Aunt Peg was annoyed to have missed the imprudent argument that revealed the Brody cousins' true colors.

Now she said stoutly, "I like to think that I'd have knocked that stupid boy on his ear."

"Or maybe he'd have done the same to you," I pointed out.

Sam was pragmatic about the loss. "You can always rebuild if you want. It's been a while since you used that kennel, though."

"I haven't used it to house dogs." Aunt Peg continued to gaze at the pile of smoking debris. "When Max was alive and we had more Poodles to care for, he and I spent hours there each day. There was nowhere else we would rather have been."

Far be it from me to point out that Aunt Peg's husband had also died in that building.

"I know it's been years since those pens were full," she said with a sigh. "But I still liked to go out and visit sometimes. The kennel was a wonderful place to sit and reflect upon everything that had gone before."

"I bet you looked at all your trophies," Davey said.

"No, not really." Aunt Peg glanced at her nephew. "It was the photographs that drew me back time and again. I remember each and every one of those wins. I know the Poodles' names and how they were bred. I think about the competition that Max and I had faced. Generations of Cedar Crest Standard Poodles were born and lived their lives within those walls, and I still feel a connection to every one of them."

Aunt Peg turned away, deliberately averting her gaze from the destruction in front of us. "The kennel might have looked like just another building, but it was home to many wonderful memories. Now it feels like they're gone too, as if they were just as fleeting as the smoke that carried them away."

"I'm so sorry," I said.

Aunt Peg's spine stiffened. "This wasn't your fault."

I wasn't entirely convinced of that. "There were hints I should have picked up on. And clues I should have noticed sooner. It never should have taken me so long to realize how toxic that family is."

Aunt Peg managed a grim smile. "I wouldn't be surprised if Leo was looking down on us right now and thinking much the same thing."

Harley Jones and I had an appointment with Detective Young later that morning. Harley even shaved and put on a suit and tie for the occasion.

The detective listened intently as I outlined everything I'd learned over the past week. Then Harley and I described the previous night's encounter with the three Brody teenagers. When we were finished, Detective Young promised to put the information we'd given him to good use.

I didn't know if he'd be able to get an investigation opened, but at least I knew I'd done all I could. Harley, meanwhile, was sitting on the story of the decade. I didn't ask what he planned to do with the material and he didn't offer to tell me. He was probably considering which of his media connections to approach first. At least I hoped he was.

That afternoon, Aunt Peg had a long talk with Libby Rothko. It ended with Libby proposing that the Brody family pay for replacement of the kennel and other related costs. The offer sounded suspiciously like a bribe to me and Aunt Peg rebuffed the offer politely but firmly.

Though Libby was the one who'd initiated the process, now that it had reached its conclusion she seemed to remember that she was a Brody too. Either that or they'd purchased her cooperation. In any case, the family had closed ranks and mostly disappeared from public view.

Ron Brody filed for divorce less than a month after his father's death. Libby mentioned to Aunt Peg that the split had come as a surprise to her. She wondered whether the turmoil between their parents had been the catalyst that had led to Ashley and Megan's acting out.

I thought that was an incredibly insipid euphemism to describe a joint, premeditated action that had led to the death of a very good man, but I told myself that I'd already devoted more than enough time worrying about the Brodys and their issues. I needed to get back to the things that really mattered: my family, my Poodles, and the fact that summer vacation was passing by in the blink of an eye.

At the end of August we held a small party for Bud and declared him officially ours. By then the little spotted dog was beginning to look like a new man. His eyes were bright and curious, his ribs were covered with flesh, and his coat had begun to shine. Even better, Bud no longer cringed when he heard loud noises or hid behind the couch when our family life became too hectic.

He'd adopted Kevin as his child and followed him everywhere. Once—not by parental design—the two of them had even shared a bath. That had been a bit of a mess.

So I was surprised when Davey came to me one day and told me he thought we might want to make some changes. Specifically with regard to Bud's name.

"It doesn't suit him anymore," he said.

"What do you mean?" Davey and I were sitting outside on the deck. Kevin and Bud were rolling around on the lawn. "I thought you chose that name because compared to the Poodles, Bud's a bit plain. So you gave him a name to match."

"No, you have that all wrong. I named him after a *bud*. You know, like in your garden?"

Davey looked at me and grinned. I'm a terrible gardener and we both knew it.

"You named that dog Bud to remind me of my failures?"

"No, I called him that because when we found him, it felt like his new life was just beginning. I knew he was going to grow and develop and become a totally great dog. And now he's almost there."

"Darn it, Davey." I sniffed loudly. "Don't make me cry."

"Geez. Why would you want to do that?"

I gave him a watery smile. "Because even when I think I know almost everything about you, you still manage to surprise me."

Davey looked perplexed. "Is that a good thing?"

"It's a very good thing."

"So do you think we should change his name?"

"No way. Bud is just the right name for him. In fact, it's perfect."

The little spotted dog heard us talking about him. His head lifted and his tail began to wag. He opened his mouth in a doggy grin. Kev hates to be ignored. He stood up and stamped his foot. Then he added a loud squeal.

Davey winced slightly. He looked at me and shook his head. "I hope you're planning to train those two."

Not me. I knew when I had it good.

"I'm not going to change a thing," I said.

As owner of prize-winning Poodles, Melanie Travis knows how to handle fierce competition. But when a conformation show turns deadly, it'll take every trick in the book to outsmart a murderer who refuses to lose . . .

With the excitement of the spring dog show season sweeping Connecticut, Melanie is determined to help her son finally lead his Standard Poodle toward a championship title. Aunt Peg even skips the judging panel to exhibit a pup of her own, and she's set on standing out from the pack with a handmade leash from Jasmine Crane, a talented canine portrait artist who also crafts stunning accessories for discriminating show-goers. Jasmine's handiwork is to die for—but Aunt Peg didn't expect to discover the woman murdered behind the concession booth, strangled by one of her dazzling custom creations . . .

Another shockwave ripples through the close-knit show community when Amanda, Aunt Peg's longtime dog sitter and a renter on Jasmine's property, ominously vanishes that same day. While nosing around for clues, Melanie suspects a dangerous connection between Amanda's disappearance and the homicide case—a hunch that grows as her investigation reveals sketchy secrets about the late artist. Juggling a demanding teaching job, the pressures of the show ring, and a daunting suspect list, Melanie finds herself entangled in a mindboggling murder mystery . . . and hot on the trail of a desperate killer . . .

Please turn the page for an exciting sneak peek of Laurien Berenson's next Melanie Travis mystery RUFF JUSTICE coming soon wherever print and e-books are sold!

Chapter 1

It is a truth universally acknowledged that a Standard Poodle in possession of eleven points toward a championship must be in want of a dog show.

Okay, Jane Austen didn't use those exact words. But if she had been a member of my family she might well have because dog shows are a way of life for us. I met my husband, Sam, at a dog show, and our blended canine crew currently includes five black Standard Poodles and a small, spotted mutt named Bud.

All our Poodles are retired show champions, except for one: Kirkwood's Keep Away, more casually known as Augie. He belongs to my thirteen-year-old son, Davey. A novice dog handler with plenty of other interests to keep him busy, Davey had been working on finishing Augie's championship for nearly two years.

Now we were all in agreement that it was time to finally buckle down and get the job done. Which had brought us to yet another dog show. Like all exhibitors, we were eternal optimists.

Connecticut weather in early April was notoriously fickle. Though the show scene had moved back outdoors for the spring season, the day was chilly enough for everyone to be bundled into warm jackets. Still, after a winter spent at often cramped indoor venues, we were all delighted to be outside in a spacious park. The air might have been unseasonably brisk but at least it wasn't raining. Or snowing.

Twelve large rings had been set up in the center of the big field. They were positioned in two rows of six, with a wide alleyway between them, covered by a green-and-white striped tent. At each end of the competition area was another, smaller tent where exhibitors set up their grooming equipment and completed their preshow ring preparations.

By the time we arrived midmorning, most of the available space under the grooming tent nearest the Poodle ring had already been claimed by the professional handlers who'd been at the show site since dawn. Sam pulled the SUV into the unloading area beside the tent. I got out and had a look around, hoping to find a small spot to wedge our gear in.

The scene beneath the tent was hectic. I saw dozens of wooden crates stacked on top of each other, and rows of rubber-matted grooming tables squashed into narrow aisles. I heard the loud, persistent whine of free-standing blow dryers. Some exhibitors were working on their dogs while others were dashing back and forth to the rings.

To the uninitiated, it might have looked like pandemonium. To me, it looked like home.

Suddenly a familiar head popped up. A hand lifted and waved in the air. "Melanie!" Aunt Peg called. "Over here."

Even in the midst of all that chaos, Margaret Turnbull was hard to overlook. She stood six feet tall and had a direct gaze that missed nothing. Her posture was impeccable, and her demeanor was that of a woman who knew exactly what she wanted and almost always got it.

Over the decades, Aunt Peg's successes in the dog show world had earned her a reputation for excellence and the lasting respect of her peers. Her Cedar Crest Kennel had not only produced a number of the country's best Standard Poodles, it had also provided foundation stock for those discerning breeders who'd followed in her footsteps.

Now nearing seventy, Aunt Peg had scaled back her involvement in breeding and exhibiting to concentrate on her busy career as a multi-group judge. She'd had a litter of Standard Poodle puppies the previous fall—her first in several years. I knew she'd retained the best bitch puppy for herself, but now I was surprised to see Aunt Peg standing in the middle of her own setup. The Poodle, Cedar Crest Coral, was sitting on a grooming table beside her.

It looked as though Aunt Peg would be showing today too. Somehow she'd neglected to mention that.

Aunt Peg had a word with the puppy, then left

her sitting on her monogrammed towel. She slipped through the setups between us and came to help unload the SUV.

The four of us worked together with a practiced ease born of repetition. By the time Aunt Peg and I reached the vehicle, Sam already had the hatch open. He'd pulled out the dolly and he and Davey were loading Augie's crate onto it.

In my sometimes crazy world, Sam was my rock. We'd known each other for nearly a decade and been married for half that time. I loved that he was smart and perceptive. I also loved that Sam had sun-bleached blond hair, a killer smile, and a body buff enough to draw second looks from girls half our age.

As I reached around him to grab the wooden tack box, I trailed my fingers across Sam's back. He shifted slightly in my direction and winked.

Davey was threading a noose carefully through Augie's thick neck hair before hopping the big Poodle out of the car. He caught the interaction between his stepfather and me and shook his head. Thirteen was a tough age for kids and parents both.

"What about me?" asked a plaintive voice. "What should I carry?"

Our younger son, Kevin, had turned four in March. He was enrolled in preschool now. As a consequence, he was feeling very grown up. I looked around for something to hand him and settled upon a small, soft-sided cooler.

"You can take this," I said.

Kev thrust out his lower lip. "I want something big."

Aunt Peg leaned down and examined my choice. "Don't lose that, it's very important. The cooler has Augie's bait in it. Without it, Davey will be in trouble when he goes in the ring."

The thought of his brother in trouble immediately brightened my younger son's face. Kevin had his father's sandy hair and slate-blue eyes. When he smiled it was like looking at a version of Sam in miniature.

"I have Augie's bait," he echoed happily. "Cool."

We moved Aunt Peg's equipment to one side and squeezed our own stuff in next to it. Sam wedged the crate up against a tent pole. Then he and Kev went to move the SUV to the parking lot. I put the tack box within easy reach on top of the crate and stashed the cooler and Kevin's toy bag behind it.

Davey set up the grooming table. When it was ready, he lifted Augie up into place. I saw him cast a glance in Coral's direction and frown. Aunt Peg's pretty puppy had already been brushed out. With her dense black coat and soft, dark eyes, she looked like a perfect, plush doll. When Davey looked her way Coral stood up and wagged her tail.

"What's the matter?" I asked him.

"Aunt Peg is showing."

I understood his consternation. It had been a long time since I'd seen Aunt Peg in a ring with a Poodle on the end of her leash. "Now we'll have two chances to win," I said brightly.

"Now I'll have to beat her too," Davey grumbled.

"You have a dog and I have a bitch," Aunt Peg reminded him. "We won't meet in the classes. And besides, Coral is only six months old. We're only here today for the experience."

I leaned down and whispered to Davey, "You should be happy Aunt Peg has her own entry to concentrate on. That'll give her less time to worry about what you and Augie are doing."

"I heard that," Aunt Peg snapped. The woman has ears like a fox.

Ignoring her, I opened the tack box and took out the tools Davey would need to start preparing Augie for the ring. A fully mature Standard Poodle dog, Augie was wearing the continental clip, one of three trims approved for AKC breed competition. His face and throat were clipped to the skin, and he had a dense coat of long, shaped hair covering the front half of his body. His hindquarter and legs were mostly shaved as well, leaving only rounded rosettes on each of his hips, bracelets on his lower legs, and a large pompon on the end of his tail.

Beginning the grooming session required a pin brush, a slicker brush, a greyhound comb, and a water bottle for misting the coat. I lined up the equipment along the edge of the tabletop.

Davey looped his arms around Augie's legs and gently lowered the Poodle into a prone position. Augie knew what to expect. He relaxed and lay quietly on his left side. Hands moving quickly through the hair, Davey started line brushing the Poodle's mane coat.

"I see the gang's all here," said Terry Denunzio. Sweeping past me with a Japanese Chin tucked beneath each arm, he aimed an air kiss in my direction. "*Finally*," he added with a smirk.

That last part was a dig at Aunt Peg, who always beat us to shows, then complained vociferously that we were late, even when we had hours to spare. Assistant to top professional handler Crawford Langley, Terry was one of my best buddies. Nearing thirty, he was ten years younger than me and impossibly cute. He was also flamboyantly gay. Terry's antics were the perfect foil for Crawford's calm, dignified manner. The two of them made a great couple.

Terry often entertained himself by taking potshots at people. And since it wasn't unusual for me to be the target of his biting wit, now I couldn't resist having some fun at his expense. Terry's hair color seemed to change with his moods. Or maybe the time of day. But this tint was something I hadn't seen before.

"Red?" I said incredulously. "You've got to be kidding."

"What?" He stashed the two toy dogs in a pair of crates and straightened and twirled for effect. "You don't love it?"

"I don't even like it." I wrinkled my nose. "You look like Howdy Doody."

"That's what I told him." Crawford entered the neighboring setup from the other side. He was carrying another Chin and a fistful of ribbons.

"And I said"—Terry paused and looked around to make sure we were all listening—"who the heck is Howdy Doody?"

Back at her own grooming table, Aunt Peg barked out a laugh. "Good for you, Terry. It's wise to be impervious to insult."

"Who are we insulting now?" Bertie Kennedy

came flying into the tent towing a Bearded Collie. Another professional handler, Bertie was married to my younger brother, Frank. The couple had two children: six-year-old Maggie and a son named Josh, who'd been born the previous September.

Crawford had been showing dogs successfully for decades. Bertie's experience comprised only a fraction of that time. But she was talented and worked hard. The fact that she was tall and gorgeous didn't hurt either. As she hopped the Beardie onto a nearby table, I leaned over to give her a hug. Apparently the setup on our other side belonged to her.

"Terry," I told her. "We're laughing at his hair."

"Hey." She pulled back and gave me a stern look. "I could be offended by that." Bertie's hair was a deep, rich shade of auburn. Terry's was flaming red.

"You tell 'em, doll." Terry plucked a Mini Poodle out of a crate and went to work. "We redheads have to stick together."

"At least until Tuesday or so," I said. "By then he'll probably be blond again."

"Somebody woke up on the wrong side of bed this morning." Terry fluttered his fingers in Aunt Peg's direction. "Competition a little tough for you today?"

"I might ask the same of you," I shot back. Davey was showing one Standard Poodle. Crawford and Terry had three. And as Aunt Peg had pointed out earlier, since the initial classes were divided by sex, it was unlikely that Augie and Coral would meet in the show ring.

"You two quit fussing." Aunt Peg was busy putting

up her puppy's topknot. "Coral is a baby. She's just here to learn what dog shows are all about."

"A puppy of yours needing experience?" Sam said. He and Kev had returned from parking the SUV. "That sounds unlikely."

Sam released Kevin's hand and I handed my son the bag of toys. He sat down in the grass, took out a pair of Matchbox cars, and began to zoom them around the table legs.

"I can't believe how much I've missed this," Aunt Peg said with a smile. "It's been entirely too long since I had a Poodle to show. Judging is a wonderful way to give back to the sport, but this . . ." She waved a hand to encompass all the activity under the tent and the other exhibitors around us. "This is what it's really about. The dogs, the grooming, the competition, the camaraderie—"

"The smell of hairspray in the morning?" I teased.

"Laugh if you will, but I'm perfectly serious. Judging is a fruitful occupation and agility is loads of fun. But nothing can compare with the satisfaction you feel, walking into the breed ring with a beautiful, home-bred dog on the end of your leash."

"Here, here," said Crawford.

The rest of us nodded in agreement. Dog shows had an addictive quality and we were all well aware of it. The competition was always interesting, and occasionally even rewarding. But that was only part of the equation. Exhibiting gave breeders the opportunity to form relationships, to compare notes, and to analyze the results of their efforts. We came to the shows for the dogs, but the people were every bit as important.

"Speaking of judging," said Sam. "When are you going to apply for a license, Crawford?"

The handler gave him a sideways look. "Is that your way of saying you think I'm of an age where I ought to be slowing down?"

Sam reddened. I'd rarely seen him at a loss for words, but now he looked as if he wished he'd never asked the question.

I quickly intervened. "What Sam meant, Crawford, is that the judging pool would be enriched by your experience and expertise."

"That's what I thought." The handler cracked a grin. "But the judging pool will have to wait. I'm too busy doing what I do best." He swept a Toy Poodle off a tabletop and exited the tent. Terry picked up two more ring-ready Toys and followed.

"That's my cue," said Bertie. She left with a Duck Toller.

"And mine as well," Aunt Peg announced. "Keep an eye on Coral for me, will you? I'll be back in just a few minutes."

"Where are you going?" I asked.

"I decided that a return to the ring deserved a nice new piece of equipment. I ordered a beaded show leash for Coral from Jasmine Crane. She told me it would be ready for pick up today."

Sam and I exchanged a look. We were both remembering that most of Aunt Peg's old equipment had burned up in a kennel fire the previous summer.

"That sounds perfect," I said. "Jasmine's leashes are beautiful."

Every dog show drew a variety of canine-centric concession booths, offering all manner of dog-related products. I'd seen everything from sheep-skin beds and squeaky toys, to canine books and figurines. In vendor's row, there was something for every dog lover to drool over.

Jasmine Crane's specialty was canine art. Working in oils and pastels, she created original paintings and took commissions for pet portraits. Jasmine was a skilled artist, deft at capturing both her subjects' looks and their personalities. When passing by her booth, I'd often admired the merchandise she had on display.

Recently Jasmine had expanded into the growing market for custom-made collars and leashes. Her eye for color and symmetry lent her products a special flair, and her strapworks were quickly becoming as popular as her art.

Like all show Poodles, Coral was table trained. When Aunt Peg left, Coral lay down on the table-top with her head between her front paws, patiently waiting for Aunt Peg to return.

Davey had finished line-brushing Augie and put on his slender show collar. Now Sam supervised as Davey parted the long hair on the Poodle's head and banded together the numerous ponytails that would support Augie's towering topknot. Davey and Sam were spraying up Augie's coat when Aunt Peg reappeared ten minutes later.

"Let me see." I held out my hand. "I bet it's gorgeous."

"I'd be delighted to show it to you," Aunt Peg replied unhappily, "except I don't have it. Jasmine wasn't in her booth. I even waited a few minutes, hoping she'd return, but she never showed up."

"That's odd," Sam commented. "How does she expect to make sales if she isn't there for her customers?"

"I haven't a clue." Aunt Peg sounded huffy. "And it's very disappointing. I had that leash made specially, so I could start Coral's career off right. Now we'll have to do without."

Davey looked over. "I can lend you a lead, Aunt Peg. I have extras."

"Thank you, but no." She walked over and dug around in her tack box. "I have a leash. It's just not the *right* leash."

Aunt Peg reveled in her dog show superstitions. Heaven forbid you wished her luck before she went in the ring. She would react as though you'd driven a dagger into her heart.

Davey looked at me and shrugged. I returned the gesture.

Aunt Peg sighed. Loudly. "There's nothing to be done for it. We shall simply have to rise above."

My sympathy for her plight was muted. Trust me, if anyone was capable of rising above, it was surely Aunt Peg.

She took out her scissors and applied the final finish to Coral's trim. Over in our setup, Sam and Davey were doing the same to Augie. Crawford and Terry came running back to the tent with their Toy Poodles. They exchanged them for the Standards and quickly got ready to leave again.

Aunt Peg lifted Coral off her grooming table and set her on the ground. Davey followed suit with Augie. In a procession of Poodles, we all headed over to the ring.

Following behind with Kevin, I felt a frisson of excitement in the air. Things were about to get serious. It was time to find out if all the hard work we'd done to ready Augie for the show had been worth it. For Davey's sake, I really hoped today was going to be his day.

Chapter 2

Poodles come in three varieties, divided by size. From the tiniest city apartment to the expanse of a rural ranch, a Poodle can fit in anywhere. Despite their differences in stature, all Poodles share the same whip-smart, eager to please, fun-loving disposition. Plus, they're people dogs. So most are kind enough to hide the fact that they can out-think their owners. There's nothing a Poodle enjoys more than a good joke, especially one at their person's expense.

Though the breed was originally developed to retrieve, the gaiety of the Poodle temperament is uniquely suited to the show ring. Poodles are natural entertainers. In the breed ring, a judge is looking for a sound, typey dog with correct conformation. But Poodles bring something more.

They walk into a dog show ring and make it their own. They play with their handlers. They flirt with the spectators. They charm the socks off the judges. Poodles understand that dog shows are supposed to be fun. And they want everyone else to be having a great time too.

We crossed the short expanse between the handlers' tent and the show ring in the company of more than a dozen other Standard Poodles. Davey kept Augie close to his side. His right hand was holding the end of the lead, his left was cupped beneath the dog's muzzle. His arm, looped around Augie's mane coat, prevented anyone from stepping too close and jostling the carefully coiffed hair.

By contrast, Aunt Peg was letting Coral play at the end of her leash. The rambunctious puppy briefly dropped her head to sniff at something enticing in the grass, before bounding back up like a gazelle. Her pomponned tail, held high in the air, wagged back and forth with delight.

I watched the boisterous display with surprise. Aunt Peg was a formidable competitor. And this carefree behavior—on the way to the show ring, no less—was very unlike her.

"I guess you really *are* here for the experience," I said.

"Every puppy should have a good time at her first dog show," Aunt Peg replied. "Besides, it's not as if she has any real hair to muss."

Augie's regal topknot towered nearly a foot in the air. Coral's resembled a wispy black bottle brush. The fringe on her ears barely reached the end of the leathers. In her puppy trim—with a blanket of shaped hair covering her entire body—

Coral was more cute than imposing. Compared to the other Standard bitches, Coral would look like a baby. Which was exactly what she was.

Aunt Peg reached over and poked Davey in the shoulder. "There's a major today in dogs. I expect you to look sharp. Augie should be very competitive in this company."

Davey nodded but didn't reply. He already knew what was on the line. And unfortunately, pressure from Aunt Peg was nothing new.

In order to attain its championship, a dog needed to earn fifteen points in same-sex competition. The judging began with the classes for unfinished dogs. As she had yet to turn a year old, Coral was entered in the Puppy Bitch class. Augie, a mature dog ready to take on the toughest class competitors, was in Open Dogs.

When the class judging had been completed, each individual class winner returned to the ring to vie for the titles of Winners Dog and Winners Bitch. Those two were the only entrants to receive points. The number of points awarded ranged from one to five, and was determined by the amount of competition beaten.

Two majors—awards of three or more points—were required to complete a dog's championship. Major wins were highly sought after and always difficult to attain. Augie had previously accumulated eleven points toward his championship, including one major. Coral, about to make her show ring debut, obviously had yet to earn even one.

The area near the in-gate of the Standard Poodle ring was already crowded with handlers and dogs. Inside the ring, the judge was quickly working his way through a small entry of Löwchen. Aunt Peg stopped to talk to someone she knew. Davey paused at the fringes of the activity, eager to keep Augie out of the fray. While Sam remained with him and kept a firm grip on Kev's hand, I slithered between people and Poodles and made my way to the steward's table to pick up our numbered armbands.

As I waited my turn, Terry appeared beside me, intent on the same mission. In Standard Poodles, he and Crawford had a class dog, a class bitch, and a champion "specials dog" who would be competing for Best of Variety.

Terry sidled closer and said out of the side of his mouth, "How is Augie's bite?"

"Fine," I whispered back.

"He's not missing any teeth?"

"No. Why?"

"Mr. Logan is a real stickler for correct dentition."

Some breed standards disqualify dogs for an incorrect bite or missing teeth. The Poodle standard wasn't one of them. But even so, every judge carried his own preferences and idiosyncrasies into the ring with him.

"You can't blame him," Terry said.

That piqued my interest. I turned and stared until he continued.

"Mr. Logan once stuck his hand into a Doberman's mouth and cut his finger on the dog's braces. He had to go get stitches."

I reared back in surprise. Missing teeth were a minor infraction compared to *braces*. Artificial enhancements were strictly forbidden.

"You're making that up," I accused.

"No, really." Terry was all innocence. Like butter wouldn't melt in his mouth. That was the problem with Terry's gossip. I never knew how much to believe. "Ask Peg, she'll tell you."

Aunt Peg was all the way on the other side of the ring. As Terry knew perfectly well. I grabbed our numbers from the steward and went back to join my family.

"Mr. Logan hasn't even started judging Standards yet and already you look outraged," Sam said mildly. "What is Terry up to now?"

"Apparently an exhibitor once took a dog into Mr. Logan's ring that was wearing braces on its teeth."

"Oh yeah." Sam didn't even blink. "That's old news."

Even after all the years I'd been involved, when it came to showing dogs, I still sometimes felt like the new kid. Why did everybody always know this stuff but me?

"The judge had to get *stitches*," I said.

Sam still wasn't impressed. "I wouldn't worry about that. I'm sure the cut is healed by now."

"Mom, Puppy Dogs are in the ring," Davey said urgently. "I need my number."

Oh. Right. Time to get back to business.

Davey held out his arm. I ran two rubber bands up the sleeve of his jacket, then slid the cardboard square securely underneath. Inside the ring, Mr. Logan was taking his last look at four Standard puppies before pinning the class. Aunt Peg came around from the other side of the ring to watch the remainder of the dog judging with us. I handed over her armband and she slipped it on.

"Crawford should win that class handily," she remarked. "That's a nice puppy he has. He'll give Augie a run for his money in Winners."

"Augie has to get out of the Open class first," I reminded her.

Aunt Peg waved a hand as if that was a given. I wished I had even half her confidence.

As usual, however, it turned out that Aunt Peg was right.

Crawford's white puppy topped his class easily. And after a prolonged battle, Davey and Augie prevailed over three other dogs in Open. Davey accepted his blue ribbon with a grateful smile. Then he hurried Augie back into position as Crawford brought his puppy back into the ring so the two could be judged against each other for Winners Dog.

Mr. Logan made it look like a close decision. And it probably was. He left Augie at the head of the line until the very last moment. Then, as the two dogs circled the ring one final time, the judge looked back and pointed to Crawford's puppy for the win.

My heart sank like a stone. Sam was standing beside me. I felt his shoulders slump. The fact that Davey had been so close to nabbing Augie's elusive second major made us both feel even worse.

"Did Davey win?" Kevin asked. He had yet to master the intricacies of the judging system.

"No," I said glumly. "Not this time."

Looking resigned, Davey moved Augie back into line. The dog who'd placed second earlier to

Crawford's puppy returned to the ring to be judged for Reserve Winners. This time the decision took only a few seconds. Mr. Logan quickly motioned Augie over to the marker and handed Davey the purple-and-white-striped ribbon.

Davey exited the ring with a frown on his face. He wasn't upset, just disappointed. We all were.

"I really wanted to win that one," he said dejectedly.

"I know you did, sweetie." I looped my arms around his shoulders and pulled him close for a hug. Davey usually objects to PDAs from his parents. This time he didn't even murmur a protest. "But you'll have another chance next week. Augie looks great and he was really showing well for you."

"That puppy of Crawford's is a star in the making," Sam added. "It was just bad luck that you and Augie ran into him today. I'm pretty sure the win finished him, so at least you won't have to worry about him in the future."

"That's pathetic," Davey muttered. "That dog finished as a *puppy*, and I've been showing Augie forever."

"Pathetic, is it?" Aunt Peg inquired. The judge was still busy marking his book, so the Puppy Bitches had yet to be called to the ring. "I thought you wanted to show Augie yourself."

"I do," Davey protested, but Aunt Peg wasn't finished.

"If all that mattered was getting the job done, we could put that dog with a professional handler and have him finished in no time. Would you prefer that?"

"No, of course not."

"That's what I thought," Aunt Peg sniffed. "Now give your nice Poodle a pat and let me go take my turn."

Mr. Logan had returned to the center of his ring. The steward called out the numbers of the two Standard Poodle Puppy Bitches. Aunt Peg went sweeping past us with Coral bouncing at her side.

The fact that Aunt Peg won her small class didn't come as a surprise. Coral might have been immature and inexperienced, but she was still a very pretty Poodle. But what happened after that was totally unexpected.

The Bred-by-Exhibitor class had only a single entry, but there were five nice bitches in Open. A lovely brown Poodle with a professional handler prevailed, and I assumed she would go on to take the points.

That decision looked like an easy one to me. But apparently not to Mr. Logan.

He motioned Coral forward to the head of the line and turned the contest into a duel between the puppy and the Open Bitch. Judging by the expression on Aunt Peg's face, she hadn't anticipated this turn of events either.

Aunt Peg is a competitor to the core, however. I could see the exact moment she put aside the notion of Coral using the dog show for experience—and got to work beating that other bitch. All at once, she began presenting Coral to the judge as if she was offering the rarest of diamonds for his perusal.

The best handlers are skilled at showcasing a

dog's good points and drawing the judge's eye away from its faults. Coral was a bit small. Her tail set could have been higher and she was somewhat lacking in under jaw. However those flaws were more than offset by her lovely face and expression, her well-angulated shoulder, and her solid topline. When the puppy settled down and moved right, she appeared to float over the ground.

And suddenly Aunt Peg was doing everything she could to make sure Coral was settled and showing effectively.

Mr. Logan waffled and wavered for what seemed like an inordinate amount of time. Usually when that happened it meant a judge didn't particularly like either offering. But Mr. Logan had two nice bitches in front of him. He also had two Poodles who couldn't have been more different in age and condition. Under those circumstances, most judges would opt to reward the mature entry. So what was this judge spending so much time thinking about?

"Aunt Peg's going to win," Kevin said. Sam had picked him up so he could see the ring better.

"I think you're right." I sounded shocked. I *was* shocked.

And I wasn't the only one. When the judge pointed to Coral for Winners Bitch, Davey released his breath on a long exhale. "How did Aunt Peg *do* that?" he asked.

Sam shrugged, looking equally bemused. "Magic?"

When it came to Aunt Peg's powers, anything was possible.

After that, the Best of Variety judging proceeded in a more conventional manner. Crawford's handsome special was awarded BOV over two other champions. His white puppy, now being handled by Terry, was Best of Winners. Coral, the only bitch in the ring, was awarded Best of Opposite Sex.

With an auspicious debut like that, I assumed Aunt Peg would remain at ringside to have Coral's picture taken with the judge. But when the rest of the family went trooping back to the handlers' tent, Aunt Peg and Coral fell in behind us. I started to ask her about a win photo, then saw the expression on her face and thought better of the idea.

Aunt Peg appeared to be seriously disgruntled by the outcome.

Crawford and Terry had stayed to have their winners' pictures taken, but Bertie was standing in her setup when we returned. There was a Sheltie on one of her grooming tables and a Smooth Collie on another, but Bertie was taking a break to consult her program and drink a soda. Her gaze slid over us, one by one.

"I'm guessing it wasn't your best day," she said.

"Augie was Reserve," Davey told her. He put the Poodle back on the tabletop. Augie would now need to have his tight topknot taken down and the hairspray brushed from his coat. "But Coral won."

"Congratulations!" Bertie cried. Then she looked at Aunt Peg, who was glumly slipping Coral into a crate. The puppy didn't have enough hair to even need brushing out. "Wait. That's good news, isn't it?"

"You would think," I said. "If Augie had won, we'd all be dancing in the aisles."

Well maybe not Davey, who rolled his eyes at

that. But hey, he's thirteen, so that's par for the course. The rest of us would have been doing a serious jitterbug.

Bertie watched as Aunt Peg silently pulled the two ribbons out of her pocket and tossed them into her tack box. "Coral was Best Opposite too? That's terrific. Did you get a picture?"

"No." Aunt Peg frowned.

"Why not?"

Instead of replying, Aunt Peg turned to Sam. "Suppose you were judging bitches today. Who would you have put up?"

Sam answered without hesitation. "The brown bitch. She deserved the win."

"Yes, she did," Aunt Peg agreed. "Coral never should have beaten her."

"So what?" I said. "We've all had days when we should have won, but didn't. It's nice to have things go the other way for a change."

"It's not *nice*," Aunt Peg grumbled. "Walter Logan should have known better. He should have *judged* better. That result never should have happened."

"So why did it?" I asked.

"I have no idea. I suppose I'll have to ask him the next time I see him."

Bertie snorted under her breath. We all looked her way.

"What?" asked Aunt Peg.

"You're kidding, right? Your puppy won the points on a day when she shouldn't have and you honestly don't know why?"

"Certainly not," Aunt Peg said sharply. "Please enlighten me."

Sam cleared his throat. Suddenly I realized he also knew what Bertie was thinking. "As Melanie said, we've all been beaten when we shouldn't have been. Sometimes because a judge plays politics and puts up a professional over an owner-handler."

"I certainly don't see how that applies." Aunt Peg looked nonplussed. "*I'm* an owner-handler."

"Oh please," said Bertie. "If you're a normal owner-handler, I'm Winnie the Pooh."

Aunt Peg's eyes narrowed. She was not amused. "Are you saying that my win was due to politics?"

"Think about it," I said. "You're a judge yourself. And you obviously know Walter Logan—"

"I know *everybody* in the dog world," Aunt Peg sputtered.

"Precisely my point," I affirmed.

"And don't forget about the intimidation factor," Bertie added.

"What intimidation factor?" asked Aunt Peg.

Davey laughed out loud. After a few seconds the rest of us—except for Aunt Peg—followed.

"But it shouldn't matter who is showing the dog." Aunt Peg's tone bordered on outrage. "They're supposed to be judging the other end of the lead!"

"That's how it works in your ring," Sam replied mildly. "But not everywhere."

"But . . ." Aunt Peg was sputtering again. "That's not fair."

"Maybe you should hire a professional handler for Coral, Aunt Peg," Davey said innocently.

Okay, that was fresh. But it was also pretty funny.

Sam spun away to hide a grin. Bertie abruptly got busy digging in her tack box. I swallowed a laugh and bent down under the grooming table to see how Kevin was doing.

Aunt Peg drew herself up to her full height. She glared around at us as if we'd suddenly morphed into a bunch of back-stabbing traitors. "You people are all annoying me," she announced. "I'm going to go pick up my new leash. Hopefully by the time I return, you will have realized the error of your ways."

"Fat chance of that," Davey muttered under his breath.

Thankfully I appeared to be the only one who heard him.

Aunt Peg hadn't even been gone five minutes when my cell phone rang. I showed the name on the screen to Sam and Bertie and said, "Do you think she wants to apologize?"

I should have known better.

Aunt Peg was already talking before I even got the phone to my ear. "Melanie, run quickly to the ambulance at the end of the field. It's needed right away at Jasmine's booth."

"Is somebody hurt?" All at once I felt guilty. "It's not you, is it?"

"I'm fine," Aunt Peg snapped. "More or less, anyway. But Jasmine Crane isn't. She appears to be dead."